BB

The Girl on the Landing

Also by Paul Torday

Salmon Fishing in the Yemen
The Irresistible Inheritance of Wilberforce

The Girl
on the Landing

PAUL TORDAY

Weidenfeld & Nicolson
LONDON

First published in Great Britain in 2009
by Weidenfeld & Nicolson

3 5 7 9 10 8 6 4 2

© Paul Torday 2009

A CIP catalogue record for this book
is available from the British Library

ISBN 978 0 297 85525 5 (cased)
ISBN 978 0 297 85533 0 (trade paperback)

Typeset by Input Data Services Ltd, Bridgwater, Somerset

Printed in Great Britain by Clays Ltd, St Ives plc

The Orion Publishing Group's policy is to use papers that
are natural, renewable and recyclable products and made
from wood grown in sustainable forests. The logging and
manufacturing processes are expected to conform to the
environmental regulations of the country of origin.

Weidenfeld & Nicolson

An imprint of the Orion Publishing Group
Orion House, 5 Upper St Martin's Lane,
London WC2H 9EA
An Hachette Livre UK company

www.orionbooks.co.uk

I

The Picture

The last few miles of our journey took us through a region of fields of golden wheat, now being harvested as we drove past. The sky was golden too, ramparts of cumulus catching the late afternoon sun.

As we moved south the colours in the sky changed. Dark grey infused the clouds, and a corona of yellow light formed around their edges. A wind got up, bringing down a first handful of autumn leaves, and I could feel the vibration of distant thunder. That should not have been possible from inside a car, but I felt it all the same: a sense of huge charges of electricity building in the upper atmosphere, an intensity to the light where it gleamed between the darkening clouds. My perceptions had become so much sharper in the last few weeks; it was as if I was rediscovering the world.

I felt certain that a thunderstorm was coming, but it did not come that afternoon: it remained somewhere grumbling in distant valleys. It was late August and we had been invited to stay for a few days in a country house in Ireland. The house was an attractive example of the Georgian period, with large bay windows and walls covered in creeper, now turning from green to red. It stood in parkland of a hundred acres or so, and beyond the pastures lay dark woods on every side. Behind the house, beyond the walled garden, were the remains of a tower house, roofless and ruined.

We had never been to the house before, and I did not know the owner very well. We were members of the same club in London. Somehow my wife and I had received an invitation to come and play golf on a well-known course not far from the house. Of course I accepted.

I had just finished dressing for dinner. While Elizabeth sat at a table, examining and adjusting her appearance with the help of a cheval mirror, I stood at the window and looked out. The room was at the front of the house and had a view of green pastures and mature trees: antique oaks and limes of great size and girth, their trunks gnarled by age. The leaves on the trees were just beginning to turn and the air was soft, but with that first chill of autumn that comes as the sun sinks lower in the sky. The threatening clouds had now lifted and the pale blue evening sky was streaked with pink, a promise of fine weather for the next day.

It was so quiet. The nearest main road was miles away. The house lay among woods and small rivers that drained into the larger valley where we were playing golf the next day. The fields of wheat that were being harvested as we had turned off the main road were some miles distant and the tractors and the combines we had seen on the way could not be heard. Around the house, the only sound was the cawing of rooks that fluttered into the sky – wheeling in strange patterns – before settling back into the branches again.

Elizabeth completed her preparations and then came and inspected me. With a look of dissatisfaction she adjusted my bow tie and flicked invisible dust from the lapels of my smoking jacket. We set off down the corridor towards the great staircase that led to the ground floor.

As we walked I looked at the pictures out of idle curiosity. We had been in the house only for an hour or two and I had not had time to examine any of them yet. It is just a habit of mine: I know nothing about pictures, but I gaze at them all the same. They are windows into other worlds: if I stand in front of a seascape of a breezy foreshore, I can almost feel the wind on my face, the faint pinpricks of spray on the moving air. This house was full of pictures: scarcely an inch of wall space remained uncovered.

There was the usual collection of brown paintings, badly in need of cleaning or restoration; landscapes that suggested classical antiquity; one or two Venetian scenes; farther on, a few portraits of the owner's ancestors, gloomy-looking men in black coats or frowning females clad in dresses of dark stuff. Large canvasses filled the spaces between elderly glass-fronted display cabinets containing dusty Dresden shepherdesses, but slightly lower down there was a smaller picture that caught my attention.

The painting was of an interior that showed a shadowed landing. On one side of the landing was an old linen press; its drawers and doors were clearly drawn. On the other side, the only object of note was a white marble statue of an angel, mounted on a column of black basalt. The angel's wings were unfurled, as if it had just alighted in that position. Its chin was poised upon the palm of its hand, and one elbow was resting on its knee. The whole aspect of the angel was curious: it might have been weeping, or it might have been watchful, admonitory.

The landing ended in an archway that led to another landing, the vaguely sketched outlines of which receded into the hinterland of the picture. This second landing was bathed in a silvery light, as if pictured by moonlight. If there were windows, the artist had not bothered to define them. One simply had an impression of a transition from darkness into light. Here, at this junction, was a female figure clad in a green dress. Whether it was a girl, or a woman, was hard to say. The artist may perhaps have been idle, or maybe it was a question of technique. The foreground of the picture was drawn with great precision and attention to detail: the bare floorboards of the landing denoting austerity, if not actual hard times; the faintly asymmetric linen chest suggesting its origins in the best sort of domestic cabinetmaking. The farther into the background the artist went, however, the less he appeared to care about detail. The female figure was merely sketched in and she was dark, so dark one could make out only the merest suggestion of a face, but she was surrounded by a nimbus of light. A mass of sombre colour behind her hinted at a large vase with a fan of branches in it. As I looked into the picture I could imagine the rustling of silk as the girl continued her walk along the landing towards the vantage point of the artist.

'Darling, are you coming?' asked Elizabeth, in the exasperated tone of someone who had taken nearly an hour to get changed for dinner while I had stood looking out of the window. She was waiting for me at the top of the staircase, reluctant to go down and meet these people we hardly knew without me beside her.

'Just a minute,' I replied. 'There's rather an odd picture here.'

There was a faint snort in reply, but she made no attempt to come and look, merely tapping her foot as she stood and waited.

I decided the figure was a girl, rather than a woman: there was something in the slim erectness of her posture that suggested a person not yet challenged by age or child-bearing; an undefeated attitude, I thought. Was she looking at the angel? The juxtaposition of the two figures was curious, even unsettling.

I decided to come back and take a look before breakfast the next morning, when maybe the light in the corridor would be stronger.

I straightened up and went to join my wife. We descended the stairs together in sedate silence.

Dinner was no worse than any other occasion when people who are more or less strangers meet for the first time. The usual game of who knew whom was played, quite successfully. The food and wine were good. The owner of the house was reserved, but at the same time had a natural courtesy. I decided I liked him; I had not seen enough of him on the occasions we had met before to form any clear opinion. Elizabeth and his wife got on all right, and the other couple were relaxed and talkative.

After dinner the owner took me out on to the gravel at the front of the house so that we could smoke our cigars without censure from our wives. The two of us stood together, puffing away in easy silence for most of the time. I complimented the owner on dinner, and on the wines, and received only the briefest of replies. Then I asked, 'Have your family always lived here?'

This time my companion replied with some animation.

'We have lived here for quite a while, in that old tower house, you know, and then we built this place when things appeared to be settling down. The old tower house was built in 1560, and the new house was built in 1780, but the tower has rather fallen down, as you may have noticed. There has been a dwelling of some sort on the land for a lot longer than even the old house. There is an ancient burial mound in the woods.'

'How fascinating . . . and were you brought up here?'

'Not at all. I inherited quite by chance. It should have gone to a cousin, but he died in a car accident, and so the house came to me. We've only lived here for ten years. But you've brought a dog with you?'

This non sequitur was caused by a sudden movement in the back of my car, as my old black Labrador woke up and looked out to see whether I was near by.

'Yes. He loves coming everywhere with us. He's too old to race around now, but he's never happier than when he sits by the side of a river or follows me around on a golf course, when he's allowed to.'

'I quite agree,' said the owner, 'I always take one of our spaniels golfing or fishing with me. They're such good company, aren't they? But don't leave him outside. There's a clear sky and it will be a chilly night. He'll be very stiff in the morning. Take him up to your bedroom if you like. I'm sure he'll be much happier there. We've a spare dog basket we can lend you. Dogs rule this house, not people. He's very welcome inside.'

After demurring for some time I finally agreed to his suggestion, and later, when the other couple had left and we were going to bed, I let Rupert out of the back of my old Range Rover, and walked him around the gravel a couple of times, then took him indoors. He sniffed the air as he entered the house, and paused for a second. But the owner's spaniels had been shut up in the kitchen for the night, and so Rupert eventually followed me up the great staircase. I turned right towards our bedroom, with Rupert padding at my heels. Then a strange thing happened. He froze. I turned to see why he was not beside me and saw that he was half crouching, as if threatened. His hackles were up, and a low, rumbling growl came from deep within him.

'Come on, Rupert,' I said. Some new smell had upset him, I supposed. It was not surprising in a house full of strange dogs. But Rupert would not come on.

Elizabeth appeared at the bedroom door, now clad in her silk dressing gown, and when she saw what the problem was, she came and spoke gently to Rupert. It made no difference. He would not move an inch.

Puzzled, I gave up. If he was not going to be happy in the house there seemed little point in dragging him into our bedroom. I took him back to the car and he scrambled in, his tail thumping once or twice as if to reassure me that he would be much better off out here.

At last I went to bed.

The next day was spent golfing. I played a very moderate game as my concentration had gone, and I felt I was not living up to my host's expectations. Nevertheless, it was a beautiful soft day, and the outing was generally agreed to have been a success. There was some teasing about my poor form, which I took with a restrained smile, and I had to admit it was deserved. My mind had been wandering all day, as if new pathways were opening up inside my head. But outwardly I smiled, and laughed at the jokes.

It was late afternoon when we arrived back at the house, and tea was brought to the drawing room, where we were all sitting. We were chatting about the day when a thought struck me and I stood up. 'Do you mind if I go upstairs while it's still light? I want to get a better look at that picture of the girl on the landing. I couldn't make it out very well last night.'

The owner and his wife looked blank.

'I'm not sure which picture you mean,' he said, after a moment.

'You know, the one with the girl standing looking at the marble angel. It's hung quite low down.'

'Oh, that one,' said the owner's wife. 'It's a funny little picture. We got it with the house. I keep meaning to put something a bit more cheerful there. But there's no girl in it. It's just a rather badly done interior, as far as I remember.'

'Oh,' I said. 'I thought there was. I'd better go and have another look.'

I went upstairs, followed by the owner and Elizabeth. We bent and examined the picture. Now, in the light of day, I could see they were right. There was no human figure in the picture, only a mass of something – was it a shadow? a stain? a blemish in the canvas? – at the juncture of the two landings, where last night I had seen, or imagined, a girl standing. That was what had tricked my eye. As I straightened up I saw recent scratch marks in the varnish of the floorboards of the corridor. Beside them lay a few leaves from a rowan tree that must have blown in from somewhere. It looked as if Rupert had, quite literally, dug his toes in when he stopped here last night. Something had disturbed him.

That visit to Ireland was a while ago. I still remember the melancholy woods around the house, the flocks of rooks fluttering among the trees, or wheeling in great arcs above the dewy pasture of the park. I can remember how I lay awake that night, unable for some reason to sleep, listening to the harsh screeching of an owl, perhaps in the ruined tower. A wind got up and the house creaked, as old houses do, and I imagined, half awake and half asleep, that people were passing up and down the corridor outside. I looked at my bedside travel clock and saw that it was two in the morning. I willed myself to ignore the sounds of the strange house. I fell into uneasy dreams, while Elizabeth breathed steadily beside me, sound asleep. Just before dawn I sank into a deeper slumber, and awoke later than I had intended. We had to rush to catch the ferry back to England.

2

There Was Something Different
about Michael

The morning we returned home from our golfing trip – it was too short to be called a holiday – I had enormous trouble waking Michael up. It was as if he had taken a sleeping pill, maybe several. I had to poke him and even then he lay back on the pillow again, his eyes unfocused, muttering incoherently about dreams.

If there's one thing I can't stand, it is listening to other people talk about their dreams. You know, 'and then I was standing on a roundabout and there was a number fourteen bus coming straight for me, only it wasn't a number fourteen bus, it was a big yellow fire engine'. Dreams are rubbish thrown out by the brain, and should be treated as such.

I finally made Michael understand that we were late for breakfast, and had a ferry to catch. We managed to get up, packed and downstairs, where we had a quick cup of coffee with the people we were staying with. They were very nice; well, he was. The awful thing is, I can't remember their names any more. He was one of Michael's club friends, which means nothing to me. Why should shared membership of a club, which probably has a thousand members, mean that you have anything else in common? But that was typical of Michael. He unquestioningly assumed that every other member of Grouchers was a kindred spirit, which, of course, most of them were very far from being. We had been on some very odd visits to some very odd people which had all started with Michael saying something like, 'The Smiths have asked us shooting. I've accepted. I've heard it is a very good partridge shoot. You haven't met James Smith, but you'll like him, I'm sure.' Then I would be dragged off to some dreadful old pile filled with the most ghastly people, to spend a day trudging across ploughed fields up to my ankles in mud. Afterwards we would return home without me having formed any clear impression of who our hosts actually were.

So, the Irish visit was probably better than most. It had been a comfortable house, full of rather pretty furniture, and the wine and food had been good. I liked the people more than most and when we said goodbye I even asked them to come one day and stalk at Beinn Caorrun. What a joke! I hated going to Beinn Caorrun.

On the journey back from Ireland, I began to feel that there was something different about Michael. I first noticed it on our way to the ferry terminal at Rosslare. But what it was that I had noticed I couldn't exactly define.

'Why do you keep looking at me?' he asked, after another sideways glance from me.

'No special reason,' I said. Then, 'Are you feeling all right?'

'Of course I'm feeling all right,' he said rather snappishly. 'Don't I look all right? Is there a spot on the end of my nose?'

There was no spot. He looked paler than usual, otherwise he appeared as he always did: an untidy mop of prematurely grey hair on top of an angular face with a long, aquiline nose and a good chin. He had grey eyes, to go with his prematurely grey hair, which were now directed at me in a not very friendly glance. He was wearing a grey cable-knit jersey over scruffy brown corduroys. This was the way he always dressed when he wasn't fishing, or golfing, or shooting, or stalking – activities that took up most of his free time.

'You haven't shaved very carefully this morning,' I said.

'If that's what's bothering you, then all I can say is that I am deeply sorry,' said Michael. 'I will try to do better in future.'

I could see we might be on our way to having one of our rows. They used to come out of nowhere, like a squall on a summer's day, about once a month, but lately their frequency had been increasing. So I said nothing. It's not a good idea to have a row in a car. You can't walk out of the room and slam the door when the room is travelling at seventy miles an hour.

I'm making it sound as if we had an unhappy marriage. That's not true. It was what my mother used to call a 'workable' marriage. When I married Michael she warned me not to expect too much.

'These men with too much money and not enough to do can be very self-centred,' she told me. 'I hope you didn't choose him just for his money.'

I didn't choose Michael for his money; not only for his money. I met him at a dinner party about ten years ago, when I was in my early twenties; well, my mid-twenties. Michael was sitting on my left. The man on my right was the host, Peter Robinson, whose wife Mary had been my best friend since school days. I chatted to Peter through the starter and halfway through the main course, rather dry roast pheasant with gravy that tasted like dishwater. Mary is one of the sweetest people I know, but you don't go to her dinner parties for the cooking. I don't normally remember food unless it is very good indeed, but I remember everything about that night, when my life began to change.

I decided I ought to turn my head in the opposite direction towards my neighbour, who was sitting in silence while the girl on his left was listening to a joke being told by someone across the table.

'So what do you do with yourself when you're not at one of Peter's parties?' I asked in a bright voice, after we had reintroduced ourselves.

'Do?' he asked, as if I had accused him of being a drug dealer. 'I don't *do* anything.'

This was not a promising start, but Peter was now busy talking to the girl on his right, so I was stuck.

'You must do something?' I repeated.

'Must I?' he said. Then suddenly his face creased into the most charming smile. 'People keep telling me that.'

'You seriously do have to do something,' I told him. 'Otherwise how on earth do you get through your day?'

'I manage my affairs,' he said, still smiling. 'They aren't very interesting, but managed they must be.'

This was hard work.

'Do you live in London?' I asked.

'Some of the time,' he said. I thought he was going to stop there, in which case I would probably have to pretend to faint, or run screaming from the room. Then he added, 'But I live in Scotland some of the time too, in Perthshire.'

'That sounds very nice,' I said encouragingly.

'It is. It's God's country.'

'What do you do up there?'

'I look after things. We have some land ... and things to look after. What about you? You obviously expect everyone to be busy, so I imagine you are?'

'I work for a woman's magazine,' I said, and told him the name.

We talked for a while about life on magazines, and the London property market, which is mostly what I write about. I had only recently started my career as a journalist, and already lived in weekly fear of being sacked by Celia, my capricious editor. My neighbour made an impressive effort to appear interested, and I decided my first reading of him as a Triple A star bore might have been a bit harsh. Then Peter made all his guests do a manoeuvre, which normally I hate, but on this occasion I was grateful for. The men stood up and moved two places to their left and I found myself sitting beside someone different for the pudding course.

After dinner, the men stayed behind in the dining room with a decanter of port, and I sat with Mary and the other girls in the drawing room. I managed to get a quick briefing on the guests I hadn't met before. The second man I had sat next to I already knew from a previous evening at Peter and Mary's flat, so I asked instead about the first one.

'Michael Gascoigne?' Mary said. 'I saw you struggling a bit.'

She smiled and I said apologetically, 'Was it that obvious?'

'No, but I know what he's like. He's really very nice if you get to know him.'

'What does he do?' I queried. 'He was very offhand when I asked him.'

'He's embarrassed because he really doesn't do anything at all, and in London everyone does something. That's why he lives most of the time up in Perthshire. His family owns some land up there. There are a lot of trees, some sheep and deer, and I think he may have a few holiday cottages as well. Then there's the house. It's a very cold place. I've been there with Peter and I nearly died of damp and hypothermia. He mopes about up there, looks after his holiday lets and changes the light bulbs when they pop; generally keeps the show on the road. I think he gets an income from that.'

'And he has a flat in London?'

'Yes, near Baker Street. Peter's just put him up for membership of Grouchers, so he must be thinking about spending more time in town.'

'What's Grouchers?' I asked.

'It's a very pompous men's club that Peter goes to when he's fed up with me.'

Then the men came into the drawing room and that was the end of that.

I thought no more about Michael that night, and by the next morning he had almost faded from my memory. Nevertheless, when I bumped into him outside Selfridges after work a week later, I recognised him almost at once. The first thing I saw was a tall, stooped man in an old waxed jacket and scruffy cords being tugged along the pavement by a black Labrador puppy. The man, even more than the dog, looked so out of place and un-London-like that he caught my attention, and then I recognised him.

He did not recognise me. I heard him say, 'Oh, for God's sake,' as the puppy wound the lead, one of those extendable affairs, around a lamp-post. He started to untangle the dog. I could have walked straight past and almost did, but for some reason I stopped. I don't know why. There was something rather hopeless and vulnerable in the sight of such a big man being towed around by such a small dog. I put a hand on his arm and said, 'Hello. Do you remember me?'

He straightened up and looked at me, then smiled.

'It's Elizabeth, isn't it?'

'That's clever of you.'

'Not at all. I enjoyed meeting you. This is Rupert.'

The puppy, already quite well grown, jumped up and put muddy paws on my skirt.

'Oh, I'm so sorry,' said Michael. 'Get down, Rupert.'

'Don't worry,' I said. 'It'll brush off.'

'At least let me pay for the dry cleaning,' he said, 'or let me buy you a cup of tea? He looked at his watch. 'Or how about a glass of wine? It's after six.'

'It gets better,' I said. 'I'll go for the glass of wine.'

That is how I started seeing Michael Gascoigne. He was probably the least exciting man I had ever gone out with, yet, after a while, it was as if there had never been anyone else. He was very solid and dependable. I soon learned that whatever Michael said he would do, he did. He never boasted, or told an untruth, or made a promise he could not keep. He was the most utterly reliable man I had ever met, contrasting vividly with two or three hopeless boyfriends and indeed my own father, who had sauntered out of the family home when I was sixteen to go off with a girl half his age and live in the South of France. Yet there was a melancholy quality to Michael, a sense of bewilderment about him, as if at some point in his life something had happened to him that he didn't quite under-stand. Sometimes I noticed a strained, puzzled look in his eyes which made me feel sorry for him, and want to look after him.

I also learned that Michael was nowhere near as idle as he pretended to be. His mother had died when he was sixteen, his father five years later. (That was rather a tragic story: his father had been caught out in a snowstorm on Beinn Caorrun, the family mountain, and had never been found.) Since Michael had inherited at the age of twenty-one, he had been acting as his own factor, running the estate in Perthshire that had been in his family for the last hundred years or more. At the foot of the mountain is a valley through which the River Gala runs, and along its banks there were a good number of cottages, which had once housed foresters and shepherds and other estate workers. These Michael had done up and let out as holiday cottages. Then there were several hundred acres of forestry, and a bit of trout fishing on the hill lochs; and stalking, which Michael mostly let, although he kept a couple of weeks for himself and his friends, as it had always been a passion of his. All in all, the income from Beinn Caorrun had kept Michael comfortably off since he inherited it, and even marrying me did not cramp his style too much. But then he was never very extravagant in the first place.

Caorrun Lodge was another matter. It was ghastly, and I wouldn't go there unless I absolutely had to. Michael refused to spend a penny on it, and it was as close to falling down as a house could be while still standing.

When I told my mother that Michael had proposed to me she raised an eyebrow. She had met him by then, of course.

'He won't set the world on fire,' she said. It was one of my mother's favourite phrases.

'I don't think the world needs to be set on fire,' I said mildly. 'Michael's all right as he is.'

My mother searched in her handbag and extracted her cigarette holder and a packet of cigarettes. She stuck a cigarette in one end of the holder and lit it with a small gold Dunhill lighter. The smell of Turkish tobacco filled the air as my mother exhaled, arching her eyebrows to emphasise her resemblance to someone in a play by Noël Coward.

'You won't be poor, at any rate,' she said. 'I knew the parents a long time ago. They were very dull and very rich. I dare say Michael has inherited some money as well as his Scottish place.'

'That's not why I'm marrying him,' I said, blushing. My mother saw my blushes and smiled, but spared me further comment. After all, while I was (more or less) independent from a financial point of view, my mother herself depended on a very erratic alimony payment and a trickle of dividends from some shares my grandfather had left her. It would be a relief for her to take me off her worry list.

'And you'll be marrying the dog, as well.'

'I adore Rupert,' I said. I was on more certain ground there. My mother leaned back in her armchair and drew on her cigarette again. Through the wreaths of smoke she looked at me. This time the brittle tone of voice that was customary to her was gone, and she spoke gently.

'You don't really love him, do you?'

She meant Michael, not Rupert.

'I don't know,' I said. 'Mummy, I wish you wouldn't ask me about such things.'

'It's something parents tend to do,' she said. I could see, without her needing to say anything, that she was thinking not of me, but of her own marriage, which had once been full of promise yet ended in desertion. She sighed.

'I suppose you'll be happy enough.'

'Michael will look after me,' I said confidently. 'And I'll look after him. It'll work out, Mummy.'

I was not quite sure myself why I had accepted Michael's proposal of marriage. It had taken me by surprise when it came. I had thought, if I had ever thought about it at all, that my affair with Michael would one day just fade away. He would forget to ring me, or I would forget to ring him, and that would be the end of it. Sometimes I thought that our relationship was like lying in a warm bath; it is very agreeable for a while, but when the water cools down you have to make an effort and climb out.

The evening that Michael proposed to me he had asked me out to dinner at the Italian restaurant just around the corner from his flat. We had been there several times before, and they knew us. The food was average, but the people were friendly and knew what we liked. At some point in the evening, Michael refilled my glass of wine, and then raised his own and said, 'To us.'

This was rather theatrical for Michael, so I raised my eyebrows. 'And what is the occasion?'

He put his glass down and said, very seriously, 'You know, since my father went missing, I've been an orphan. I need someone to look after me, Elizabeth.'

I went rigid. He couldn't, could he? He wouldn't, would he? What the hell would I say if he proposed?

'Oh dear, put like that, you probably do need looking after,' I said, or some such rubbish.

His face assumed a contorted look as one hand dived into his trouser pocket. Men can be so clumsy. I hoped he might be about to sneeze, and was looking for his handkerchief, but out came a small blue leather box. He put it down carefully on the table, then opened it. We both stared at the ring inside. It was a rock, a seriously large diamond in a pearl setting.

'It was my mother's,' he said. 'Thank God she wasn't wearing it when she drowned.'

Michael had mentioned his mother's accident before but had never gone into actual details of how either of his parents had died. Now did not seem like the time.

'Elizabeth,' he said, looking straight at me, with his steadfast, boring look. There was no mistaking it now. My past started racing through my head.

'Elizabeth, will you marry me?' he asked.

Time slowed down. On the one hand, could I really face spending the next forty or fifty years with a man whose idea of an adrenalin rush was playing bridge at his club? On the other hand, Michael was kind. He would, I felt sure, never mistreat me or betray me, or wander out of my life with a girl half his age as my father had done. And he was well off. How well off I did not know, but there was evidence of real wealth in his life: the pair of guns he had inherited from his father which he once told me were insured for fifty thousand pounds; the ring in front of me, with its enormous diamond; the estate up in Perthshire which I had not seen at that point. My own life was precarious enough. I didn't need to get married yet. I was still young – although several of my friends had already married. I had a job that I had a love–hate relationship with, but it was anything but secure; people were fired in my office for turning up at work in the same coloured dress as Celia. One's subconscious mind, however, makes all the real decisions and I must have weighed all this up a good while ago, for it took me only a moment or two to answer, even if it felt like days.

'Yes, Michael,' I said. 'I'd love to marry you.'

He beamed all over his face and leaned across to kiss me. There was a burst of cheering from the Italian waiters who were clearly in the know, and then one of them came forward with a huge bouquet of white and crimson roses which had been hidden behind the bar. Suddenly everyone in the restaurant was laughing and talking, swept up in the occasion, and Michael was even laughing out loud.

Yes, I thought to myself, I'll probably be happy enough with Michael.

I *had* hoped that my father, for once in his life, would make some gesture of recognition that I was his daughter, and come back to England for the wedding. He did at least write, which was something. My mother read the letter out loud, as we sat around the table in her kitchen. I did not trust myself to speak after I had opened the letter, so I scanned it quickly and then handed it to her.

'"Darling Betty,"' my mother read, '"I was so pleased to hear that you are at last about to be wed. I remember John and Mary Gascoigne quite well, although I am not sure I have ever met Michael. He was never on parade when I encountered them, which was usually racing somewhere. The parents were very rich and rather dreary, so you are probably getting the best part of the bargain by not having living in-laws. I am sure Michael has turned out to be an excellent fellow, my darling Betty, otherwise you wouldn't be marrying him, would you? Sadly the date you kindly mentioned when your dear old Pa was to have given you away is not free. We have asked the Billancourts down from

Paris to stay that week and I simply won't be able to get away."'

Here my mother raised her head and actually snorted with annoyance. The Billancourts were the parents of Marie-Claire, the girl my father had run off with, and her parents were about the same age as my father.

'"I will of course be thinking of you and I hope the enclosed cheque will be useful when you come to set up home. Your loving Pa."'

A cheque for one thousand francs had fluttered out of the envelope and lay upon the table.

'Well,' said my mother when she had read this, 'Your father is running true to form, I suppose. I never really thought he would come. Don't cry, darling, he's not worth it. You might be able to get a few coffee mugs for the kitchen with the money.'

'I'm not crying,' I said, angrily wiping away a tear.

In the end, Henry Newark gave me away. He was one of my mother's grander friends, and as my only other living male relative, Robert Fenham, my mother's brother, had Alzheimer's, we had to ask someone from outside the family. Henry was, I think, bemused by the request, but he was a kind man and enjoyed parties, so he accepted. The wedding was held in the church of Stanton St Mary, a pretty medieval building in Cotswold stone, and afterwards the reception was given in a marquee in what my mother called the Park, a rough paddock of a few acres that lay to the south of the house beyond a ha-ha.

My mother's house was her family home, inherited from her parents and was a charming, if not particularly large, dwelling of six bedrooms or so, which might once have been a farmhouse. Now it was what estate agents call a 'gent's res', with a dining room and a drawing room and a small study-cum-sitting room where my mother actually spent most of her time. Outside was a stable block built around a cobbled courtyard although the ponies had disappeared the week my father left all those years ago, and the stalls were now used as potting sheds. On the west side of the house was a small garden surrounded by herbaceous borders, and then the paddock on the far side of the ha-ha; a strip of coppiced beech wood marked the boundary.

The house stood on the edge of Stanton St Mary, suggesting a squierarchical detachment from the rest of the village which my mother relished, although by no means did she have the income to support such aspirations. Stanton St Mary was a quiet village, surrounded by mournful water meadows often covered in low mist. A small tributary of the Severn wound its way around the edges of the village. Today the paddock was brightened by the presence of a large marquee and, as I looked out of my bedroom window, I could see that the caterer's van had already arrived.

'Come *on*, darling!' called my mother from the foot of the stairs. 'You mustn't be late for your own wedding.'

The truth was, that that morning I was having a bad attack of second thoughts. Perhaps everyone does on such occasions. I had spent a long time, between three in the morning and breakfast, wondering why on earth I was marrying a man I hardly knew, despite having been in a relationship with him for several months. It hadn't occurred to me to wonder why I knew so little about him, why he appeared to be without family or without friends other than fellow members of Grouchers, the club he had recently become a member of. There had even been times when I wondered whether there was not something wrong with Michael; quite badly wrong. From time to time he would retreat into a mood that seemed very like a dull kind of despair, as if life were altogether too much for him. When those fits overcame him, I wasn't sure whether I could stand being with him for the rest of the day, let alone the rest of my life. But then the mood would pass and he would be almost normal again; almost. We didn't laugh a lot together, though. I wasn't at all sure that, if for some reason Michael himself failed to turn up at the church, I would really mind that much, once the initial embarrassment was over. I almost hoped he wouldn't. What would we *do* with ourselves for the next fifty years or so?

But Michael would turn up. That much I did know about him. He always turned up if he said he was going to.

Henry Newark was there at the entrance to the church, resplendent in his grey morning suit, and when we marched down the aisle together Michael, who was waiting in front of the altar with Peter Robinson standing next to him, turned to look at me. Then his whole face lit up in the most brilliant smile I had ever seen and, for a moment at least, everything was all right.

It was after the wedding that something odd happened. The reception in the marquee was in full swing, the speeches were over and everyone was enjoying themselves and making a lot of noise. The guests were an odd mixture of my friends, quite numerous, my mother's friends, almost as many, a few of what my mother called 'the locals' from the village, and a very sparse scattering of members of Grouchers and their wives. This last group, invited by Michael, huddled together in a corner, looking over their shoulders with disdain at the other guests, and clearly wondered why on earth they had got caught up in this rout. They were Michael's 'friends'; of his family, there was none. The whole mixture was being entertained by a really dreadful string quartet my mother had insisted on hiring, who were sawing away at Mozart's Hundred Greatest Hits in one corner of the marquee.

Michael and I had slipped away to the house to change into our going-away clothes. For some inexplicable reason, I was downstairs first. I stood in the hall and saw, through the front door, which was open, that someone had parked a Land Rover in the yard. Then a tall, grey-haired man came out of the kitchen.

'Oh, I'm sorry if I startled you. I was looking for Michael. You must be Elizabeth.'

He was wearing an old tweed suit, and was not in any way dressed for a wedding reception. He had a full head of crinkly grey hair and a strong face that looked as if its owner spent a good deal of time out of doors.

'I'm Alex Grant,' he said. 'I'm an old friend of Michael's parents. The family doctor from Glen Gala. I've been staying with friends in Oxfordshire, who told me that you and Michael were getting married today. Wonderful news. I hope you don't mind me dropping in like this, but I had to come and congratulate you both and drop off my wedding present. I've left it on the kitchen table. It's not something I would trust to the post.'

Alex Grant? I had never heard his name before and felt sure he was not on the invitation list. So this man must be a gatecrasher. He was a very polite gatecrasher, although I would have preferred it if he had not kept on staring at me.

'Thank you very much,' I said, not knowing what else to say.

'And how is Michael?' he asked. 'He must be a very happy man today.'

'Michael is very well,' I said. 'He should be downstairs in a moment. I don't know what's keeping him.'

Alex Grant glanced in the direction of the staircase and then said, in a lower voice, 'I'm glad to hear it. I haven't heard anything from him, or from Stephen Gunnerton, for quite a while, so I assumed that everything had settled down. And when I heard he was getting married, I couldn't have been more delighted by the news.'

I didn't know what to make of this. Who was Stephen Gunnerton? What, or who, had settled down? I felt I had to say something.

'Thank you,' I replied. 'Michael will be down in a minute. Why don't you go across to the tent and get yourself something to drink? We'll come over in a moment and say hello properly.'

'Oh, I don't think I will,' he said. 'I'm not really dressed for a wedding, and I daren't have anything to drink as I have to drive back to Oxfordshire in a minute; I mustn't abandon my friends for too long.'

I wished Michael would come downstairs. What on earth could he be doing for all this time? Then Michael did appear and when he saw Alex Grant he stood stock still.

'Hello, Michael,' said Alex Grant. 'I hope you don't mind me looking in unexpectedly like this – I was staying nearby and thought I would come and say hello.'

'Hello, Dr Grant,' said Michael slowly. He did not smile. 'I am very well. How are you?'

Michael's voice was at its most wooden, as if he were really a cleverly constructed automaton. For a moment, although it felt like half an hour, the two men looked at each other. It was very strange: I felt as if some unspoken communication passed between them, an acknowledgement of something unsaid. Then Alex Grant looked at his watch and shook his head.

'Well,' he said, 'I mustn't keep you from your guests. Elizabeth, I'm delighted to have met you, and I hope you will look me up when you come to Glen Gala. Michael, many congratulations on your ... on your new life.'

Then he was gone, and a moment later I heard the sound of the Land Rover as it drove out of the yard.

I looked at Michael. His face was expressionless.

'Who was that?' I asked.

'Our local GP up in Perthshire,' said Michael. 'I should have asked him, I suppose. He was a very good friend of my parents. I forgot.'

'He brought us a present,' I said. 'That was nice of him. He left it in the kitchen.'

In the kitchen, unencumbered by wrapping paper, was a rather beautiful antique crystal decanter, with a card propped against it bearing the inscription: 'To Elizabeth and Michael'.

I showed the present to Michael.

'Isn't it lovely?' I said. 'You can keep your whisky in it.'

Michael glanced at the decanter without comment. Then he steered me out of the house and together we walked back to the marquee to say our goodbyes.

So, we were married, and Michael, Rupert and I began our life at number 2, Helmsdale Mansions, not far from Baker Street. Despite my not infrequent doubts, I knew I had done the right thing in saying yes to Michael. There was something different about him: some quality, like a placid river at night whose dark and even surface is suddenly ruffled by a breeze and turns quicksilver in the moonlight. He was solid, dependable, steady and respectable: all those things. Dull as ditchwater might be another way of putting it, only he wasn't dull: just when you thought he was going to be, there was that smile, which made him look years younger than he pretended to be; or an unconscious flash of poetry in his language; or that far-off look, as if he were trying to remember a dream he had. He was, I soon realised, a very intelligent man who read widely and thought deeply; but as he never told anyone what he was reading or what he was thinking about, people tended to write him off as a bore.

But he never did anything out of the ordinary. Instead his life became ever more a matter of routine. Perhaps I had not noticed before we were married how Michael always rolled up the toothpaste tube into a tight scroll to make sure he got out every last drop. My toothpaste tube had always looked as if someone had jumped on it. Michael was the only man I had ever known who put shoe trees in his shoes every night, and folded his trousers in a trouser press. At breakfast, when he boiled an egg, he would almost be driven to distraction if I spoke to him while it was cooking, in case he left it in for too long. His routines were impressive, unvarying and claustrophobic.

He had become a member of Grouchers not long before we were married. Now, to keep himself amused while he was in London, he accepted the position of part-time membership secretary, a ten-to-four job for a few months of the year. Grouchers was one of those institutions that could only have been invented in Britain, where men left the regimentation of their offices for a regimentation of their own invention.

And so our life went on. Our winters were spent together in London. In the summer Michael spent time at Caorrun, and I went up for the odd weekend, but only when he made a scene about my never going there. We had no children; a matter of choice, rather than biology. I found I needed to keep going with my job, as sitting around in number 2 Helmsdale Mansions waiting for Michael to come home and tell me about the bridge tournament results might have shrunk my world a little more tightly around me than I could bear.

I enjoyed my job, writing about the property market in central London, with occasional pieces about completely unaffordable country houses. The prices always went up, the flats and houses grew smarter every year, and it was not hard to find something to say about them. The magazine and its spurious glamour and genuine spite and gossip kept me amused, and enabled me to cope with the predictable nature of our domestic life. I suppose the income, slight as it was, gave me the illusion of independence as well.

We varied the monotony of London life with frequent excursions, occasionally to stay with fellow members of Grouchers, or with visits to Michael's estate in Perthshire. Proper holidays abroad seemed to be out of the question. Michael could never see the point of 'abroad', and disliked the heat and foreign food. He never described our absences from London as holidays. To him, one went up to Scotland, or down to London. One was either away, or in Town. The concept of a holiday was offensive to him, as if all his golf and fishing and stalking were stolen moments, instead of the main purpose of his life. And I went with him. I sat shivering on river banks while Michael stood in the middle of a river casting; or else I sat in the car with steamed-up windows, reading my book. In the end I learned to fish, and even to golf a bit, although I drew the line at stalking. How anyone could shoot those poor animals was beyond me, but Michael told me that if he didn't cull the deer, the Deer Commission would do it anyway, to prevent them from starving to death in the winter.

The one thing I could say about my marriage to Michael was that in those first years it was exactly as I had expected it to be. I had a large and comfortable flat not too far from the centre of London; a big improvement on the two-roomed affair well to the north of Ladbroke Grove where I had previously lived. I had the pleasure of saying to people, when they asked what I was doing that weekend, 'Oh, we're going to spend a few days at our place up in Perthshire' in a way that made people who had never been there feel rather envious.

It was a modern marriage. I didn't have very strong feelings for Michael, but I liked him. It wasn't the romance of a lifetime, but I'd had romances and they tended to end up looking rather shabby. Marriage was about commitment, not love; wasn't it?

I still remember the day my mother found my father in the hall at home. I was on the landing at the head of the stairs; they did not see me, so when they started speaking, I stopped where I was. My mother came in from the garden with a trug full of cut sweet peas, and saw my father, suitcases packed, bending down to check his appearance in the oval mirror that hung above a small side table. He was wearing a tweed suit and looked rather smart, as if he were going racing. He straightened the knot in his tie and then turned and saw my mother. For a moment neither of them said anything, then my mother spoke, so softly and slowly I could only just make out her words.

'You really are going,' she said. 'I thought it was just talk.'

'Oh, darling, there you are,' he said. 'I've been looking for you. I was going to leave a note. I think the talking has gone on long enough, don't you? We don't seem to be getting anywhere.'

'You're going to go off with that girl, aren't you? She's barely older than Elizabeth.'

'We've been through all of that.'

'It's disgusting. I can't believe you really mean to do it. How could you?'

My father took his old silver cigarette case out of his pocket and extracted a cigarette, then closed the case again with a click. He took his lighter out of another pocket and lit his cigarette. After a moment he exhaled, then said, 'I have a romantic nature.'

My mother gave a small scream, and then put her hand over her mouth. She made no further sound but I could tell she had begun to sob because her shoulders were shaking.

'You said you would think about it,' she whispered in a trembling voice quite unlike her normal speech. I realised this was the tail end of a conversation that must have been going on for weeks, or months. My father shrugged. He did not say anything else for a moment. Then there was the noise of wheels on the gravel outside.

'That'll be the taxi,' he said. 'I must go. Say goodbye to Elizabeth for me, will you? I couldn't find her either.'

'What will we do?' asked my mother. 'What do you expect us to live on? How do you expect us to survive?'

'Well,' said my father, stubbing his cigarette out in an ashtray on the hall table, 'you've got this perfectly nice house, which is your own property and unmortgaged. I dare say you can find a solicitor to talk to about extracting some alimony from me. Apart from that, I really don't have any suggestions. You know I hate goodbyes. I'm going now.'

He picked up his suitcases and walked out of the front door. My mother stood quite still and said not another word as he left. As I stood in the shadows at the top of the stairs, swallowing to try to get rid of a lump in my throat that had grown bigger and bigger as I listened to my parents talk, I knew that my life was about to change for ever.

I never saw my father again after that day, although he did, now and then, remember my birthday and send me a card with small gifts of money. That was years ago, but I still remember with perfect clarity every second of that brief, scene. I didn't want a marriage that was going to end the way my mother's had. I wanted someone I could trust.

I thought I sensed in Michael a determination to make our marriage work, and last, which meant more to me than any romantic declarations or passionate embraces. There had been very little of either. I felt – perhaps with very little concrete evidence – that Michael really loved me and that he just had more difficulty than most men in expressing his emotions. When he proposed to me it was with every appearance of sincerity, albeit in the tones of someone reading the weather forecast. The day after I had accepted, he took out his diary and tried to find a date for the wedding that was free from golfing, fishing, shooting or committee meetings at his club.

Anyway, that was then and this is now. Since we came back from Ireland at the end of August, there has been something different about Michael. All the way from Fishguard to London he hardly talked at all, except once, as we sat in a queue on the M4. It was dark, and a column of red brake lights stretched ahead of us into an infinite distance. Michael turned to me and said, 'Lamia.'

I heard it distinctly but I did not know what the word meant: I had never heard it before. It sounded like the Latin name for a plant, or some uncomfortable skin condition, or even a foreign country; there are so many new ones these days. His eyes were wide open and he was staring at me, or through me, in a way that made me feel uncomfortable. His face looked thinner somehow, as if he had lost weight. It was all planes and angles in the light from the dashboard. Then he turned away again to look at the road.

'Lamia? What do you mean?' I asked.

Michael said nothing, just hunched over the steering wheel, tapping it with a forefinger as the car moved forward another six inches.

'What do you mean?' I asked again.

He heard me and turned back.

'What do you mean, what do I mean?'

'You said a word, a foreign word. I wondered what it meant.'

'I don't recall saying anything,' he said.

'I'm sure that you did.'

He said nothing.

'Michael? Did you?'

'Perhaps I was clearing my throat,' he said. 'I really don't remember saying anything to you. Will that do? This damned traffic jam is beginning to drive me mad.'

There was definitely something different about Michael that day.

3

Mr Patel's Membership
Application

The morning after we got back from Ireland, Elizabeth was up early. I found her in the kitchen reading emails and text messages from her office on her mobile, which I had not allowed her to take to Ireland, because she would have spent the entire time taking calls. The previous night she had been too tired to do anything except crawl into bed.

She was stalking up and down the kitchen with a mug of Nescafé in one hand and her mobile in the other, muttering to herself.

'Everything all right?' I asked, appearing in the doorway in my dressing gown and slippers.

'No, everything is *not* all right,' she said. 'I go away for a few days and not one thing – not *one single thing* – that I asked to be done has happened. Celia will *kill* me. I probably won't have a job by tonight.'

'Oh, dear,' I said, pacifyingly. I had never actually spoken to Celia, Elizabeth's editor and boss, but she appeared to be a strong-minded woman.

'It's all right for you,' she said, turning on me. 'You can wander into your blessed club at any time you like and have a long lunch and be home in time for tea. If I get away from the office before eight tonight, I shall be very lucky.'

'Shall I book a table at the Italian?' I asked.

'If you want something to eat tonight, then yes. I won't be doing any cooking.'

She drained her mug of coffee, slammed it down on the sink, and left, banging the front door behind her.

It wasn't just the office. Our relationship had not been easy of late. Sometimes I wondered whether it had ever been easy; I wondered why Elizabeth had even married me in the first place. Because I'd asked her, I suppose. I knew why I had married Elizabeth. She was my chance. She was my one chance at happiness, normality, and all the things I wanted. If I was capable of love, I loved Elizabeth. But my version of love wasn't always enough to keep her happy.

I went back to my dressing room, and put on a dark grey suit, a pin-striped shirt and a dark blue tie, and then came back into the kitchen and made myself a slice of toast and a pot of coffee. While I bit into the toast and sipped the coffee, I read the front page of the *Daily Telegraph*; then I folded it and put it in my briefcase to finish later in my office at the club.

Grouchers was a quarter of an hour's walk from the flat, and as it was a dry morning I decided to risk leaving the umbrella at home. The streets and squares were bright with the luminous light of early autumn, the leaves in the small park I walked through just beginning to turn, the air warm and exhilarating without the stuffiness of a summer's day in London. I walked at a leisurely pace down Baker Street, across Oxford Street and into the outskirts of Mayfair.

Here was my place of work for a few months every year: a private members' club called Grouchers, after its founder Emmanuel Groucher, a successful wine merchant who had lived near Oxford Street towards the end of the nineteenth century. The club was established in a town house, at the corner of a small mews, which was held on a long lease on very generous terms from the estate of a Duke of Rotherham who had once been a member. Grouchers did not have the political or social connections of some of the better-known clubs farther south, in and around St James's Street. It aspired to be nothing more than a club where members could lunch or dine together, and escape for a few hours from their wives by playing bridge or backgammon. There were no bedrooms. There was a pretty dining room, a bar, a morning room, a couple of card rooms, and a vast marble space occupied by gentlemen's lavatories equipped with mahogany and porcelain furnishings. There was a hall with a porter's lodge, a cloakroom, an extensive wine cellar in the basement, and that was Grouchers.

It suited me. I found its dignified spaces reassuring: the committee rooms lined with leather-bound volumes; the dining room with its oil paintings of racehorses or still lives featuring dead pheasants; the morning room where the only sound was the rustle of pages being turned as members considered their sporting bets for the day. I was comfortable with most of the other members too. No one ever asked a personal question; indeed, few questions were ever asked. Most conversation was in the form of grunted affirmations when another speaker execrated the latest remarks of some politician or other, or else the performance of the English cricket team. I appreciated the calm routines and pre-dictability of life at Grouchers.

When I joined the club – or, more truthfully, was pushed by Peter Robinson into taking out membership – it was like putting on a uniform that said everything about me that anyone needed to know: I was simply a member of Grouchers. What I might have been before I joined, no one cared. I had passed the entrance requirements, and therefore I was one of them.

The only qualification required to join Grouchers was the support of six members – which Peter Robinson organised without any need for effort on my part – and an understanding that the candidate was 'a gentleman'. Emmanuel Groucher had once memorably defined the concept of what a gentleman was by saying: 'Whatever it is, it's not the sort of damned fellow who talks to everybody at breakfast.' In fact it was impossible to get breakfast at Grouchers, so there was no practical way of carrying out this test on aspiring members. Nevertheless, the idea was understood at Grouchers, and most of its members barely talked at all, let alone during meals. Conversation in the dining room tended to focus on requests for the butter dish or the salt to be passed. In the bar, or in the gaming room, one was allowed to be more loquacious as long as it was within measure. No female, apart from Mrs Thornton and the waitresses that served us at lunch or dinner, had ever set foot in Grouchers.

The members were mostly Londoners: solicitors, accountants, chartered surveyors, retired soldiers. They all dressed and behaved with the greatest degree of respectability. One never saw brown shoes being worn with a blue suit, or a loud tie. Most members erred on the side of sombre in their dress. Now, as I walked through the small squares and side streets that lay along my route to Grouchers, I was conscious of different feelings about the club. It no longer seemed, as it once had, a haven or refuge. I was conscious, for the first time, of a question forming itself in my mind: what was the point of Grouchers?

When I arrived at the club James, the day porter, was in his lodge and he greeted me.

'Morning, Mr Gascoigne. Did you win your game of golf in Ireland, sir?'

'Lost it, I'm sorry to report, James.'

James shook his head and smiled sadly, whether in commiseration or in despair at my obvious lack of technique, one could not say. I went down the corridor and through the door marked 'Private' that led to the offices. Here was a room occupied by Mr Verey-Jones, the club secretary, who dealt with every aspect of club life except one. I had worked with him now for several years and had no idea what his first name was or, indeed, if he had one.

Verey-Jones employed the staff, and managed the wine cellar, and worked out the menus with the chef; stored the cigars and organised for the decorators to come in once a year to smarten the place up when we closed in August. He chaired the Club Rules Committee, a small group that was more enigmatic than the Druids. Every five or ten years the committee produced a minor amendment to the rule book, which was studied with the closest attention by all members when it was finally posted on the noticeboard.

When Verey-Jones saw me come into the office, he stood up, brandishing a slip of paper.

'Ah, Gascoigne. I think we've got it. I think we've finally got it.'

He waved the slip of paper in front of me, looking as Neville Chamberlain must have looked when he got off the plane on his return from Berchtesgaden. I took the paper from him and studied it. It said:

'Bye Law no. 31: the words "members are requested not

to have their mobile phones switched on and should not use them on the club premises" have been replaced by "members shall not use their mobile phones (or other electronic equipment) on the premises"'.

'Ah, yes,' I said, 'very good.'

'The use of the word "shall" is so much more prescriptive, I feel,' said Verey-Jones. 'It took us a long time to come up with the right word, but I feel it has been worth it.'

'Yes, indeed it has,' I said.

Verey-Jones looked at me for a moment to see whether I might be a little more enthusiastic but when I said nothing further, he commented, 'There's post for you, Gascoigne. I hope you're with us for a day or two, as there's quite a backlog. Mrs Thornton has the letters for you.'

Mrs Thornton was the secretary who did the typing and bookkeeping for the club and really, if anyone kept the place going, it was her. My role as membership secretary was a relatively new position, created to relieve Verey-Jones of his excess workload, about which he had been inclined to complain in recent years. I think I was of some help to him, in a minor way. We both knew that I didn't need the money, which was a fairly small stipend. We also both knew that I had the confidence of the membership, an important point if one was to be entrusted with managing the process by which applicants for membership to the club were admitted – or were not admitted. So when I said to Verey-Jones, 'I'm here for two or three days, but then I've got to go up to Scotland to check up on things there,' I knew it would irritate him, but there was nothing he could do about it.

He grunted, and withdrew behind his desk. I walked across the office and straightened a picture that was hanging slightly crooked, a drawing of Oxford Street in the 1890s featuring Emmanuel Groucher's wine emporium. Mrs Thornton greeted me with a friendly smile and a cup of coffee, and then handed me a sheaf of post. I thanked her and started to go through the letters. About half came from the sons of members being put up by their fathers or uncles, and admission was almost automatic unless the family had a history of falling behind with subscription payments. There were a couple of names I did not know, but the members introducing them I did, and I felt confident they would not put forward anyone who would not fit in. There was one letter I put to one side: it was from a man I knew to be a recruitment consultant, and he wanted to introduce a colleague as a member. I imagined them turning the dining room into a place where they interviewed people; something that had to be stopped. I decided to have a word with Verey-Jones later, to see how we could knock the idea on its head. Then there was a letter whose handwriting I recognised immediately. It was from Peter Robinson, my barrister friend.

'Dear Michael,' it began, and ran on through a few lines about what an outstandingly good member his proposed candidate would be, and how he had found six members to support him. My eyes skipped over all this and came to rest on the candidate's name. It was Vijay Patel.

This gave me something to think about. On the one hand, if Peter Robinson was putting Mr Patel forward, then I could be sure that Mr Patel would be in every way an excellent future member of the club. Peter's judgement was impeccable. On the other hand, if Grouchers had any defining characteristic it was as a refuge for prejudices of every sort that could not be aired in public. Indeed, it might be said that Grouchers was a fantasy world, where perfectly normal middle-aged, middle-class men were transformed for a few hours by a collective mania into behaving and speaking as if they were inhabiting some last outpost of the British Empire in the 1950s.

I thought I ought to have a word with Peter about his candidate when he came in at lunchtime. Before then I had time to finish the rest of my post, dictate some letters to Mrs Thornton, and still have quarter of an hour to spend doing the Sudoku puzzles in the newspaper.

During lunch I spotted Peter coming into the dining room and gave him a nod. When he had finished eating I came up behind him at the coffee urn. 'Peter. How nice to see you. Can we have a quiet word?'

Peter turned and smiled. He filled two cups of coffee, one for each of us, and then we repaired to a far corner of the morning room that was reserved by tradition for confidential conversations. We sat opposite each other in two huge armchairs covered in cracked brown leather.

'It's about Mr Patel, isn't it?' said Peter, as soon as we had sat down.

'Yes, it is. Tell me a bit more about him.'

Peter shrugged and said, 'Not much to tell. He's the son of a Ugandan Asian businessman who came here in the 1960s to get away from Idi Amin. Vijay's an investment banker, very successful. He has beautiful manners. He is by far the best amateur spin bowler in our part of Hertfordshire. That's how I know him.'

Peter and Mary Robinson lived in Hertfordshire at weekends and Peter was mad about cricket. When I said nothing, he went on, 'And yes, he would be the first member of this club who didn't have white skin.'

'Some members might feel a little uncomfortable about your choice, Peter,' I said gently. 'You know it is my job to mention possible difficulties. The last thing we want is to have a member's candidate blackballed. Especially a member as widely respected as you.'

'That's bollocks, Michael, and you know it,' said Peter firmly. 'Vijay is as English as any of us.'

'That's not how some members might see it, Peter,' I replied. He smiled. Tall, thin and rather overfull of nervous energy, Peter was a leading light in a high-powered set of chambers specialising in human rights legislation. He enjoyed a fearsome reputation among judges and I could see why he was considered to be good at his job: the smile was intimidating. Peter was, I suppose, my closest friend: I had known him for over ten years.

'My name's Robinson,' he said. 'Some people might I say I was descended from a Polish Jew, and that my name means "Rabbi's son".'

'Are you?'

'I might be. Gascoigne means you come from south-west France. You might well be more of a Gascon than you are an Englishman, whatever that means. Few of us know who we really are.'

'Well, of course I'll put him in the book,' I said. 'If that's what you want.'

'This place needs waking up,' said Peter. 'Otherwise members such as myself, much as we love the place, are going to start resigning.'

Before I could think of an adequate reply Peter stood up, and patted me on the shoulder.

'I never got round to hearing about your golfing trip in Ireland, old boy. I'll have to leave it to another time. It doesn't seem to have done you much good. You look peaky.'

Then he left, and a moment or two later I stood up and went over to the membership book, which sat on a table near the door. In the column marked 'Candidate's Name' I wrote 'Mr V. Patel' and in the column marked 'Introduced By' I wrote Peter's name. The last column left space for the minimum requirement of six signatures of men who had been members for at least five years. Then Mr Patel would become a member of Grouchers – unless someone put a black ball in the box.

The last candidate for membership to be blackballed had been a cashiered former major in the Royal Artillery whose application to join had nearly succeeded, until the story about his misappropriation of mess funds had been circulated. That was in the 1980s, and on the day of his election a single black ball had been placed in the box. His application had thus been unsuccessful, and the member who had proposed him had felt compelled to resign.

I went back to the office and began dealing with some correspondence about preferential rates for Welsh and Scottish members. The argument being advanced was that, as they used the club less often, being farther away, they should pay lower subscriptions. English members were objecting, saying that this meant they were subsidising, for no good reason they could see, the Welsh and Scottish members. It was the sort of argument Grouchers excelled at: incapable of ever being resolved to everyone's, or indeed anyone's, satisfaction and likely to rumble on for at least the next generation while filling up several filing cabinets' worth of correspondence. Verey-Jones's own comment summed up the dilemma.

'Of course,' he said, as he handed me the latest file of members' letters on the subject, 'I have Welsh ancestry and a London address. So the question is one about which I find I am peculiarly sensitive.'

I resisted pointing out to him that I had a Scottish address. My sensitivities were obviously not considered to be in the same league as his.

At about four o'clock I decided I had had enough. Verey-Jones was doing the monthly stocktake in the cellar, so I straightened all the letters and papers on my desk, told Mrs Thornton that I would be back in the morning, put my news-paper in my briefcase, and went out past the porter's lodge.

'Mr Gascoigne, sir?' said James, as I passed. 'There's a lady waiting outside to see you, sir.'

'Is it Mrs Gascoigne?' I asked, surprised.

'No, Mr Gascoigne. The lady has been waiting since two o'clock.'

'Why wasn't I told?' I asked in amazement.

'She didn't want to disturb you, Mr Gascoigne.'

This was awful. Some poor woman had been waiting outside to see me for two hours. What on earth could it be about?

'It's an Indian lady, sir.'

James could barely conceal a smirk. I knew no Indian ladies. There could only be one possible explanation, bizarre as it might seem.

'You should have told me anyway, James,' I said angrily, and strode outside. A small, attractive woman in a sari was standing at the foot of the club steps. She was not tall, but stood very upright, and wore a sari of dark green flecked with red. Her long dark hair fell to her shoulders. Her eyes had beautiful dark brown irises, surrounded by a white so

44

white it looked almost blue. Her face was heart shaped, and olive skinned.

'Mr Gascoigne, sir?' she asked. It occurred to me that she must have been asking everyone who left the club since two o'clock the same question. That meant that half the club would know about this.

'Yes, that's me,' I said.

'I am Mrs Patel,' she said. She was clutching a small parcel in her left hand and did not put out her right. I did not know whether I should offer to shake hands with her or not. I made a slight bow instead.

'I'm very pleased to meet you,' I said. 'I have just been hearing about your husband from Mr Robinson.'

'It would mean so much to Mr Patel to be a member of this club,' said Mrs Patel suddenly. 'His father would have been so proud. Please, please, Mr Gascoigne. You are a person of great influence, I know. Do your best for him, I ask you this favour.'

I started to mutter something about how it was up to the members, but she was not listening. She had said what she had come from Hertfordshire to say. Instead she thrust the small parcel into my hand.

'This is burfi. It is an Indian sweet, most delicious, with silver almonds. Please take this gift from me.'

I had no choice but to accept the parcel. Then she turned, and walked off with surprising speed. I looked down at the silver foil and sniffed: an odour of boiled milk came from it. When I looked up, Mrs Patel had gone.

That evening, as Elizabeth and I sat in the Italian restaurant around the corner from Helmsdale Mansions, I told her about Mr Patel. She was not amused.

'You men at Grouchers,' she said. 'You ought to be locked up. Half the House of Lords are Ugandan Asians these days, and you worry there'll be a fuss if even one comes into your miserable club.'

'How was *your* day, darling?' I asked. Elizabeth's tirades on the subject of Grouchers made me uncomfortable. Grouchers had become an important part of my world in recent years. It was my anchor, the rock upon which I stood. One needed a firm footing upon something solid. There were too many treacherous quicksands and strange currents in the world.

'It was hell,' said Elizabeth. 'And, to cap it all, Christine's pregnant.'

I was going to ask who Christine was but remembered just in time that she had been Elizabeth's PA for the last three years.

'She'll want maternity leave, of course, and then I'll have to put up with temps for God knows how long until she decides whether or not she wants her job back.'

'I'm going to ask Peter and Mary up to Caorrun to stalk and play golf next month,' I said to Elizabeth. 'I'd like you to be there. Can you get some time off?'

I knew she would be able to. Although Elizabeth complained endlessly about her job, she seemed to be able to extract a remarkable amount of free time from her employers.

'Do I have to?'

'You can ask Anna and David Martin as well, if you like,' I said. Anna was Elizabeth's new friend. Her husband, David, was another member of Grouchers, one I knew rather less well than Peter. But the Martins would help make up a party; I didn't care, as long as Elizabeth would be entertained, and would overlook the deficiencies of Beinn Caorrun for a few days. I just needed to get away from London. I wasn't feeling myself at present.

We finished our pasta and decided to have coffee back at home, so I paid the bill and we walked back to Helmsdale Mansions. Elizabeth's mood had mellowed after a couple of glasses of wine. I had drunk nothing with dinner, but decided that I would have a malt whisky as a nightcap. Then I remembered the burfi, that Mrs Patel had given me. Bribe or not, it might as well be eaten.

'I've got a treat for you,' I told Elizabeth, and told her the story about Mrs Patel, and her strange offering.

'How very peculiar,' said Elizabeth. 'I don't normally like Indian sweetmeats. I find them sickly.'

'Those are the ones you get in restaurants,' I said. 'This is home-made. I bet it will be delicious.'

But when we got back to the flat I could find no trace of the little package in silver foil. I looked everywhere, in the kitchen, even in the bin, in case I had absent-mindedly thrown it out, but it was nowhere.

'You must have dropped it on the way home,' suggested Elizabeth.

'I could have sworn I put it down on the hall table,' I said.

'You're becoming very odd, darling,' said Elizabeth. 'Perhaps you ought to see someone about it.'

I went and poured myself a large whisky, and turned on the ten o'clock news. I was growing tired of people telling me I wasn't myself.

In the middle of the night I awoke and sat bolt upright. The bedroom curtains stirred in a soft breeze that was blowing in from somewhere. Something had awoken me, I thought at first; something like a whisper. Then into my mind came the words that had been in my dream, a dream in which the wind made the green tops of the trees bend before it, and in which bright red berries glinted.

Few of us know who we really are.

Somehow this thought made me feel profoundly uneasy and excited at the same time. Where had the words come from? I lay awake thinking about them. Where did one's sense of self come from: was it one's upbringing, or genetics, or from belonging to a club like Grouchers? I felt there was an answer out there, not far away, in the darkness. It was almost as if I could reach out and touch it. Then I remembered that those were the words Peter Robinson had used at lunchtime the previous day, when we were talking about Mr Patel. At once I was calmer, and settled back on my pillows, feeling sleep returning. Elizabeth slept soundlessly and deeply beside me. As I fell asleep the whisper returned.

None of us knows who we really are. None of us knows who we really are.

The next morning, before lunch, I went into Grouchers' bar and ordered myself a dry sherry. Someone touched me on the arm as I took it from Pierre, the barman, and I turned to see Peter Robinson. Beside him stood a tall, good-looking, dark-skinned man with jet-black hair brushed back from his forehead. He smiled at me, waiting to be introduced.

'Michael, this is Vijay Patel,' said Peter. 'I thought I'd let him see for himself what Grouchers is like. Can you join us for lunch?'

'I'm Michael Gascoigne,' I said, taking Mr Patel's outstretched hand. 'Delighted to meet you.'

'Likewise,' said Mr Patel. 'This is a treat for me.'

I could not really refuse the invitation, so I sat with Peter and Mr Patel at lunch. Mr Patel turned out to be everything Peter Robinson had said: urbane, intelligent, charming. At the same time, he looked slightly bewildered, as if he was not quite sure why he was there. I suspected that Peter had strong-armed him into applying for membership, as he had done in my case, as part of his campaign to make the club conform more with his own view of what it should be like.

'By the way,' I said, 'please apologise to Mrs Patel. I'm afraid I lost the cake she very kindly gave me yesterday, and so never got the chance to taste it. Please thank her from me in any case. It was such a kind thought.'

Vijay Patel put down his knife and fork and looked a little confused. He smiled uncertainly.

'Cake? Mrs Patel?' he said. 'I'm sorry, I'm not sure I understand you correctly.'

'Burfi, it was called, I believe,' I said, remembering what Mrs Patel had told me.

'Yes, burfi is a well-known Indian sweetmeat. Most delicious. But who is this Mrs Patel, please?'

Now it was my turn to feel confused.

'Mrs Patel? I assumed she was your wife?'

Peter said, in a tactful voice, 'Vijay is not married.'

'Not yet, I'm afraid,' said Vijay Patel. He laughed, but still sounded uncertain.

'Your sister?' The lady I had seen was too young to be the mother of this man.

'I have no female relations in this country,' said Vijay Patel. 'All boys in our family, you know. Now who could you have met? It is beyond me to explain it, Mr Gascoigne.'

Now I was more than confused; I was embarrassed. I felt myself beginning to colour.

Peter said, 'Why don't we go next door and have a cup of coffee?'

'I'd love to join you,' I replied, 'but I really must get back to my desk. So nice to have met you, Mr Patel. I look forward to seeing you here again soon.'

I stood up, and so did Vijay Patel, and we shook hands. Then they went into the morning room, and I went to the porter's lodge to find James.

'James,' I began, 'do you remember that Indian lady who came to see me yesterday afternoon?'

James looked at me in surprise.

'Indian lady?' he asked. 'I'm sorry, sir. Are you sure? There were no ladies here yesterday, except Mrs Thornton.'

4

The Hill of the Rowan Trees

I love Beinn Caorrun. The name means 'the hill of the rowan trees' and the place and I are indivisible. When I drive up north, up the A9, and then turn off on to the long, steep-sided valley that leads to my other home, my real home, my heart leaps within me. Everything is different up here. The quality of the light is different, and it changes all the time. One moment it is as dark as night, the next, soft white clouds fill a sky of limpid blue.

The air is different, too. As I drive along the valley road, a single-track affair with passing places, I always open my window unless it is snowing. Then I hear the stony voice of the Gala as it rushes down towards its junction with the Tay. I smell the air and the fresh coolness of it always hits the back of my throat, then travels to the very base of my lungs, filling me with a sense of being connected to the world again, no matter how grey and weary everything might have seemed when I left London.

The shoulder and then the grey and green ramparts of Beinn Caorrun begin to appear, as the road crests an incline and enters a hanging valley. High up on the hillside are fields of stone and the occasional white dot of a sheep. Lower down its slopes the forest begins. Dark woods now rise above each bank of the Gala and I drive through them: twisted alder, fir, Caledonian pine, birch, rowan and larch. The woods are full of mossy stones and fallen branches from the understorey of the trees, lying here and there like discarded spears. By this time of the year, the colours in the wood are turning to gold and brown, and the clusters of red and yellow berries on the rowans catch the eye. It is years since anyone bothered to manage these woods and the timber no longer has any value. At the two white-painted stones that form the drive entrance, I turn gently uphill and drive for a mile along the track covered in pine needles, winding between the tangled wood and green-covered boulders, until the house comes into view.

Caorrun is where I was brought up. This glen, these woods, these hills, bounded my world for many years. I went to school at the Bridge of Gala as a child. For most of my life I have spent more time here than anywhere else. When I come home, I can feel the life of the place flowing back into me as if I was bloodless before, but am now being infused with life. The noise of the Gala and the wind in the trees speak to me in many different voices.

Caorrun Lodge sits on a shelf of land, slightly raised above the surrounding forest. Around the main house and its two attendant cottages are great banks of rhododendrons. My grandfather, like many of our branch of the Gascoignes before him, had been an eccentric loner: his particular obsession was collecting species of rhododendrons. He once went to China before the Second World War, to Yunnan, to collect seeds. The idea was to have a display of plants that flowered right through from January to August, but what you see these days is mostly *Ponticum*, the common woodland rhododendron that has by now smothered all the plants my grandfather collected. For a few weeks in June and July the sombre dark green plantations are bright with purple flowers, and then their moment of glory is over.

Beyond the lodge is the stalker's cottage and a second cottage where Mrs McLeish lives. Mrs McLeish comes in and looks after the house while I am away and does the bookkeeping and administration for the holiday cottage rentals. The house itself could not be called beautiful. Built from dark stone, and three storeys high, it has an air of neglect about it The lawns around it are always shaggy with moss and are strimmed once a month by Donald the stalker; the window frames should have been repainted years ago and are now beginning to rot; the gutters need cleaning out, and the stonework of the house is covered in dark stains and green moss where the gutters have overflowed. Why people ever built houses that cannot be looked after without a cherry picker or a sixty-foot ladder is beyond me. I know I really must do something about it before the house gets dry rot. It would stink of damp, except that I leave every window in the place open to keep the air moving. The truth is, the house is exactly as it was when my father disappeared on the hill years ago. He was out hind-stalking by himself and got caught in a fierce January blizzard that blew in from the Arctic on a sudden north-westerly wind. Somehow, although reason tells me that he has been dead for over ten years, I have always been expecting him to come back. I want him to find the house as he left it, I suppose.

But that is, of course, ridiculous, and I decided this time, as the car came to a stop on the gravel, that I would ask Mrs McLeish to get a firm of builders to quote for a proper makeover for the house, top to bottom, inside and out. I opened the tailgate and Rupert stirred in his basket, then scrambled out on to the gravel. He wandered over to the edge of the lawn, cocked his leg for a few moments, and then stretched himself luxuriously, sniffing the air in the same way I had done.

Inside the house, I put my bags down in the hall and shouted for Mrs McLeish. She appeared instantly at the drawing-room door.

'I've lit a fire for you, Mikey, and put the hot water on. There's a venison stew in the oven for your tea; it just wants heating through.'

Mrs McLeish had known me since I was a small child, and sometimes forgot I was grown up now. She had worked for the Gascoigne family since she herself was little more than a child and was first employed as a maid by my parents. They once told me that she had turned up at the door, looking for work, a few days after the nurse my mother had hired decided to leave, unable to bear the gloom and remoteness of Glen Gala.

My parents did not spend all their time at Caorrun, preferring to spend the spring and early summer watching my father's various racehorses running, and the winter in the South of France. Mrs McLeish was my constant companion from almost as soon as I could walk. She cared for me, fed me, made sure I was properly dressed, and otherwise let me do anything I wanted to. She was not a warm or an affectionate person, but I knew that she watched out for me, all the same. I sometimes used to think that Mrs McLeish understood me better than I understood myself.

Her cooking was famously bad: Elizabeth wouldn't eat it. I found it quite acceptable, but I knew that if we had people staying for the stalking it wouldn't do, and we used to get a girl from Dunkeld to come up and cook for us. She was coming up that weekend, because we had the Martins and then Peter and Mary Robinson arriving to stay for a few days. Elizabeth was taking the train up to Perth on Friday morning, because she liked Anna Martin, and it meant she would have someone to talk to. Mary Robinson was, of course, Elizabeth's oldest friend. Elizabeth and I had met at one of Peter and Mary's dinner parties. I didn't know David Martin very well.

Elizabeth was coming here less and less. It pained me that she disliked Caorrun so much and took so little trouble to do anything to improve the place, or even hide her feelings about it.

I thanked Mrs McLeish and, knowing my routine, she left me and went back to her cottage. I checked the fire in the drawing room and then took my bags up to the bedroom. The floorboards creaked as I went up the stairs; the threadbare runner had long ago worn through to its canvas backing. The landing itself was uncarpeted and the air outside our bedroom was chilly. I don't like warm houses; I can't sleep in them. I never sleep well in London, because Elizabeth always has the central heating on, except in July and August. Some people complain Caorrun is a cold house, and so I had to put electric radiators in all the bedrooms except ours. Our own bedroom is a cold room, but it has a wonderful view.

Although it was near dusk, I went straight to the window and looked out across the tops of the trees to the Falls of Gala. A long thread of white shimmered above the trees, and I could just make out the faint hues of a rainbow as the spray caught the last light from the sun. The head of the waterfall was concealed in mist and so it looked, almost, as if the white thread of water was coming straight out of a dark sky and disappearing into the darker trees. I opened the window a little: it was difficult, because the sash cord was rotten, but I managed to lift it a few more inches, and listened until I could distinguish the note of the falls. There was water running off the hill. It must have rained a lot while I was driving up here. I left the window open; I wanted to hear the sound of the falling water in my sleep.

I started to unpack, and hang up my clothes. A large cobweb had been built inside the wardrobe. I flicked it off and the spider dropped to the floor of the wardrobe and scuttled into a crack. I checked the bed. The linen felt damp, but it would do. The room contained our double bed, a dressing table that had been my mother's, a wardrobe, a tallboy that held a few things of Elizabeth's and a couple of old wooden chairs. There was a small rug on the floor on one side of the bed, as Elizabeth complained she got splinters in her feet whenever she got out of bed, but otherwise the room was bare of any decoration. I like bedrooms to be simple.

I went downstairs to the drawing room. In the firelight it looked quite welcoming. The furniture was old and scuffed, the upholstery almost worn through on some of the arm-chairs, and the sofa collapsed beyond redemption into a sagging pile of fabric and worn cushions. A few pictures hung on the walls – unashamedly Scottish scenes, mostly Highland cattle beside lochs with their reflections etched in the water, or improbably large stags on misty hillsides. Elizabeth disliked them, but for me they were windows into the world beyond the walls of the house. Then there were a couple of estate maps, and that constituted the entire decor, except for a vast model of a steam yacht that had belonged to a previous Gascoigne and which had been moored at Dornoch, never used, until it sank in a storm many years ago.

I went to the sideboard and mixed myself a whisky and water from the decanter and jug that stood there, then went and sat at my desk and looked through the post that had accumulated since my last visit. Mrs McLeish dealt with all the bills, and anything that looked urgent or personal she forwarded to the flat in London, so most of the post was junk mail. I noticed, however, that a magazine I had ordered had arrived. I decided to take it into the kitchen and read it while I ate my supper.

I sat in the kitchen eating a few forkfuls of watery stew and sipping my whisky, while I turned the pages of my new magazine, careful to avoid any gravy getting on to the pages.

When I had finished my supper, I washed up, and then put the magazine away, out of sight. I have interests that I don't share with Elizabeth or any of my Grouchers friends: I don't feel I want to discuss such matters with people who wouldn't understand.

I went into the drawing room and picked up some of the magazines I had brought with me from London so that my guests would have something to browse through and wouldn't feel obliged to talk all the time. I had bought *Golfers Monthly, Trout & Salmon, Fly Fishers Weekly, Country Life* and *The Field*. I poured myself a second whisky and water, and glanced at a few pages of *Trout & Salmon* while the fire burned low in the hearth. Then I stood up and stretched and went outside with Rupert.

The mist and cloud that had shrouded Beinn Caorrun and the Falls of Gala had gone. It was a clear night, with a full moon rising. The silver light gave the forest an ethereal look and glinted on the rock faces of the mountain far above. The air had a sharp feel to it. I thought we might get a frost that night. In the absolute stillness I could hear the distant sound of the waterfall. Then a fox barked in the wood, and Rupert raised his black head for a moment. I heard a rustling noise. Was that something moving in the trees at the end of the lawn – a fox, or perhaps a deer? But it was only the wind.

'Come on, Rupert,' I said. 'It's time for bed.'

We went upstairs and I got undressed and climbed in between the sheets. They *were* damp. Rupert climbed into his basket and began to snore. I lay awake for a few moments, listening for the sound of the waterfall. When my ears had tuned into it, I felt a warm peacefulness steal over me, and was asleep almost instantly.

In the night I was awoken by Rupert whining. I sat up in bed. A strong wind had got up. I had left the curtains undrawn, as I always did when Elizabeth was not there, and I could see the full moon now high in the sky shining straight down on me. Racks of black cloud scurried across its face, driven by the rising wind. The house creaked like a ship in the wind, and it was easy to imagine that someone was dancing on the bare wooden floorboards on the landing outside. Rupert climbed out of his basket when he sensed my movement, and came across to the side of the bed. I sat up for a moment. Rupert's restlessness made me feel as if there was something alien in the house. I never locked the front door at Caorrunn. Perhaps I ought to go and make sure everything was all right. Then Rupert nudged my hand with his wet nose, asking for a stroke on the head. I did as he asked, and the gesture reassured us both. After a moment, he went back to his basket and I lay down and sank into sleep.

In the morning, the wind had dropped, but when I looked outside I could see it had been a wild night, and a cold one too, for despite the wind there were traces of frost on the lawns. The grass was now scattered with leaves and small branches that had been snapped off the trees. Indeed, a branch of rowan with some berries on it had even managed to blow in through the window at the far end of the landing. It lay outside my bedroom door, and I picked it up and looked at it. Rowan leaves and berries are meant to protect you from the spirit world, someone had once told me. No wonder the wind had woken me in the middle of the night.

I cooked some bacon and made a pot of coffee, and then I heard the sound of Donald's Land Rover coming down the track from his cottage a few hundred yards away. I went outside to meet him.

'How are you, Donald?' I asked. Donald was a small, dour man, who could climb the steepest hills like a goat. He might have been about forty.

'I've been waur,' he said. 'We need a proper frost to get the rut started. There's a few stags coming on to the hill now, right enough, but we need more.'

Beinn Caorrun was what they call a hind forest. Most of the time we had far more hinds than stags, but as the autumn went on and the nights became colder, stags started coming in from neighbouring forests. Soon we would hear them roaring in the woods around the house, and then the rut would begin.

'Hell of a wind last night,' I said, to keep the conversation going while I decided what I was going to do today. There were a lot of chores around the house to get it ready for our visitors, and I ought to go through the estate accounts with Mrs McLeish. But I decided what I needed first was some fresh air and exercise. I felt stale and liverish. I hadn't been feeling right for some days, since we got back from Ireland three weeks ago. For a moment I almost thought about going to see Alex Grant, for a check-up. He was a good doctor; but there was too much history. Most of the time I avoided him. A day on the hill would do me more good than anything else.

Donald said, 'Well, there was no wind with us last night.'

I smiled. Donald had probably hit the whisky bottle, and when he did that, he could sleep through a hurricane.

'Donald, go and get my rifle from the gunroom, please, and if you'll give me half an hour to get ready, we'll try to find a stag. Or if we can't, at least I'll get a look at what's on the place before our guests arrive.'

An hour later we were driving up the bumpy hill road in the Land Rover, with the tracked all-terrain Argo Cat loaded on to a trailer behind us. The road became more and more like a track until it petered out among great boulders. We parked the Land Rover behind one of these and then unloaded the Argo Cat and drove a few hundred yards farther up the hill towards a rocky knoll. Beyond this the land was boggy and strewn with stones, the remnants of an ancient moraine, so we had to get out and walk. First we climbed to the top of the knoll and spied for deer through our binoculars. Donald found a group of about twenty, way out on the western march of the estate, but it looked as if there were only hinds. Then I picked out another group, higher up on the face of Beinn Caorrun itself. I tapped Donald on the arm and said, 'I think there are some stags in that group.'

Donald got out his telescope and had a closer look.

'Aye, there's three stags there. We'll see if we can get close to them.'

We set out. Small though he was, Donald was a difficult man to keep up with, and while he might go easy on my guests, he made no concessions for me. I was breathing hard after a few hundred yards, but I was damned if I was going to ask him to slow down. There had been a time when Donald could not have kept up with me; that was long ago.

It was a frustrating stalk. Twice the stags started moving, but instead of moving into the wind as deer usually do, they cantered downwind, as if something had spooked them.

'It'll be a hillwalker,' I said.

'Aye, but I canna see anyone,' said Donald. The unpredictable movements of the deer meant we had to walk in a great circle and climb about a thousand feet in order to approach them from a direction from which they would not pick up our scent. The wind wasn't helping, either. One minute it was flat calm, the next moment there was a stiff breeze, now blowing from the east, now veering around to the north.

We traversed the great screes below the summit of Beinn Caorrun. Below us were ridges and corries that fell away steeply to the bogs and pools on the flats below. The colours were constantly changing: at times everything was grey and bleak, the crags around us dripping with water as we were enveloped in a streamer of cloud; at others the sky was bright and the flats below woven with brown and gold and bright green.

Towards four o' clock we spied another group of deer far below, and carefully picked our way down the steep crags until we lay on a ridge above the place we had last seen them. But when we peered over the ridge, they had moved on again.

'What's the matter with the blasted animals today?' asked Donald. 'Something keeps moving them, and I canna see what it is.'

'Is the shepherd out today?' I asked. But we would have heard the quad bike, or the shouts as he worked his dogs.

'He gathered in most of the sheep last week. There's only a few left on the hill now.'

It was not until after five that we finally caught up with the stags we had been following. Donald wriggled forward on his stomach to find a good firing position, set up the rifle and then beckoned to me. I crawled forward, keeping as flat as I could, and raised my head carefully to look through the scope.

'That big black beast that's just looking in our direction now,' whispered Donald. 'He's an auld animal and a good one to shoot. Quick now, I think they've seen us.'

All the deer that had been sitting down or grazing in a brown hollow about a hundred and fifty yards downhill now scrambled to their feet and looked upwards. They were not looking at us, but slightly to our right. Perhaps we had startled a sheep on our way in but I had no time to think about it. My stag slowly turned until he was broadside on, and then he looked straight at me. I saw his haughty, innocent face gazing at me in the scope, as if he could see every detail of my own face, and read every thought in my head. I breathed out, until the cross hairs were rock steady, and squeezed the trigger. There was a bang, and then a loud smack as the bullet went in.

'Got him,' said Donald. I reloaded just in case, and

watched the rest of the deer take off in flight. The beast I had shot was stone dead. We jumped to our feet and walked down to him.

'About sixteen stone,' said Donald. 'Look at the wear on his teeth, he's an auld stag. He wouldna have been able to feed himself much longer. Wouldna have lived through the winter.'

'Won't be much good to eat, either,' I said.

'Ach, the game dealer will take him off to Gairrmany. Those Gairrmans will eat any venison they can get.'

Donald gralloched the beast, and left its innards on the grass for the foxes and eagles to eat. Then we got the dragging rope out, tied it around the stag's antlers, and dragged him downhill to a place where we could drive the Argo Cat, then loaded him on to it. It was six o'clock before we got back to the Land Rover. The wind had dropped again, and the sky had cleared. It had turned into a beautiful evening. The peaks of Beinn Caorrun were silhouetted against a rose-coloured sky, and the tops of the trees below, along the banks of the Gala, were turning gold in the setting sun. I had an hour's daylight left and decided I would walk back to the Lodge.

How often had I walked these hills as a child, and as a teenager, before circumstances had separated me for a while from this place? Then I had heard the voices of the place in my head, telling me things, teaching me. That was long ago and I was different now. I was 'better'. The voices had gone. I had heard in those days – I don't remember who told me or how I came by the news – that there was a boy in this valley who had been taught, or who had taught himself, to stalk deer. He could approach animals unseen, undetected, better than any stalker of twenty years' experience: noiselessly, without alarming them, as if he were invisible, as if he controlled the movement of the air around him so that it carried his scent away from their nostrils. Then he killed them with a pointed stick or a knife; I don't remember now. I had heard all this a long time ago, although the memories lingered faintly in this place.

It was a beautiful evening and I wanted to be by myself for a while.

'Donald, I'm going to walk back,' I told him. He nodded, got into the Land Rover and started the drive back downhill, the stag lying in the well of the Argo Cat, his antlers poking over the side. When Donald got back he would have to hang the stag and butcher it in preparation for the game dealer calling. It would be an hour or two yet before his day was over.

I often felt like this after a good day's stalking: a mixture of melancholy guilt at killing such a beautiful animal combined with the intense satisfaction of concluding a difficult and demanding stalk. Reason told me that the stags had to be culled every year; instinct said otherwise.

It had been a difficult stalk, too, I thought. We must have gone up and down over three thousand feet and walked several miles over steep and sometimes dangerous ground. Yet I felt well on it, not tired somehow, and more full of life than when I had started the day. I wondered what had spooked the deer: we didn't often see hillwalkers on our ground. If they came to climb the peak of Beinn Caorrun it was usually from the other side.

Home is the hunter, home from the hill.

That was what my father used to say after a good day's stalking, when he came back to the house and pulled off his

64

boots, put the rifle on the hall table, and poured himself a whisky and soda. He did not know the truth of what he said. We are all hunters: we can never be separated from our origins. Civilisation has developed our social brain, and taught us other skills. But beneath that overlay, somewhere at the back of our brains, is the genetic imprint of an ancient hunter, who stalked far bigger animals than deer: aurochs, perhaps mammoths, perhaps other humans. We are all hunters, whether we like it or not.

As I walked down the track towards the forest below, the wind sighed around me, ruffling the grass like a woman stroking a man's hair. I smiled as the image came unbidden into my mind. The grass around me bent in waves, then straightened again, and then the wind touched me. Every hair on the back of my neck stood up.

I stopped for a moment, wondering what had alarmed me. I looked uphill, expecting perhaps to see a fox staring down at me, or a buzzard wheeling above me in the sky. The sensation of being watched was now so powerful that I could scarcely prevent myself from breaking into a run. A prickle of sweat broke out on my forehead. All of a sudden, I was seized by a feeling of horror, as if something from outside had come into the world.

I tried to reason with myself. This was panic: I had heard one or two old stalkers talk about it, a feeling of otherness that can overtake you out on the hill, alone at dusk, with not another person, nor any house, for miles around. As the colours fade from the hill and the stars begin to appear in the sky comes that feeling of utter isolation. But it was more than that: a feeling of having strayed, by accident, into someone, or something, else's world, of being followed by something you cannot see. I had heard them speak of it, and had dismissed it as the kind of story it is good to tell after a day on the hill, when you are sitting by the fire and have a dram of whisky in your hand to comfort you. I shook my head and tried to get a grip of myself, but the feeling would not go away. It was not as intense as it had been a moment ago, but the sense of quiet watchfulness was still very strong. I stepped up my pace and before long I was striding downhill so fast that from a distance it must have looked as if I was running.

As I entered the forest, and the road became more like a road and less like a track, the feeling began to fade. I did not slow down, though I was wet with perspiration. The sooner I was indoors, the better. The road turned a corner and there was the house, the light from the drawing-room windows casting pale rectangles on to the grass. Mrs McLeish had been in to light the fires and cook the supper. I was never as glad to get inside the house before. Rupert met me in the hall, wagging his tail and asking to be taken for a walk. I let him out into the garden for a few minutes, but couldn't bring myself to go outside again. I stood in the doorway and whistled for him until at last he came back, looking at me with reproach.

When he was back inside I did something I had never done before at Beinn Caorrun: I locked the doors.

That night I sat by the fire late, drinking more whisky than I usually allowed myself, and reading articles about golf matches, and a new type of graphite driver, until at last a sense of my old, safe self returned to me. Tomorrow night Elizabeth and the others would come, and we would laugh and joke, and make plans for playing golf, and I would be

Michael Gascoigne, member of Grouchers and dependable husband, once more.

At last I found the courage to go upstairs, across the poorly lighted landing, and so to bed.

5

Serendipozan

Michael sounded awful when I rang him.

'Oh, hello, it's you,' he said.

'Who were you expecting to ring?' I asked.

'I wasn't expecting anyone to call at this time of the morning. I'm half asleep.'

I looked at my watch. It was half past eight. By this time Michael should have been up and about for a couple of hours, if he had followed his usual routine.

'Have you been hitting the whisky?' I asked. It sounded as if he had been hitting something, or else something had been hitting him.

'No, damn it. I had a bad night, that's all.' Then he muttered something away from the speaker that sounded like 'lama'.

'I didn't catch what you said.'

'I didn't say anything,' he answered, now definitely awake and also sounding as if he might lose his temper. 'What do you want?'

I almost hung up the phone then. If there had still been such things as telegrams I would have sent one saying 'NOT COMING STOP YOUR BEHAVIOUR ON TELEPHONE BOORISH AND AWFUL STOP LOOK AFTER OUR GUESTS YOURSELF STOP'.

'Well, we could start with you saying something along the lines of "Hello, darling, how are you, can't wait to see you",' I suggested. There was a silence and I could visualise him trying to pull himself together.

'I'm sorry, Elizabeth,' he said. There was a faint suggestion of gritted teeth, but he carried on: 'I really did have a bad night and I'm ashamed to say I didn't know what time it was when you rang. How are you?'

'Too late for that,' I said, but he could hear in my tone that I wasn't going to make him suffer any more, at least not right now. 'I just rang to say I will be at Perth at six o'clock and Anna and David Martin will be with me. The Robinsons are supposed to be leaving London about midday. They're driving up, and bringing some of our kit, which is very nice of them: your golf bag, for instance, which you forgot.'

'Oh God, so I did,' said Michael, now sounding quite himself, even contrite.

'Yes. What are friends for, if not to act as couriers? Heaven knows when they will arrive. About ten, I should think, so I said we wouldn't wait for dinner. Clare the cook should be there about two o'clock. Now, will you remember to come and meet us at the station?'

'Yes, darling.'

'And is there anything you want me to bring? Anything else you've forgotten?'

There was a pause and then he said, 'Bring some Nurofen in case this headache doesn't go. It will save me having to go into Perth to get some when I drive down.'

We spoke a few more words to one another and then Michael hung up. I put the telephone down, frowning. I hoped he wasn't going to be in poor form this weekend, and leave me to make all the running. It would be hard enough work as it was, trying to be bright and jolly and make people forget that they were staying in a house in the mountains practically in the depths of winter, with no central heating. Michael would provide reasonable drink; he couldn't be called mean, and his wine never gave anyone a sore head. Thanks to Clare and me, the food would be good. But was that enough to get people to overlook peeling wallpaper on the stairs, lino with holes in it in the bathroom, and spiders in the bath? I know Scottish lodges are meant to be good for the soul, rather than being renowned for their luxury, but Caorrun Lodge was at the extreme edge of what could reasonably be regarded as habitable.

I went into the bathroom. My taxi would be arriving soon so it would be as well to have a final check through what I was meant to be taking. First, I would find the Nurofen. I opened the cabinet above the washbasin, and found a family-sized packet of the stuff. Michael was prone to headaches; more so in recent months. As I took the Nurofen out another small packet fell out and I caught it, to my surprise, on the way down. It was a prescription medicine. I looked at the label. It said: '*M Gascoigne Serendipozan*'. Underneath the name of the drug was the name of the manufacturer: '*Tertius AG*'. The packet was intact, so I couldn't tell whether it was something Michael was taking now, or had taken in the past. I was puzzled for a second. In all the years of our marriage I could not once remember Michael going to the doctors. Never in London, at any rate; I remembered I had once had to drive him to the surgery at the Bridge of Gala, when we had been staying up at Caorrun. But that had been in order to remove a fishing fly that had got stuck in Michael's cheek, just below his left eye, when a gust of wind had taken him unawares while he was fishing. That was one of the few occasions when Michael had been to see Dr Grant, the man who had turned up unexpectedly at our wedding. It was almost as if there was some bad feeling between them, except that on the one occasion we had asked Alex Grant up to the house for a drink, he had been friendly and courteous. In fact, he was an agreeable and civilised neighbour who I wished we saw more of.

I decided that, if Michael hadn't mentioned these tablets, then he didn't want them. I thought I ought to check what they were for, just in case, went into the little room we used as a shared study and switched on my laptop. I had a few minutes before the taxi was due. When the computer had booted up, I Googled the word Serendipozan and clicked on the entry at the top of the list. It read:

Serendipozan is one of the new generation of neuroleptics. While we must concede that extrapyramidal symptoms (e.g. acute Parkinsonism) and neuroleptic malignant symptoms (sometimes resulting in mortality) have been observed in control groups, we believe that these occurrences are statistically insignificant. This must be balanced against clear evidence of the effectiveness of Serendipozan and the significant improvement it can give to the quality of patients' lives, allowing in many cases for them to live within their own communities without the need for medical supervision. That is why we are recommending this treatment for licensing by the Federal Drugs Agency and the National Institute for Health and Clinical Excellence (NIHCE) in the UK.

Dr Hans Bueler, Tertius Corporation AG,
International Symposium on Clinical, Psychiatric
Medication, Basle, 2002

I stared at the screen. None of it made any sense at all. What did this have to do with Michael? I was about to click on another entry when the doorbell buzzed. I switched off the computer, went back into the hall and answered the door. It was the taxi driver.

'Two minutes,' I said. I went back to the bathroom and collected the Nurofen, then went and got my suitcases.

At King's Cross I met Anna on the train.

'Where's David?' I asked.

'He's stuck in a meeting in the City. Something came up. It always does, and usually on a Friday.'

Anna is one of my greatest friends, but her husband David is rather a trial. He is a stockbroker, and one of those men who always greets you with an enormous, cheesy smile and is very touchy-feely. David makes me feel uneasy, and I don't think he makes Michael very relaxed, either. His other defining characteristic, when a few men are around him, is to make outrageous, ultra-right-wing remarks about anything and everybody. I think he sets Michael's teeth on edge sometimes.

On the other hand, David is a crack shot, an excellent golfer and a very good trout fisherman. He never minds being woken at dawn to go and kill something, and never complains about the weather. So, while sometimes a pain in the dining room, he is an acceptable playmate for Michael on the hill or the golf course.

'How's David going to get to Caorrun?' I asked, feeling relieved that I wouldn't have to spend the next seven hours in his company, which I had been slightly dreading.

'Fly-drive. He's going to get the five o'clock from Heathrow to Edinburgh, and then pick up a hire car. He should be with us in time for dinner.'

This was perfect. I could chat to Anna as much as I wanted, and we could share a bottle of wine, and then I might try to kip for half an hour.

So Anna and I chatted. She was about my age, in her mid-thirties, medium height, dark haired and beginning to put on weight, as indeed am I. The Martins have two children at boarding school, but thankfully Anna has little inclination to talk about them; or perhaps she is just being tactful, knowing that Michael and I have a childless marriage.

Instead, we usually talk about people we know. Anna works for an upmarket estate agency near Sloane Street – and that's how we met, when I interviewed her a few years ago for the magazine. She's one of those people who actually understands what I do, knows what is going on in my world, but is less likely than the people I work with to plant a dagger in my back.

After about half an hour of this, and our first glass of wine, Anna said, 'How's Michael, Elizabeth?'

'Oh, much the same,' I replied.

'David said that he hasn't been looking himself recently. David never normally notices what other people look like, so I thought I ought to ask.'

I considered this.

'Truthfully, I don't know that there is anything wrong with Michael, not physically. He's been a bit moody recently, but then that's probably because he's been away from his beloved Scottish mountain for too long. He hasn't spent as much time there as usual this year, and I think he's been missing it. London gets him down after a while.'

'But you've only just got back from Ireland.'

I considered that, too. It was true that, if Michael was not himself, overwork was not the cause. The fact is, Michael had always been distant, slightly detached from everyday life. Sometimes he gave me the impression of a man fumbling through fog. I knew it would be like this when I married him; what I hadn't allowed for was that it grew no less painful as the years went by, watching a grown man so ill equipped for dealing with the world. In fact, if anything, it became even more painful. I used to find myself grinding my teeth and quietly muttering 'Come *on*, Michael' when he suddenly faded into silence in the middle of a sentence, as if the clockwork inside him had wound down. I didn't realise that the fact we never sat and giggled about anything, never got drunk, never, ever did anything unexpected together, would matter more to me as time went by, not less.

I never thought about leaving Michael; not for very long, at any rate. I think some instinct within me told me it might kill him. But since we had come back from Ireland, something had changed in him – maybe it had been going on for longer than that. He was different: he had lost weight; there was a change in his expression from time to time that worried me. I didn't think it was anything to do with me. Our married life was no worse, if no better, than it had been for the past few years. Then another idea occurred to me.

Oh God, I wonder if he's having an affair.

I didn't speak out loud but Anna caught the thought, as close friends will. She asked, 'Everything is all right between you two, isn't it? I mean, you know you can tell me anything. I would never repeat a word to anyone, not even to David.'

She poured two more glasses of wine, inviting me to tell all with an expectant look.

'No, Anna, nothing like that,' I said.

At least, not that I know, I thought. Anna paused for a moment, to see whether I would say anything more. I was surprised by the sharpness of the pang that the thought gave me. When I said nothing, she gave an imperceptible shrug and we talked about something else. I could see she didn't believe me.

After a while we stopped talking, and watched the east of England go by in the pale sunshine, which glinted on stubble fields and the autumn colours of the woods. We both read our novels for a bit, and then I slipped into a doze, mostly asleep, but remembering to keep my mouth shut and not to snore.

The train reached Perth on time, and Michael was waiting for us there. He seemed his old self, and almost pleased to see us. He kissed me, then Anna, on the cheek, and put our bags in the back of the Range Rover. Once we were inside the car I asked, 'Has Clare turned up?'

'Yes,' said Michael, 'with a carload of food. She's cooking away, Mrs McLeish has lit the fires and all the rooms are ready.'

He made Caorrun Lodge sound almost cosy, even though Anna had been there before and knew what to expect.

We drove up the A9 and then turned off up the single-track road that ran beside the Gala. As usual I was dreading the next few days. I would be cold, uncomfortable and bored. It helped that the Robinsons and the Martins were going to be there too. At least the evenings would be lively, as long as David didn't go over the top, and not full of the long silences that occurred when Michael and I were on our own. But that was the contract I had entered into when I married Michael. I was marrying him, and I was marrying Beinn Caorrun. It was where he felt he belonged, and for as long as I could manage I had to put up with it. Michael knew how I felt, and to be fair he often went up there without me, knowing I would be happier staying in London. During the last three or four years this had become more frequent, and for months at a time we now led separate lives.

We arrived in front of the Lodge and Anna got out of the car. I saw her put a jolly smile on her face, bracing herself for the worst. In fact, once inside, the house was much warmer than I had expected. Fires were lit in the drawing room, the hall and the dining room, which made the whole house feel more welcoming. Upstairs our bedroom was, as usual, like the dormitory in some spartan nineteenth-century boarding school or, indeed, workhouse. But when I opened the bedroom door to show Anna where she and David were sleeping, Mrs McLeish had managed to create an illusion of cosiness in the guest bedrooms.

Once Anna and I had unpacked we went downstairs again to the drawing room, and drinks. Then I noticed that there were vases everywhere filled with rowan branches, still rich with red and yellow berries.

'Did Mrs McLeish do those?' I asked Michael, thinking that they looked very odd.

'No, I thought they might brighten up the place a bit,' said Michael.

'Oh, how sweet!' cried Anna. 'It would never occur to David to do anything like that.'

We heard the sound of a car pulling up and went outside. It was David, in a bright red BMW. Anyone else would have hired a Fiat Panda for a journey of sixty miles, but not David. He was standing by the boot unloading some cases when we came out, and immediately roared, 'The beautiful Elizabeth, how wonderful to see you!'

I allowed myself to be embraced in a tight hug, and became conscious that the atmosphere had rather more gin in it than a few moments ago.

'And my own dear wife,' he added, as Anna gave him a cold look.

He kissed her, and she said, 'You've been drinking on the plane.'

'Of course I have,' said David. 'Gascoigne! How are the stags! Fit and well?'

'Welcome to Beinn Caorrun,' said Michael, rather stiffly.

David is about six foot, quite large and meaty looking, with tight, curly blond hair that is beginning to go grey. He has the watery blue eyes of someone who wouldn't say no to a bottle of wine at lunchtime, and a very loud voice. He's not without charm, though. Not altogether.

Once inside David handed me a box of After Eights, which I loathe, and a bar of soap I think he had picked up at Body Shop in the airport. He gave Michael a litre of Bell's whisky, saying, 'Small contribution, old boy, hope it's the kind you like.'

Then, instructed to help himself from the drinks tray, he poured a good two inches out of the same bottle into a large crystal tumbler and splashed it with soda.

*

The evening passed without excitement. The combination of the gin on the plane, and then the whisky, and then quite a lot of red wine over dinner, made David soporific rather than noisy. After dinner he sprawled in an armchair next to the fire, a nightcap clutched in his hand, trying to stay awake. In the end, he took himself upstairs before the Robinsons arrived. That was close to midnight: they had been stuck in a tailback on the M74 for an hour, and by this time all they wanted to do was go to bed.

The next morning there was a leisurely start to the day while the men made plans. It was decided that David would go up on the hill and try to get a stag, while Michael and Peter would play golf. Anna and Mary and I would go shopping at the House of Bruar, an upmarket department store just off the A9, north of Pitlochry. It was very much like most other visits to Beinn Caorrun. The men golfed, or killed things; the women shopped. It was at dinner that evening that we departed from the usual script.

David Martin had enjoyed an easy day's stalking on the hill, got his stag about three o'clock and was back at the Lodge by five. He had a bath and then probably grew bored waiting for us all to return. By the time we came back, and Peter and Michael had returned from their game of golf over in Fife, I think David had already had one or two sharpeners.

When we came down from our baths, we all slumped into armchairs and chatted for a while. My legs ached with weariness: I might not have been up on the hill, but men don't understand how physically tiring shopping can be. Then Clare put her head around the door and announced that dinner was ready.

The dining room at Caorrun is, I find, always a challenge

to one's appetite. It is partly the colour scheme: crimson flock wallpaper of a pattern once much admired by Chinese restaurateurs; gold-fabric-covered chairs that are so heavy they are almost impossible to move, with black mahogany feet and arms; a dining-room table that would have fitted in well at Stonehenge, also dark mahogany and massive. Around the walls are more pictures of stags. I have tried to persuade Michael to redecorate, but he won't. He says that his parents liked those colours and they have a period feel. That's one way of putting it.

At dinner we first had to listen to a detailed account of David's day on the hill; and then a few amusing anecdotes from the putting green, related by Peter, although the amusement was mostly to be gained at Michael's expense. This was acceptable: Michael was rather flattered to be the centre of any story, even if he was being teased. Tonight he smiled and even laughed at Peter's jokes about how he had sliced the ball, and how he found the water hazard, but I could see that he was making an effort. However he said very little, and it was perhaps in a misguided attempt to liven him up that David said, 'Now then, Gascoigne, what about this Patel affair?'

'What "Patel affair"?' asked Michael. I knew from his tone that he hadn't the slightest idea what David Martin was talking about, and was somewhere off in a world of his own. So David Martin helpfully reminded him.

'You know, the Sooty that Robinson here has decided to put up for membership of Grouchers.'

There was a deathly silence. I think David realised he had gone too far, but men of that sort, when they get themselves into a hole, generally keep on digging. Anna giggled nervously. Michael looked up from his plate, where he had been chasing a prawn about, and Peter Robinson said in his most icy barrister's tone, 'I wish you would use less offensive language, David.'

'Don't take me so seriously, old boy. And don't be so politically correct. The fact is, he's a different colour to the rest of the members. We're all what you call white Anglo-Saxon British. He's not. Might make it a bit awkward for him, don't you think?'

Michael put down his knife and fork and said, 'But if you are, as you put it, British, the chances are that very little of you is Anglo-Saxon.'

Everybody looked at Michael, but before anyone could comment he returned his attention to his plate, as if he had just settled the argument. I glanced over at my husband, impressed that for once he was managing to change the subject and defuse a rather tense moment. But David continued.

'I don't follow you, old boy. That's what we are if we're British: Anglo-Saxon or Norman French, with a few odds and ends thrown in.'

Michael shook his head. 'No, David. The Romans, and the Saxons, and the Danes, and the Normans were just colonists. Their influence on the genetic make-up of the population was relatively slight. They didn't kill all the local inhabitants when they arrived. They weren't ethnic cleansers like Genghis Khan, or Tamerlane. They colonised and, where they could, they ruled the locals, and to a small extent they intermarried with them. But the chances are that your true identity is not Anglo-Saxon, but something else. Your mitochondrial DNA, your maternal genetic inheritance, most probably resembles that of the ancient Britons who originally populated this land at the end of the last Ice Age.'

'My what?' asked David.

My mouth had fallen open. Everyone else around the table was staring at Michael with varying degrees of surprise. I had never heard Michael speak about anything remotely like this. Michael talked about golf, and bridge, and stalking, and sometimes, if he was feeling very adventurous, the iniquities of the Scottish Executive and the Land Reform Act. To hear him talking about DNA was like living with someone for ten years you thought worked in a tobacconist's shop, and then finding out that he was a nuclear physicist. It wasn't just what Michael had said: his expression had suddenly become combative as he spoke, quite different from his usual style of avoiding argument whenever possible.

I said, 'Darling, that's riveting, but isn't it a very heavy subject for dinner?'

'No, no,' said Peter Robinson. 'This is good stuff. Let him go on. I'll put up a white flag if it gets too much for me. Michael, where did the aboriginal inhabitants of this country come from? I thought they were Celts?'

Michael shook his head. He spoke again, this time in a trance-like tone that, for some reason, made the hairs on the back of my neck stand up.

'Yes, the Celts were here before the Angles and the Saxons and the rest of them. But there were others here before the Celts. Long ago, a wall of ice came south from the polar ice cap. It covered all of Britain as far south as central Wales and the Midlands in hundreds of feet of ice. As the ice moved south, it absorbed so much fresh water and seawater that the ocean level dropped, opening up land bridges between Ireland and Scotland, northern Germany and eastern England, Cornwall and Brittany. Everything for hundreds of miles south of the ice wall became polar desert.

Life, for the few humans that existed there, was impossible, so they fled south, or east across the land bridges to refuges farther south, where a few humans survived.'

Michael stopped, as if he had run out of words. There was a silence. David Martin had shown signs of becoming irritated by this conversation, which was quickly turning into a lecture.

'Old boy, I'm not sure I am following your every word, but it sounds like complete bollocks—'

'*Then listen!*' shouted Michael suddenly, and his tone was so savage that everyone fell silent. I had never heard Michael raise his voice like that before. It was as if a completely different person was sitting at the head of the table, someone I didn't even know.

'The main refuges were cave systems in the foothills of the Pyrenees. A few humans survived there. Then, ten thousand years ago, after a final advance, the last ice walls retreated. That was called the Younger Dryas Event, which preceded the last great episode of global climate change. The first sign was a carpet of white flowers, the Dryas flower, that sprang up in the polar desert. As the planet warmed up, the ice retreated back towards the polar ice caps, leaving barren earth where before there had been hundreds of feet of ice. The plants returned: first lichen and mosses, then grass. Then the animals began to move north again. After them came the hunters, also migrating north to colonise Britain.'

I think that by now we all knew something was very wrong with Michael. David, big though he was, had been intimidated by the ferocity with which Michael had curtailed his interruption. He sat looking sulky, with his head down, giving an occasional ostentatious glance at his watch. I knew

I had to do something, but I was paralysed by a mixture of embarrassment and concern. There might be dining rooms in Britain where this sort of conversation was the daily staple of life, but not at Caorrun, and we all knew it. At Caorrun we talked about golf, and stalking, and gossiped about our friends. We did not talk about global warming or mitochondrial DNA. Only Peter had the presence of mind to keep the conversation moving, knowing that Michael would have to reach his conclusion sooner or later.

'So where did we come from, Michael?' he asked gently.

Michael, still in the same tone of voice that so worried me, said: 'The first humans to come back to these lands were all the genetic descendants of a woman who lived, probably in a cave, somewhere in the Pyrenees. She is a principal ancestor of the people who arrived in this country at the end of the last Ice Age: a woman from the Mesolithic era. These were the aborigines who first populated our country, and as the ice melted and the sea rose again, they became insulated from subsequent migrations for thousands of years. The arrival of the Anglo-Saxons and the Vikings made little difference. Her blood is our blood. Our brains are her brain.'

Michael then said to David, 'Now we are entering another period of climate change, and the migrations have started again. From Africa, from eastern Europe, from Asia. There's nothing the membership committee of Grouchers can do about it.' He speared the prawn he had been chasing around his plate, ate it and then gave a smile that was both unsettled and unsettling. 'So you see, David, if we took a sample of your blood or saliva and identified your Y chromosomes and your mitochondrial DNA, we might find you were more Ancient Briton than white Anglo-Saxon.'

David had no reply to offer; he remained staring down at his plate.

Michael had finished speaking, and put his knife and fork neatly together on his plate. In the silence that followed, I realised why convention requires that we talk to each other at dinner parties. It is a preferable alternative, however tiring the effort may be, to a deadly silence broken only by the scrape of metal on china, or the intimate sounds of one's neighbour chewing.

The next morning, after breakfast, which was just like any other breakfast, David cornered me in the drawing room while Michael was out getting the rifle from the gunroom for Peter.

'That was an extraordinary outburst of old Michael's last night,' he said.

It was difficult to disagree. After Michael's little speech about DNA and cavemen, the evening had ground to a halt. No one had wanted to do very much after dinner, and our guests had disappeared upstairs as soon as they decently could. Michael had also disappeared outside with Rupert, and didn't come back until after I had put myself to bed. I lay there waiting for him to come upstairs, wondering what on earth it had all been about. Was my husband having a nervous breakdown? A mid-life crisis, whatever that is?

Outside it was quiet, except for the sighing of the wind in the trees. Then I heard a sound, like a long, low, sobbing roar from the woods, not a hundred yards from the house. The strange noise ended in a husky cough. I sat up in bed, wondering what it could possibly be: then I realised that it was probably just a stag roaring somewhere among the trees.

Later, Michael came upstairs, just as I was drifting off into an uneasy sleep. As he climbed into the bed beside me I touched his hand. It felt icy cold.

I said, 'Darling, are you OK?'

He grunted in a way that might have meant 'yes', or it might have meant 'no'. Then he said, in a low voice, 'They used to speak to me when I was a child.'

'Who did, darling?' I whispered.

'The hunters who lived in the forest, among the pine, and the birch, and the rowan. I used to see their voices.'

There was a silence while I tried to work out how to reply to this. Then, for some reason, a question popped into my mind.

'Darling, what is Serendipozan?'

But Michael said nothing, and after a while his breathing, at first heavy, became light and regular, and I knew he was asleep.

I wondered whether I should creep downstairs and try to get hold of Alex Grant. He might understand what was going on here. It might have happened before. Then I wondered what I would say if Michael woke and found me on the phone or, worse, what he would say if Alex simply turned up. I knew I couldn't face it.

At last I pulled the sheets over my head and tried to go to sleep. I lay awake for a long time, with my eyes wide open. I felt a new feeling that at first I could not identify. Then I knew all at once what the feeling was. I was scared.

Now, confronted by David Martin, who obviously wanted to talk about last night, I said, 'Michael was just changing the subject. He thought you and Peter were going to have a row about that man, Mr Patel. He simply started saying the first thing that came into his head.'

'A pretty odd thing to come into one's head, isn't it?'

I was nettled. 'Well, David, if you don't like it, you should think about how other people might feel about your racist remarks.'

David groaned. 'Oh God,' he said. 'I'm no more a racist than you are. I just like winding people up sometimes.'

'Well, this is what happens when you do,' I said sharply.

'Yes, I'm told that I'm really a caveman.' David sighed. 'Are we going to make a threesome at golf, you, me and Anna?'

'If that's what you want to do, then yes.'

David nodded and said, 'All the same, keep your eye on Michael. It might be worth getting him to see someone. You know, it wasn't just what he said last night. It was the way he said it. It just wasn't like Michael at all.'

I didn't reply, but he was right. It wasn't like Michael at all.

6

Strangers on a Train

I sat staring out of the window of the train at the Northumbrian coast. It was a beautiful sunny day, and the white crests of the waves sparkled in the sunlight. The train ran past Bamburgh Castle and headed south for Newcastle.

Elizabeth was going to stay behind at Caorrun, a triumph of duty over reluctance, to close the house up for the winter with the help of Mrs McLeish. On the way south she planned to stop with her mother in Gloucestershire for a couple of days, so she was going to drive the Range Rover down, with Rupert in the back. Our parting had been strained. I appeared to have broken her code of behaviour by trying to hold an intelligent conversation at dinner. At least, I thought it had been intelligent. Peter had understood what I was trying to say, and it had been better than descending to the schoolboy conversation about Mr Patel that David had wanted us to have. On the other hand, I had always known it would be a mistake to talk about subjects that were of great interest to me, but not, apparently, to anyone else.

When Elizabeth dropped me off at Perth station she said, 'I hope I'm going to come home and find you are yourself again.' It reminded me of my mother saying, 'I hope I'm going to come back in a minute, and find you've eaten up all your porridge.'

'You are yourself' – what did that mean? Of course I was myself. Who else would I be? I might have said something sharp in rejoinder, but then I caught a look of worry in her eyes and held my tongue. She still cares for me a bit, I thought.

Our other guests had gone and now I was heading south, summoned to an emergency meeting of the membership committee at Grouchers, to discuss the proposal that Mr Patel should become a member of the club. Things had obviously moved on while I had been away. There was an urgency to the summons, suggesting desperate hours were upon us, as if I had been enjoined to attend a meeting in a command centre in a bunker beneath Whitehall.

It had been an unsatisfactory few days up at Beinn Caorrun. More and more these days I regretted it when I asked other people there. Their presence grated on me: even Peter, of whom I was quite fond. As for David Martin, I wouldn't care if I never saw him again. Unfortunately, I would see him tomorrow at Grouchers, when he proposed to speak to the membership committee against Mr Patel's nomination. I wasn't looking forward to any of that. The peacefulness of Glen Gala was receding behind me, and ahead of me was nothing but headaches. Indeed, I had one now. I took the packet of Nurofen out of my pocket and popped a couple of capsules into my hand. Then I swallowed them, washing them down with a sip of water from the bottle I had bought. After a while I convinced myself that the headache was getting better.

The Nurofen was a small price to pay for coming off the other stuff. Headaches I could live with, if I had to. In exchange, I felt as if I was seeing the world more as it was again. I felt energy flowing through me where before there had been only listlessness. As I looked out of the train window, everything now had a sharpness, a definition, to it that had not been there before: as if I had been gazing at the world through a dirty window for far too long, seeing only the blurred outline of things.

At Newcastle a few people got on to the train. I felt I had been sitting down for a long time so I stood up and, as soon as everyone had got past, I walked along to the vestibule between two coaches, and stayed there, looking out as the train slowly slid across one of the bridges over the Tyne. I saw the other bridges – Victorian cast iron, and modern concrete – and the great, shimmering shape of the new concert hall backed by church spires. An almost imperceptible jolt shook the carriage, as if it had been hit by a strong gust of wind, and, sure enough, when I looked down towards the river, an arrow of ripples was forming on the surface of the water, as the wind rushed down the estuary towards the sea, the bright wings of seagulls dancing in its wake.

I went back to my seat. The two aisle seats were booked from York, and remained empty. As it happened, the seat opposite me was one of the few that were unreserved, and someone was now sitting in it, which meant I would have to tuck my legs in.

'Is this seat taken?'

It was a woman; no, a girl.

'Not as far as I know,' I said.

She sat upright, looking out of the window. I picked up my newspaper, but as I did so my glance swept across my neighbour, and was arrested for a moment.

Although it was eleven o'clock in the morning, she was wearing a long dark green dress made of velvet or some similar stuff. You might have expected to see a dress like that worn at a formal dinner party, or in a BBC costume drama; but not at eleven in the morning on a train. She was dark haired, with a heart-shaped face, and large dark brown eyes, so dark as to be almost black. Two ruby earrings glinted under the dark helmet of her hair. What caught my eye, however, was her gaze. There was something familiar about her, a sense of ancient connection that was both unexpected and intense. With some difficulty, I turned my eyes away from her and looked out at the view. I was not in the mood for talking to a stranger, no matter how attractive. Then, involuntarily, I glanced at her again, and saw that she was looking straight at me. Why was she dressed in such old-fashioned clothes? I turned back to my Sudoku puzzle, but she was aware of my glance.

'Why were you staring at me?' she asked. She had a clear, silvery voice.

I looked up in surprise and mumbled: 'I thought we might have met before somewhere – but I'm afraid I have a terrible memory.'

I blushed. It sounded as if I was trying to pick her up, which was the last thing on my mind.

'You will remember me if we meet again, I'm sure.'

I could think of no reply to this and did not want to be drawn into conversation. There was something about the girl's tone of voice that hinted at instability. Her dress alone was deeply eccentric. There was a silence as the train rattled through the Durham countryside. On the skyline I could see a thicket of trees, where rooks wheeled in strange patterns in the sky, before settling into their branches. It evoked a memory, but of what I was not sure. The girl spoke again.

'As a matter of fact, you have seen me before – but I'm not surprised that you can't remember where.'

'I'm sorry?'

She gazed at me, her brown eyes looking directly into mine so that I found it hard to look away.

'Can you not picture where you first caught sight of me? But perhaps you would not believe it if you could.'

She was talking to me in that light, chatty voice that people on trains use, a tone that allows a more personal conversation to develop if things go one way, and instant disengagement if they go the other way. Yet she was talking complete nonsense. I wondered again whether she was mentally deranged and decided to change my seat. Perhaps I could say I was going to get a cup of coffee, and then find a place in another carriage. I hated personal revelations from complete strangers; I didn't much appreciate them from anyone, come to that. Just to keep the conversation going while I decided what to do next, I replied, 'I do have a feeling I've seen you somewhere before. But, as I said, I have a terrible memory. You will have to help me remember.'

'I don't help people,' said the girl, smiling. 'That's not what I do.'

'That seems a bit extreme.'

'I am extreme,' she said. 'You have no idea how extreme I am.'

I couldn't think of anything to say to this, and decided I would go and sit somewhere else. But she anticipated me and said, 'Don't go, we've only just begun to talk.'

'I wasn't going anywhere,' I lied, relaxing back into my seat. I was stuck with this madwoman now. How excruciating!

'Don't you like talking to strangers?' asked the girl. 'You should, you know. You can say anything you want. Mostly you'll never see them again, so it simply doesn't matter. That's the whole point of journeys: the strangers you meet, the lies you tell them.'

'I didn't know that,' I said. 'It's an interesting point of view.'

'Yes, isn't it? Now it's your turn. You have to ask me a question about myself. That's how conversation works.'

When she said this she sounded rather like Elizabeth, who used to hiss at me, at parties, 'Can't you make more of an effort with ...' (whoever the girl next to me was). Then I would make an effort, and it would be obvious I was trying, and things would go from bad to worse.

Now all I could come up with was, 'Are you visiting friends or family at the moment?'

'I have no family,' she said.

'I'm an orphan too,' I said.

'What happened to your parents?' asked the girl. 'Or is it too sad to talk about?'

'No.' I paused. 'At least, it is sad, of course, but it was many years ago, and I have long since come to terms with what happened.'

There was a silence. She did not ask me again to tell her about the circumstances, but looked directly at me, with a half-smile on her face, and her silence invited me, almost compelled me, to continue. However odd our conversation was, I was suddenly finding it quite easy, talking to this stranger. I realised I wanted to tell her things I had kept to myself for a long time. As I began to speak she propped her chin on her hand, resting her elbow on the table, like a child listening to a fairy story. Her expression became rapt as I spoke; there was no irony or false courtesy in it.

'My mother died when I was sixteen,' I began. 'We lived in Scotland. In fact I still do.' I wondered why I had said 'I', and not 'we'. 'Anyway, she loved fishing for brown trout in the hill lochs above where we lived. I used to row for her while she fished from the boat. One day, she got her line in a tangle, and stood up to sort it out. I think she was in a bit of a temper too ... The truth is that my mother used to drink just a tiny bit more than was good for her. She had drunk several glasses of wine with lunch, even though it was only meant to be a picnic beside the loch. At any rate, she lost her balance, and at the same moment a squall suddenly drove across the lake. It came from nowhere: a violent gust of wind and sheets of blinding rain. My mother fell overboard, but she must have hit her head on the side of the boat. I couldn't find her.'

The girl opposite me said, 'You rowed round and round in circles shouting for help, but she didn't come back to the surface?'

'That's exactly it,' I said. I stopped in confusion, for I thought I saw a hint of a smile on her face. I didn't want to talk about what happened after that, how Dr Grant had appeared, and how the police had come and divers had gone down into the loch and eventually found the body of my poor mother. I didn't want to recall how Dr Grant had sat for hours in the drawing room with my father, talking to him, while I was made to go off and walk about outside.

'That is such a sad story.' The girl sighed. 'Your life was changed for ever, by one random event.'

I hesitated. There was something liberating about talking to this girl, telling her things I had bottled up inside me for so long.

'You can tell me anything you like,' she said, as if she had read my thoughts. 'After all, what harm can it do?'

There was something so beguiling in her sad half-smile that I was tempted to tell her more. But that was a ridiculous idea: she was a complete stranger.

The train was charging past the great escarpment that leads up to the North York moors. Looking out of the window I saw the white horse that dances eternally on the slope of Sutton Bank, and when I turned back I saw that the girl had put out her hand to me. I took it, and shook it. Her hand felt cold and strong.

'I am Lamia,' she said.

'Michael,' I replied. 'I'm sorry to bore you with my personal history. I don't know why I told you all that. You must be a very good listener.'

'Oh,' said Lamia, 'I can listen for ever. You have so much to tell me; perhaps things you don't even know about yourself.'

I found myself hoping that no one would come and sit in the seats next to us, which had been booked from our next stop at York – it would inhibit the conversation if I thought other people could overhear us. The girl with the strange name – what had she said? Lamia? – had persuaded me to talk about my mother's death in greater detail than I had with anyone, even Elizabeth. When I had told Elizabeth the story I had been terse, refusing to give any real details except the barest outline of the accident. After all, she had never met either of my parents.

I wondered what Elizabeth would say if she saw me now. Would she object to me having such an intense conversation with a girl ten or fifteen years younger than she was; a girl, it had to be admitted, who was far more striking than

Elizabeth now was? When I proposed to Elizabeth, she was an attractive example of a certain type: tall, fair hair, more angular than curvaceous, a somewhat severe face that looked classical in repose, occasionally softened by a warm smile. I felt guilty making these comparisons.

'Lamia is an unusual name,' I said. 'Where does it come from?'

'It's a Greek word.'

She seemed disinclined to say more, so I asked, 'Do you have anywhere to stay in London?'

Then I thought that Lamia would think I had some ulterior motive for asking the question; that I might even be about to propose some form of accommodation myself.

'It doesn't matter, as long as I am free to go where I want.'

'You haven't got anywhere to go, then?'

Lamia gave no answer. She gazed at me with her dark eyes, but did not smile. For some reason that I could not explain, I reached into my jacket and pulled out my wallet. I extracted a card from it with my name and address printed on it. 'Well, if you are stuck, call me on this number. I might be able to put you in touch with people who let out rented accommodation.'

A member of Grouchers I knew had made a fortune from buy-to-let property investment, and owned more than one block of flats. The conversation with Lamia, which had been going so well, seemed to be faltering again. I looked at my watch and said, 'I tell you what, what about something to eat; or a glass of something? Some wine, perhaps?'

Her smile came back. 'Wine is good. I like wine.'

I smiled too and stood up. I found my way to the buffet car and managed, after a few minutes in a queue, to buy two small bottles of white wine. While I paid for these, the train started slowing down as we approached York station. By the time I got back to my carriage I was struggling against a tide of boarding passengers, but eventually I made it to my seat. To my disappointment the aisle seats were now occupied by two large men in suits, both fiddling with laptops and mobile phones as they settled down. Lamia had gone, I supposed to the loo. I struggled past one of the men, who made only a token movement of his legs to let me by, sat down and put the two bottles of wine on the table – one in front of me and one in front of where Lamia had been sitting. One of the men looked at me oddly, but said nothing.

The train pulled out of York station and I waited for Lamia to return. She did not. We went through Ferrybridge and still she had not come back. I began to wonder where she was. As we approached Doncaster, I turned to my neighbour and asked, 'Excuse me, but was there a girl sitting here when you got on the train?'

'Afraid not, mate. Have you lost one?' He wheezed slightly as he said this, in appreciation of his own wit.

'A girl in a green dress?'

'No, mate. Not one in a green dress, neither.'

She must have got off at York, then. I could hardly blame her. All of a sudden I felt angry with myself: giving her my card, inviting her to call me, offering to ply her with wine – none of this looked good. Supposing she rang, and Elizabeth answered the phone? Supposing she came round to see me, asking for a night's lodging, and Elizabeth answered the door of the flat? I must have been mad. Then I saw a little white square of cardboard on the opposite seat, and realised she had not taken my card with her. Well, that was something. I leaned over the table and picked it up.

My neighbour nudged me in the ribs with his elbow.

'Mate, if you're looking for a home for that wine, just let me know.'

His companion winked at me.

'Only too happy, if you don't want it.'

I picked up the two bottles and plastic cups and put them down in front of the man who had spoken.

'No, I don't want them now, thanks.'

'Thank *you*,' said the man who had spoken first. He and his friend untwisted the screw tops and poured the wine into the plastic cups. One of them sniffed the cup before drinking and said, 'Charming bouquet, charming.'

He winked again and tipped most of the contents of the cup down his throat.

The next morning I went to Grouchers for a meeting of the membership committee. The committee consisted of me, as membership secretary; Mr Verey-Jones; the club chairman, a position at present occupied by Major General Sir Andrew Farrell (retired); and two other club members who were elected by rotation. When I came into the room, I saw that one of them had wisely not turned up to what could turn out to be a very tricky meeting. The other member was Mark Ansty, under thirty and already making a strong impression as a charming and amusing young man, though as yet his brain gave little evidence of being connected to his mouth.

The chairman looked at his watch as I came in. I knew I was late. The truth was, I had slept very badly the night before and had struggled with the normally simple acts of getting shaved and dressed. I apologised for my lateness and sat down, extracting my papers for the meeting from my briefcase.

The committee room at Grouchers is a solemn place. There is a long mahogany table, its top inlaid with scratched green leather. Large mahogany chairs, fourteen of them, are placed around the table. The walls are lined with bookshelves that contain bound copies of the minutes of every meeting ever held in the club since the turn of the nineteenth century, and old suggestions books in which members have solemnly inscribed impractical ideas for improving the amenities of the club over the last hundred years or so. I took pleasure in browsing through these on quieter days when there was not much to do in the office. These books contain offerings such as, 'Could the Club Secretary consider providing personal humidors to allow members to store their own cigars at the club?' Last, but not least, are the volumes upon volumes of the Rules of the Club, amended every few years by Verey-Jones, and countless others before him. These books have an ecclesiastical look: bound in dark brown Moroccan leather and decorated with gold leaf, they recall scriptural works, and perhaps are invested with the same sacred qualities.

Looking down on the room, from the wall at the opposite end to the chairman's seat, is a sepia-coloured portrait of Emmanuel Groucher. He is seated in an enormous chair almost throne-like in its dimensions. His dress is not clearly depicted but hints at ermine (although he was never ennobled) or perhaps the robes of the master of an Oxford college (although he never went to university). In front of him is a half-pint bottle of wine and a glass. We all understand this reference. It is the club's most prestigious asset, an investment made by Emmanuel Groucher in the first flush of his success as a wine merchant. He acquired, some time in the early 1900s, a share in a small vineyard in Beaune. This was known, at least in Oxford Street and the club, as Clos de Groucher. It was considered a huge honour to be offered a bottle and, although the vintages of recent years have not excelled, a few bottles make their way on to the club wine list every year. It is known by the younger members of the club, rather disrespectfully, as Grouchers' Old Red Infuriator.

Andrew Farrell glanced up towards the portrait, as if seeking permission to begin the meeting, and then said: 'Well, now that we are all finally here, perhaps we might make a start. Michael, who is on our list today?'

I read out the list of names proposed for the club, concluding with Mr Patel.

The chairman said, 'Ah yes, we'll get to Mr Patel soon enough. Let's keep him to the last, Mr Secretary.'

We went through the list. For each name on it, I had to read out brief details of which school the candidate went to, what his job was, if he had one, and details of his other clubs. Then I had to read out the names of his proposer and the six members of the club who were prepared to support his election. It all went as smoothly as it usually did. There was only one objection to one name, from Mark Ansty.

'We can't allow that man in. He's a bank manager. I mean to say, Chairman, if we start letting bank managers in, half the members will never dare come here. Imagine having a drink with a fellow you've been on your knees to half an hour before, trying to get an increase in your overdraft facility.'

The chairman sighed. 'If you learned how to play back-gammon properly, Mark, you wouldn't need an overdraft.

I'm overruling your objection. In this day and age we have to be realistic in our choice of members and banking has become a perfectly respectable profession.'

At last we came to Mr Patel. I read out his details: he had been educated at Harrow and was now managing director of a big American investment bank. Peter Robinson had proposed him and there were the required signatures of six supporters in the membership book. Before the chairman could say anything, Mark Ansty, who had been looking agitated while I read out the details, spoke loudly.

'It might be all very well having bank managers in here, Chairman, if you say so, but surely we have to draw the line at a *black* bank manager?'

Andrew Farrell opened his mouth to speak, but this time I cut in.

'Chairman, David Martin has asked to speak to the committee about this application. I believe he's waiting outside.'

'Oh God, this is going to be a long morning,' said the chairman. He put his head in his hands for a moment.

'He has the right to address the Committee, under Rule 16b.'

'I know, I know. You'd better let him in. Five minutes, no longer. Tell him that.'

I stood up and went outside to find David, who was lounging about in the hall. When he saw me he took his hands out of his pockets and said, 'The moment of truth, Gascoigne?'

I could see that he was rather nervous. Andrew Farrell had that effect on people.

'You wanted to say a few words to us, I believe?'

'Yes. I mean, what I want to say is . . .'

'You can do all that inside,' I said coldly. 'You've five minutes to make your point. After that you will be asked to leave, and we will consider the matter among ourselves.'

David straightened his back and cleared his throat, then went into the committee room.

'Ah, David', Andrew Farrell said. 'You wanted to speak about Patel? The floor is yours. You have five minutes.'

David Martin looked very nervous and his normal high colour had faded. He began to speak, at first with hesitation, but as he warmed to his subject, with increasing vigour.

'I think the committee ought to consider the fact that Grouchers is a very traditional club and its members have very traditional attitudes. I don't mean that we are racist. Some of my best friends are coloured people. The desk porter at the place where I work in the City is black. He's a tremendous chap. Couldn't hope to meet a nicer fellow. But I wouldn't put him up as a member of Grouchers.' He paused and looked around the table to see what sort of reaction he was getting. Mark Ansty gave him a half-smile. The rest of us were fairly stony faced, I think. David continued in a firmer tone of voice.

'I quite understand why people like Peter Robinson take the view that Mr Patel would be a good member of the club. Peter thinks he's being progressive. He thinks he's shaking the club up, modernising it. But I've got news for Peter. A great many members here don't want to be shaken up. They don't want to be modernised. That's why they are members here in the first place. We all just want to preserve a little piece of England, here in Mayfair, where English people can speak and behave as their fathers did, without being apologetic, or politically correct, or embarrassed by each other.'

I noticed once again how difficult it was for English people to use the term 'British', at least without having their fingers crossed behind their back.

Mark Ansty said, 'I think David is making a jolly good point.'

Andrew Farrell said, 'Mark, pipe down, and let David finish. No discussion until he has concluded and left the room. Two minutes, David.'

David Martin continued.

'Thank you, Andrew. I don't have very much more to say. Just this, really: Grouchers was established as a club for English gentlemen. Mr Patel may be a gentleman – I don't know, I've never met him. But he isn't an *English* gentleman. If he is made a member, it will split the club. That might happen even if he is blackballed. I'm glad I'm not in your shoes, chaps. If you make the wrong decision here today, I honestly believe it will be the end of this place.' Then David nodded to us all and walked out, with a great deal more composure than when he had come in.

His remarks produced a thoughtful silence. Then Andrew Farrell sighed and said, 'If I was looking for someone to tell me what a gentleman was, David Martin wouldn't be very near the top of my list. However, he has made some points which, unfortunately, will resonate with some of the membership. I hope I don't need to remind anyone, Mark, that anything said inside this room must never be repeated out there.' He waved his arm to indicate the main rooms of Grouchers, although he could equally have been referring to the rest of the known universe. 'Does anyone have any comments? Michael, couldn't you persuade Peter simply to withdraw the application? I know he's a particular friend of yours, and whatever one might think of David Martin's remarks, there is going to be one hell of a row if this application stays in the book. I think we all realise that.'

I was silent for a moment, thinking about it all. Then I said, 'I see it all very simply, Andrew. The club is bound by its constitution and its rules, unless and until the members decide to change them. The rules of this club are very clear: any member may put up anyone he believes to be a gentleman, and if he can persuade six other members to support him in that view, then that candidate is clearly eligible for election. Any attempt by any member of this committee to dissuade a member from sustaining such a proposal would, in my view, be an unconstitutional act. Peter and his friends think Mr Patel is a gentleman. I've met Mr Patel and I must say, I too think he is a gentleman. Therefore this committee has no grounds to do anything other than nod this through, and the rest is up to the membership.'

There was another silence when I had finished speaking and then Verey-Jones said, unexpectedly, 'Gascoigne is absolutely correct in what he says. I support his remarks entirely.'

Andrew Farrell looked around the room as if for support, but there was only Mark Ansty and, having been snubbed by his chairman, he was not about to speak up for him.

'Very well,' said Andrew Farrell. 'Let Patel's name go through. But I fear for the future.'

7

You Think You Know Someone,
but You Never Really Do

After I dropped Michael off at the station, I drove back to Caorrun for the last time that year. If it had been the last time ever, I would not have minded. That gloomy valley and all those gloomy hills: even on this sunny morning I felt oppressed, even threatened, by the dark slopes and the grey crags like teeth. As I drove, I thought about Michael. I had seen him in a new light the night before last, and as a result I was thinking about him in a new way. You think you know someone, but you never really do.

It wasn't the words Michael had used, about genes and hunter-gatherers and things that I had never heard him mention even once in ten years of marriage. It wasn't just that. First, it was the thought that I was married to someone, slept beside him, talked to him at dinner and sometimes at breakfast, and had as a result built a picture in my mind of a solid, dull, respectable but, above all, good man. A good man who loved golf and fishing, and who talked about safe subjects with safe people: he would discuss golf with golfers, fishing with fishermen. He never had arguments with people. He hated confrontation. He liked to talk to people he knew would agree with what he had to say. He used conversation as a way of reaffirming his existence, not of exploring new ideas. That this same man had become obsessed with the idea that the British were really from the Pyrenees – was that what he had been saying at dinner? – had shaken me. Michael had never spoken about such things to me; he had kept his thoughts hidden even though this was apparently something he really cared about, mad as it seemed.

For a while I concentrated on getting off at the right exit on the roundabout that took me back on to the A9. Then I thought, if he had mentioned the subject to me, I would have been unable to hide my indifference. Maybe he realised that. But it wasn't just *that*, either.

When Michael had turned on David and snarled at him to listen, I had seen someone else looking out from Michael's eyes. It wasn't Michael any more behind them. It wasn't anyone I knew. Correction: it wasn't any *thing* I knew. The hairs had risen on my forearms and on the back of my neck, and I could feel them doing the same now, as if static electricity were running through me.

I found the turning off the A9 and drove up the single-track road. My heart, as always, sank as the great mountain of Beinn Caorrun came into view. I drove on out of the woods and into the clearing where the house stood, and I felt its desolation just as sharply as I had the first time I ever saw it.

I parked by the front door, which was open, and Rupert came out to greet me, wagging his tail. I looked in the kitchen for Mrs McLeish but there was a note on the kitchen table from her, saying she had gone back to her cottage for half an hour. Oddly enough, I had scarcely ever been in Mrs McLeish's cottage – she always came over to us. Mrs McLeish was as much a mystery to me now as when I had first married Michael. She had been here since he was a child, and through the death of both his parents she had been the one person who had kept Michael, and indeed the whole Beinn Caorrun estate, going. You would have thought that she would have become almost like a member of the family, a surrogate mother, a cosy family friend. Yet she was none of those things. Small, upright, with a pale, square face, her mousy hair touched by the first frost of age but in every other way unchanged in the ten years I had known her, she kept herself to herself. She was incredibly efficient, quite capable of keeping accounts and doing VAT returns, as well as dealing with builders and shepherds and all manner of people when Michael wasn't there. But her relationship with us, even with Michael, seemed remote and wary. She and Michael looked at each other and spoke to each other with the knowledge of many years and of a shared family history, but in my presence, at least, she called him 'Mr Gascoigne' or 'Mr Michael'. No one could tell me where she had come from, or whether she had any family. Michael simply used to say, 'She just turned up one day at the front door, not long after I was born, and asked for a job. As it happened, my parents needed a housemaid. Now she runs the place. And keeps me organised.'

There had been a Mr McLeish, of course. He had come and gone in the space of two winters. His wife threw him out when she discovered he loved Famous Grouse and Johnny Walker more than he loved her, and spent a great deal more money on them. There were no children. His name was never mentioned.

On a whim, and because Rupert looked as if he wanted a walk, I decided to go up the track to find her. Rupert followed me, stiff legged.

Mrs McLeish must have seen me coming because she met me at the door of her cottage.

'I was going to come down anyway, a bit later,' she said.

'Can I come in for a minute, Mrs McLeish?' I asked. I hadn't come that far (five hundred yards and uphill) only to walk all the way back again. And I suppose I needed company too, even if it was only Mrs McLeish. I didn't want to be in the Lodge on my own for some reason.

Mrs McLeish looked disconcerted for a second, and I wondered whether there was a frightful mess inside, but when she stepped aside and beckoned me in, the room looked immaculate. I felt that she still thought of me as an interloper, and she was probably right: it was easy to see that my heart wasn't in Beinn Caorrun. She had devoted her whole life to the place, and the family that lived in it, so I suppose it would have been a miracle if she had liked me. All the same, she was not unfriendly.

'The kettle's on. Come in and have a cup of tea.'

We walked through the sitting room to a little kitchen and I stood around while Mrs McLeish busied herself making the tea. Her movements were all briskness and efficiency. Then we took our cups – bone china, I noticed – back into the sitting room. There was rather a good kneehole desk against one wall, with photograph frames on it, and I couldn't help looking at them as I went past. My eye was drawn to the black-and-white photograph of a youth, shirtless, with tousled blond hair, standing on a wooden jetty beside some lake or loch. He was holding up a large fish – it might have been a pike – by means of a weighing hook slipped in between its gills and was smiling into the camera with eyes full of fun and mischief. He looked rather beautiful, like a young pagan god.

'Is that one of your nephews, Mrs McLeish?' I asked, for she had seen me pause to look at the photograph.

'No, dear,' she said. 'That's Mr Gascoigne when he was sixteen.'

I blushed. It wasn't one of hers; it was one of mine, and I hadn't realised. I bent and examined the photograph more closely: could that lean torso be the soft white body I occasionally glimpsed underneath Michael's pyjamas? Could that impish smile, that glint of something irrepressible in the eyes of this boy, have come from the same face that I saw staring at the *Daily Telegraph* every day? It was, as I looked again, just possible that this boy had grown into the man who was now my husband, but something seemed to have been lost along the way.

Mrs McLeish gestured for me to sit down.

'Come on, Mrs McLeish,' I said firmly. 'Tell me what he was like when he was a child.'

She put her head on one side, considering. She reminded me of a sparrow contemplating one more hop towards a breadcrumb lying by the chair of a pavement café.

'He was very wild when he was young, Mrs Gascoigne. His mother often said he would be the death of her. But everyone in Glen Gala loved Mikey.'

'Mikey?'

'That's what everyone called him. He was very popular, especially with the girls.'

My Michael hardly knew what to say to members of the opposite sex. He was a nightmare at dinner parties. The only place where he seemed to feel comfortable was at that ridiculous men's club he belonged to, although I suppose it got him out of the house. The young man – the young Mikey – did not look much like a future member of Grouchers.

'He used to come to my cottage sometimes, and tell me what he was up to. Stories I could never repeat to anyone, not to his mother when she was alive, nor to you now, Mrs Gascoigne. He trusted me and knew I would keep a confidence. He used to sit in that chair, and when I told him what a naughty, wicked boy he had been he would say, "Don't worry about it, Ellie, life is for living."'

'But what *was* he up to, Mrs McLeish?'

'Just the sorts of things that a boy running wild gets up to, especially when the parents don't keep a very close eye on him.'

'Did they not spend much time with him?' I asked. I had gathered this from Michael already, but it would be interesting to hear another point of view. Mrs McLeish's loyalty, however, was to her employers, even the dead ones.

'Och, old Mr Gascoigne had an awful lot of racehorses down in England and France, so he had to be going off to see them.'

She would not be drawn on any other details. I tried another tack.

'So his parents did not keep a close eye on him?'

'He was often left on his own here,' said Mrs McLeish. 'But Mikey hated leaving his beloved Glen Gala. He had friends here. And I looked after him, and cooked for him, and washed for him, and told lies for him if I had to.'

'Lies about what? Which friends?'

Mrs McLeish chose to answer the second question, not the first.

'Willie that has the petrol station now, Mary who runs

the pub in the Bridge of Gala: a lot of local people. He had other friends too, people I think he met when he was out walking. I never met them. Mikey was a great one for walking on the hills, and he would talk to anyone he ran into.'

When did Mikey become Michael? My Michael would cross the street to avoid meeting someone he knew and would never talk to a stranger, unless that person also happened to be a member of Grouchers. Then, often despite all the evidence to the contrary, Michael would presume he was talking to someone with identical interests, education and background to himself. He was rarely right about this, but never noticed. I did. I had to put up with them if he brought them home, or when he dragged me to their houses.

'Yes, it was his parents dying so soon after each other that made Mr Gascoigne steady up,' said Mrs McLeish. 'It's a miracle he still likes the place when it took both his parents from him.'

'He looks so different in the photograph,' I said. 'It hardly seems possible it's the same person.'

'He never smiles like that these days,' said Mrs McLeish. 'He hardly smiles at all. No wonder you didn't recognise him.'

There was a pause during which Mrs McLeish probably realised her remarks could be taken as suggesting that it was marriage to me that had made Michael the way he was. So she said, 'It started around the time his father died. Before you were married, Mrs Gascoigne.'

'He's never really talked about that,' I said. 'What exactly happened?'

Mrs McLeish gave me a peculiar look. 'It was an accident. They were behind with the hind-stalking, but Donald had slipped in the snow and twisted his knee, so Mr Gascoigne went out anyway, on his own. He knew every inch of those hills. Mikey told me that his father had listened to the weather forecast, looked at the sky, and had dressed as warmly as he could, before setting out.'

Mikey, I thought. 'Did Michael not go with him?' I asked.

'He was unwell. He sometimes was, in those days. He had a migraine, and when he was like that, he was of no use to anyone. So his father went out alone.'

Mrs McLeish interrupted her story for a moment. 'But your tea's getting cold, Mrs Gascoigne.'

'Go on with the story,' I told her. 'Never mind the tea.'

'You've never been up here in midwinter, Mrs Gascoigne. You don't know what it can be like. The weather turned at midday but by then Mr Gascoigne would have been miles from the house. He was a big man, bigger than his son, and could cover the ground quickly, even in snow.'

'It snowed?'

'Yes, but it wasn't just snow: it was a blizzard that came down from the north. The temperature dropped like a stone and the snow froze as it settled. By two o'clock the sky was as dark as night. I was sitting here in my cottage and when the storm broke I wanted to go down to the house to make sure Mikey was all right, but I couldn't even walk a few hundred yards in it.'

I didn't like her calling him Mikey. We depended on Mrs McLeish but there was something about her that repelled me now, as if she shared secrets with Michael that were kept from me.

'Mikey tried to walk up the track to see if he could meet his father on the way down from the hill but it was impossible to stand upright. The snow was horizontal. In the end he rang the Mountain Rescue, who were already answering a dozen other calls. There were climbers and walkers stranded all over those hills in that storm, and two others died that day.'

'How awful,' I said. 'Did they ever find Michael's father?'

'No,' said Mrs McLeish. 'They never found the body. The police and the search and rescue teams didn't get there until the following morning. They searched on and off for three days. Mikey took them to all the places he thought his father would have gone, but they never found him, not even in the spring, when the snow was long gone and the hill had dried out.'

There was a silence after Mrs McLeish finished her story. Then she stood up. 'I suppose we'd better get on with the job, Mrs Gascoigne. You'll be wanting to get away.'

It was true. The last thing I wanted was to spend the night alone at Beinn Caorrun. I'd done it in the past but my nerve was gone. Even with Rupert in the bedroom and all the doors locked, I knew I wouldn't sleep a wink on my own. We walked down to the Lodge together, and began the task of putting the house to sleep for the winter.

It was while I was putting away some table mats in a cupboard that I found it. A bulky-looking magazine lay beneath a pile of old newspapers that Michael liked to keep – articles he had started but not finished, incomplete crosswords and Sudoku puzzles that he never returned to – and that normally ended up being used as firelighters. Beneath this pile I caught sight of the magazine and somehow I knew from its position that it had been hidden, and that I wasn't intended to know about it. I reached down to pull it out, checking over my shoulder that Mrs McLeish wasn't near by in case I should straighten up with a copy of *Loaded* in my hand. But Michael wasn't like that, I thought, looking down at the cover page, which said *European Journal of Psychiatric Medicines*. A Post-it note marked a page, and there was an online article headed 'Bloomberg Company News' which had been printed out and inserted into the pages of the magazine as an additional bookmark.

I opened the magazine at the Post-it note and read:

High or mega-dose antipsychotic medication is now increasingly accepted as the norm in treatment of long-term mental illness. This presents the medical community with two important ethical issues. The first issue is that the chemistry of some antipsychotics, or neuroleptics as they are sometimes known, can lead to forms of ventricular tachycardia. This has in a small, but important, number of cases resulted in patient death. Other well-reported symptoms in a number of long-term studies carried out at high and medium-security facilities for the mentally ill have been akathisia, and extrapyramidal symptoms consistent with the onset of Parkinson's disease. This data should cause us to question the time frames for the evaluation and licensing procedures for some of these treatments before prescribing them to our patients.

A further and more troubling question is: what is the behavioural norm towards which we wish our patients to return? What is standard behaviour, and what is not? Clearly violent behaviour is not acceptable to society as a whole, but is that violence caused by a feeling, on the part of the patient, that we are seeking, by chemical means, to obliterate his identity ...

I couldn't understand why Michael should be reading about this, but then the article he had printed off fluttered out from the pages of the journal. I caught it and read it. It was an interview with someone, but one word in particular caught my eye:

> If I look to the product revenue streams that are going to sustain and build our share price going forward ... Serendipozan, recently approved by both NIHCE in the UK and the FDA in the US, has to be one of our stars.
>
> **Dr Heidi Schnoffler (CEO), Tertius AG,**
> **Bloomberg Financial News Channel**

I carefully put the magazine back where I had found it, and shut the cupboard door just as Mrs McLeish came into the room, with an armful of dead rowan branches.

'Mr Gascoigne's overfond of these things,' she said. 'The berries have dropped off and rolled all over the floor. It's taken me ages to sweep them all up. By the way, we're short of storage space, Mrs Gascoigne. There's an old linen press that was moved into the hay barn a few years ago because Mr Gascoigne took against it. But I think we need it back in the house, to keep all the sheets and blankets in.'

'That's fine, Mrs McLeish,' I said absently, thinking about Serendipozan and why Michael should have press cuttings about it. 'Where will you put it?'

There's room enough on the landing. Donald will move it for me. We'll give it a good spray of woodworm killer first.'

A couple of hours later, I was in the Range Rover, with Rupert snuggled up in his basket in the boot. He loved car journeys. As I started the engine, for some reason I glanced up at our bedroom window. The sun was full on it and the reflected glare blinded me, and then in an instant the sun was behind a cloud, and my heart leapt to my throat. I thought I could see a girl standing in the window, looking down at me. Then I thought it was myself I was looking at, and then the sun was out once more and I was blinded by the glare from the glass panes. When the sun went in again, I found myself looking up at an empty window.

I sat for a while with my damp hands on the steering wheel, my heart thudding. I ought to go and check, oughtn't I?

'No,' I said out loud. 'It was just a reflection of some sort.'

What else could it have been? I put the car into gear and released the handbrake. I needed to be away from this stupid place and its stupid reflections.

The journey down to my mother's house in Gloucestershire was easy enough. As I approached Stanton St Mary, it was getting late and in the headlights familiar streamers of mist were coming off the water meadows. The lights were already on in Stanton House and, as I drove up the drive, I felt an odd sense of relief. The pleasure that I felt as I arrived home (for I still thought of this house as my home, much more then Beinn Caorrun or the flat in London) usually did not survive the first half-hour with my mother, who always managed to find something quite maddening to say to me. But in those first moments, I would always have the recurring memory of how it had felt, as a small girl, to walk my pony back across the paddock to the stables, after hacking down to the village and back. Then, when the pony had been stabled, there was tea with Marmite-and-cucumber sandwiches in the kitchen and half an hour's piano practice, followed by a hot bath. Later, I would be allowed to take supper upstairs in my nursery, where I would read a few pages of a book under the watchful eye of my nanny. In those days of plenty, when my parents were still married, we had a housekeeper who doubled up as my nanny, and home felt like a place of love and security: at least, until I was sixteen. Then the pony was sold, and I was taken away from boarding school and put into a day school, all within a few weeks of my father's departure.

My mother was thrilled to see me now, but only because it gave her a chance to tell me about her new lover. This conversation began the following afternoon.

'He's *so-oo* charming, Elizabeth, darling. You'll adore him. He's renting a farmhouse in the village until he finds something more suitable.'

'How did you meet?' I asked.

'In the Stanton Arms at a quiz night. I've been dying to tell you, darling.'

'And his name?'

'Charlie Summers. I think he's related to Henry somehow. A sort of second cousin.'

Quite a lot of people liked to claim they were related to Henry somehow. Henry Newark was well off, and was generous to his friends and relations.

'And what does Charlie do?' I asked, trying not to sound too like my mother herself, when she used to ask who I had danced with at a party.

'He represents a firm that sells the most wonderful dog food. If I had a dog, I'd feed it nothing else. As a matter of fact, Charlie thinks we might get a dog. Henry's dogs all eat it and he says they are all so much better since they changed to it.'

We might get a dog? Whatever else this dog food rep was, he was a fast worker.

My mother must have seen something in my expression, because she said, 'Darling, you don't mind your poor old mother having a bit of fun, do you? I get so lonely.'

I got up from where I had been sitting and hugged my mother. Of course I didn't mind, not really. The dog food rep would be no worse nor better than the last one: charming, shiftless, middle-aged men with no steady income and a good sales pitch. They usually stayed with my mother until the point when they discovered they could not persuade her to take out a mortgage on her house, the only real asset she had, in order to invest in their computer maintenance business, or their wine business, or their dog food business.

Later that evening we talked about Michael. My mother sat beside the fire in her old armchair, smoking, with her cigarette stuck on the end of an ebony cigarette holder. I used to ask my mother why she made such a spectacle of herself: smoking was bad enough in itself, wasn't it, without drawing attention to oneself by looking like someone from the 1920s? All she ever said was that the cigarette holder ensured that the smoke would not harm her.

I sat beside my mother on the floor, with my knees drawn up, and a glass of white wine in my hand.

'And how is dear Michael?' my mother asked. I knew she didn't think much of him, and she was unconvincing in her attempts to appear interested or affectionate as far as he was concerned.

'Oh, he's fine,' I said. 'Thanks.'

My mother glanced at me. Self-absorbed as she might be,

I was her only child, and she knew every tone of my voice, every nuance and inflection of my speech.

'What's the matter?' she asked.

'Nothing's the matter,' I replied, and sipped my wine. My mother said nothing, but gave me a level stare until at last I said, 'Well, I'm a bit worried about him.'

'Worried how? Has he been a bad boy? I can't see Michael getting up to any mischief of *that* sort,' my mother said dismissively. The unspoken assumption that I was the only girl in the world who had the lack of judgement to fall for Michael nettled me.

'Nothing like that, of course not,' I said sharply.

'Then what?' asked my mother.

I paused and tried to collect my thoughts.

'It's just that he's been behaving quite oddly,' I said. 'I can't quite describe it. It isn't any one thing. Most of the time he's just his normal self. You know what a creature of routine Michael is.'

'I do indeed,' agreed my mother.

'But lately he's been different. It's almost as if some of the time he's the Michael I know, and some of the time he's an actor pretending to be Michael, and then ...'

I stopped again, not wanting to finish the sentence. My mother surprised me by finishing it for me.

'Some of the time he's someone you don't know at all.'

'Yes. That's exactly it. How did you know?'

'I didn't, except that I have always felt that Michael was slightly too good to be true. No one is as perfectly self-controlled and conventional and polite as Michael is. I've always assumed there had to be another side to him, and hoped that, whatever it was, he wouldn't be unkind to you.'

I told her about the strange conversation we had had that

night at Caorrun. I also tried to describe the articles in the journal I had found, but couldn't remember the exact details.

'Anyway, as long as he isn't beastly to you, darling,' said my mother, who was becoming bored with talking about Michael and wanted to get back to the subject of the dog food salesman.

'No, Michael has always, always been kind,' I said. 'But what should I do if it goes on like this?'

'Well,' said my mother. 'The obvious thing is for him to go and see his doctor.'

'I don't know. Michael doesn't seem to like his doctor. He seems wary of him. I'm not sure he'd agree to go.'

'Who is his oldest friend, in that case?' asked my mother. 'Is it that lawyer chap? The best man at the wedding?'

She meant Peter Robinson. I thought about this. Michael had hundreds of friends and he had no friends at all. Peter was the closest thing he had to a real friend, someone Michael might confide in, if there was anything to confide.

'Probably,' I said. 'Anyway, he's the only one of Michael's ghastly club friends I actually like.'

'Then have a word with him,' suggested my mother. 'Talk to him. Ring him when you get back to London.'

'I think I will,' I said. 'Thanks.'

My mother acknowledged this with a faint smile, and then said, 'Now, darling: do you think Rupert would like to try some of Charlie's dog food? His coat really has lost its shine, you know. I'm sure it would help.'

Two days later Rupert and I drove back down to London. I had arranged to meet Michael in the Italian restaurant that evening. He had a meeting at Grouchers that was going to run late, he thought. There seemed to be a lot of meetings at Grouchers: did none of these men have proper jobs to go to? They spent all their time forming committees about this, and committees about that.

When I returned to the flat, at first everything seemed normal. Then, after a while, it didn't seem normal at all. To start with, the flat felt cold. I checked the radiators, and the central heating had come on as it was meant to in the late afternoon, but it didn't seem to be warming the place up. I looked in the bedroom to see whether Michael had left a window open, as he sometimes did when I wasn't there – I hate draughts – but the window was closed. The bed looked as if it hadn't been slept in, although there was a slight depression in the bedclothes on Michael's side, as if he had lain on top of the bed. I went into the kitchen. There were no unwashed dishes, nothing stacked in the dishwasher, nothing much in the fridge. It didn't look as if he had eaten much while I had been away; perhaps he had eaten all his meals at his club. The standard bottle of wine that was usually in the fridge was still in the fridge: he hadn't touched that, either.

I hugged myself, shivered and went into the sitting room. The desk was covered in sheets of paper with notes scrawled on them. So Michael had been here, after all. I was beginning to wonder. I picked up one of the sheets and glanced at it. In Michael's tight, precise handwriting were the names:

Stephen Gunnerton.
Alex Grant.
Stephen Gunnerton.
Alex Grant.
Stephen Gunnerton.
Alex Grant.

repeated dozens of times. On another sheet, in a more looping straggly script, was the word 'Lamia'.

I couldn't make sense of any of it. Why would Michael write Alex Grant's name over and over again like that? And who was Stephen Gunnerton? The name rang a bell, but I couldn't remember where I had heard it before. Writing down someone's name once might serve as a reminder. Fifty times seemed a bit odd.

Why – apparently – hadn't he slept in the bed, or eaten, or drunk, in the last two days? What had he been doing with himself? Had he been out all that time? If so, where had he been, and what had he been doing? Michael's behaviour was becoming decidedly odd. I shook my head to try to dispel the feeling that there was a wrong note somewhere, a disharmony hanging inaudibly in the air.

I took Rupert out for a walk and then brought him back to the flat, put him in the kitchen and shut the door. He curled up in his basket with a sigh of relief. Home at last. Rupert was more relaxed about coming home than I was. There was something about the flat that made me feel uncomfortable, that made me want to go out and be with other people.

I tidied myself up and then went out to meet Michael. He should be at the restaurant by now. He never switched his mobile on, so there was no point in ringing him.

I walked down the street and crossed over, then took the turning that led to the restaurant. Like any girl, I hated the idea of sitting in a restaurant on my own, so I took a cautious look through the window. Yes, there was Michael. The place was already quite busy, even though it was only just eight o'clock. Michael, was sitting at a table at the back, talking to someone. I couldn't quite make out who.

Was there a person sitting at his table? I was curious as to who it could be.

I walked around to the door and went inside. Alfredo was standing by the reception desk and, as soon as he saw me, he went into his standard '*Ah, la bella signora*' routine. I didn't mind Alfredo, really.

After he had taken my coat, I went into the restaurant. There were a lot of people moving about, as another party had arrived just before me. Did I see someone getting up from Michael's table? No, perhaps not. He was still talking, only now it rather looked as if he were talking to himself. I felt hot with embarrassment. Did he not know how bizarre he looked, chatting away to an empty chair?

As I approached his table he saw me, and an odd expression crossed his face – a look of confusion or disappointment. Then he jumped to his feet.

'Hi, darling,' he said, smiling. 'How are you?' He kissed me on the cheek, and Alfredo, who had been following me, pulled back a chair. I saw that a glass of white wine had already been poured for me. Michael had drunk most of his glass, but that could not account for his sudden animation, the laughter in his eyes.

'God, I've had the most absurd set of conversations at Grouchers,' he told me. 'I've been longing to tell you.'

He started to laugh, and then checked himself.

'Let's choose something to eat,' he said, 'and then I'll tell you all about it.'

8

She Left Her Glass of Wine
Untouched

'Come into the office,' said Verey-Jones when the committee meeting had finished. 'I want to show you something.'

We went to the back of the club and into Verey-Jones's office, where he pointed at a brown paper parcel on his desk.

'There,' he said, 'look at that.'

We both looked. The parcel was an odd shape, with bits of Sellotape hanging off it, and rips in the paper covering. It had obviously been a difficult object to wrap in the first place, and this had been compounded by the incompetence of whoever had wrapped it.

'Perhaps it would be better if I took the paper off,' said Verey-Jones, after we had observed the object for a moment. With a few brisk but careful movements, he tore away the paper, revealing not one but two hideous porcelain pug dogs, portrayed in a seated position.

'There!' said Verey-Jones, triumphantly. '*Now* what do you think?'

'Very unusual,' I said. I had been through this ritual once or twice before. Verey-Jones collected early porcelain from the old German and English manufactories. He was said to have a good eye.

'Quite right,' said Verey-Jones. 'Unusual is a very good word. Braunschweig, I would think, wouldn't you?'

'Oh, I defer to your judgement,' I said.

'I am almost certain it is Braunschweig,' said Verey-Jones. 'I can't find the mark, but they didn't always put it on the very early pieces. But the colouring: these blue ribbons on the collar, the yellow bells. Braunschweig, I would say, and made around 1750. I remember seeing a similar pair of pugs sold as such at Christie's about fifteen years ago. I think that if the dealer had known what they were, the price might have been very different. Well beyond my modest means, anyhow.' He rubbed his hands together gleefully, and then cracked his knuckles. 'But that wasn't why I wanted a word. Although I am very glad you like the dogs. You should consider collecting porcelain yourself, you know. You appear to have a taste for such things.'

I made a non-committal noise and waited for Verey-Jones to get to the point. Years of service to Grouchers had rendered him incapable of direct action or speech. All subjects, and indeed, watching him as he traversed his office in the direction of his desk, all objects, had to be approached from an oblique angle. Any more obvious route would have appeared to him to be vulgar or tactless.

'Yes, I entirely agreed with what you said,' he continued, picking a porcelain inkstand from his desk and inspecting it. It was unclear whether he was still referring to the china dogs. I awaited clarification.

'You were quite right at the last meeting to point out to the general that if this black man, this friend of Peter Robinson's, has been put in the candidates book, and if six members have been found to support him, then it is very far from being our duty to interfere with the constitutional procedure. In short, I agreed with you when you argued against any attempt to influence the process one way or another.'

'I am grateful for your support,' I told him.

Verey-Jones shook his head, dismissing the idea of gratitude as an irrelevance. 'I have given it a lot of thought,' said Verey-Jones, 'and what I have concluded is that, in the first place, David Martin is correct in suggesting that the proposal of Mr Patel for membership of this club is an issue which might yet split the club in two. That may well be the case.'

'I do hope not.'

'I profoundly hope not too. But what I have concluded, in the second place, is that we are nothing if we cannot follow our own rules. And we have a very clear and precise constitution and rule book, which I have played some small part in drafting over the years. We neglect these things at our peril. Without a constitution, we are a crowd, not a club. Without a rule book, we are a rabble, not a crowd.'

I stared at Verey-Jones. There was something infinitely dignified in his delivery of this message. At the same time I felt another headache coming on, accompanied by a strange sense of detachment, as if I were seeing and indeed hearing this conversation through the wrong end of a telescope. Grouchers, and all its affairs, which for many years had been the fabric of my life, now seemed increasingly irrelevant.

Verey-Jones put the porcelain inkstand back on the desk and gazed at me. But he was not seeing me: he was seeing the endless bound volumes in which the rules and the constitution of Grouchers were written down – prescriptions hinted at, inferred, occasionally stated with brutal directness.

He said, 'I deprecate Peter Robinson's nomination of this Ugandan man to be a member of our club.'

'You don't like the candidate?'

'Don't like? My dear Gascoigne, my feelings are neither here nor there. This is a club that was founded for people who had something in common: golf, shooting, the same schools, married into the same families. Of course this Patel is a clever businessman and a talented village cricketer. I don't doubt he could charm the birds off the trees. But he is *not* one of us. I understand the feelings of the members, and my own feelings. None of these considerations matter. We have a constitution and a rule book. If we don't follow our own rules, then Mr Patel is entitled to consider us more primitive than whatever Ugandan tribe he came from.'

'I think Peter said his father was a Ugandan Asian who became a British citizen.'

'I dare say. My point remains. It is not a question of whether he is a suitable member or not. I don't think he is, but that doesn't matter. It is a question of whether we stick to our own rules, or change them every five minutes to suit the circumstances.'

Verey-Jones had missed the point, and one day I would put him right about that, but I said, 'We must stick to our own rules. You are quite right.'

Verey-Jones stared at me for a moment and then said, 'You know, Grouchers stands for a great deal. We have been going for over a century now. We are not as old as Brooks's, or White's, but we have an ambience of our own and a history we can be proud of. Our members laid down their lives in both world wars. We have had members who have played their parts with distinction on the national and even international stage. Think of General Keeping. Think of Overton-Brown.'

I recognised the name of General Keeping, who had served

in the Khyber Camel Corps in the Indian Army and had later led his men, and his camels, to destruction during the Battle of the Somme. The other name was unfamiliar to me.

'Who was Overton-Brown?'

'He was a leading contributor to the design and engineering of the tram system in Oslo, when it was installed at the turn of the nineteenth century.'

Verey-Jones shook his head. For some reason, I sensed that he was suddenly close to tears.

'Now we will have to change, because our own laws, and the laws of Europe, will force us to do so. We will have to elect Ugandan bankers as members. Polish dentists. French management consultants.' Verey-Jones turned away from me. He said, in a hoarse voice, '*Sic transit gloria Grouchers*'.

There was a moment's silence while he groped in his pocket for his handkerchief. He blew his nose and then turned back to face me.

'Anyway, Gascoigne, whatever happens, you and I must ensure it happens with dignity.'

I nodded. I did not know whether to laugh or cry myself. My conscious mind was full of sentiments, that were, if not the same as Verey-Jones's, at least an echo of them: regret, dismay, a determination to go down with the ship if going down with the ship were to become necessary. But beneath all those feelings was a growing sense that I was slipping away from Grouchers, losing my grasp on its orderly world. Maybe that was not a bad thing: it was beginning to look to me as if Grouchers itself might not survive for ever.

With an effort, Verey-Jones changed the subject.

'I say, Gascoigne, you may use my Christian name if you like. Please call me Alwyn. After all, we have been colleagues for quite a few years.'

'I will,' I promised. 'Please call me Michael.'

'Oh. Yes. Well, I expect you will want your lunch now, Michael.'

'Yes, Alwyn, I think I will go through to the dining room. You won't join me?'

Verey-Jones indicated the austere-looking lunch box on his desk and shook his head. He was noted for his sense of economy.

I headed for the dining room. Its handsome mahogany furnishings, and dark oil paintings of racehorses in the manner of Stubbs, or pictures of Springer spaniels holding down a dead partridge with one paw, always soothed me. They stood for a timeless England, an imagined England that now survived only in a few places, such as this dining room.

The room was already quite full, and dark-suited gentlemen diners were unfolding their starched white linen napkins at nearly every table; or picking up items of silver-plated cutlery to begin their noonday repast. I noticed a more audible hum of conversation than I was accustomed to hearing in this place. Animated conversation was not common to the Grouchers dining room: there was a feeling among members that any display of enthusiasm or high spirits was not compatible with the respect due to the wine and food in front of them. Yet now there was a definite buzz.

At one table I saw Peter Robinson deep in conversation with three other members. Mark Ansty and David Martin were dining together at another table. I hoped Mark was respecting the confidentiality of our committee meetings, but I doubted it. I went up to the buffet and found myself beside James Bass. I liked Jimmy. He was large and sleek, draped in a suit of shiny navy blue wool, and a waistcoat with a watch chain strung across it. He sometimes affected a monocle but was not wearing it today.

'Morning, Michael,' he said, as he noticed me. 'Ah, ham. A slice of ham,' he said to the waiter who stood by the carving board. 'No, two slices, Antonio; and a slice of tongue; a slice of that roast beef, as rare as you like; some brawn, I think; a wing – no, a drumstick from that chicken.' He accepted the plate from Antonio and then began spooning potato salad, saffron rice, some prawns, two or three eggs in aspic and a generous helping of mayonnaise on to it.

'Let's sit together,' he said, 'I want to talk to you.'

I knew it would be about the Patel affair, and my heart sank. But there was no avoiding Jimmy, so I nodded, helped myself to some salad, then went and sat at the table for two Jimmy had chosen. He was busy consulting the wine waiter when I arrived, and asked whether I would like to share a decanter of club claret.

'Just water for me,' I said. Jimmy ordered the decanter anyway, and then sent his plate back with a waiter because he had forgotten to help himself to pickled herring.

When this omission had been rectified, and Jimmy had refreshed himself with the first half-inch of his claret, he put down his knife and fork and said, 'I expect you will think this sounds funny, coming from me. I know I have Italian blood in my veins, of which of course I am very proud, even though we have lived in our part of Suffolk for the best part of a hundred years.'

Everyone knew Jimmy's grandfather had been the famous pasta trader Giovanni Basso, into whose warehouse in the East End of London had been imported spaghetti, tortellini, fusilli, penne, rigatoni, tagliatelle, and whose role in introducing pasta to a grateful British public had never been fully appreciated.

'I just wanted to let you know that I think it would be a great shame if we were to let standards slip at our club. You're sure you won't let me help you to a glass of wine?'

'Sorry, Jimmy, I'd love to, but it will send me to sleep.'

'Can't have that,' said Jimmy. 'We need you wide awake at the moment.' He diverted the decanter, which had been hovering over my empty wineglass, back to his own.

'The thing is, whatever Peter Robinson and his clever friends may think, this is an English gentleman's club. Isn't it?'

Jimmy looked at me over his fork, his eyebrows arching to emphasise his question. His face was sallow, possibly a failure on the part of his liver to keep up with its owner's varied and considerable diet.

'Yes, that was our founder's idea.'

'And he was on to a good thing. Groucher probably wasn't much of a gentleman himself, I dare say. He made too much money too quickly, for one thing. But he knew a gentleman when he saw one and those were the sort of people he liked to have around him. We ought to remain true to his ideals.'

I nodded, waiting for Jimmy to make his point.

'I mean, Grouchers is a way of life for some of us. We have hung on to our old-fashioned values here, even if the rest of the country is going down the tube.'

'I don't think things are quite that bad, Jimmy,' I said.

'Oh, but they are. You should look about you more, Michael. You should read the papers. Christ, just walk down Oxford Street and see if you can find anyone who actually speaks English. This club is an island of tradition. Without places like this, our English way of life would soon be a thing of the past. That's why we have to be so careful about who we let in here. That's why we have to stand up for what we believe in, and not be ashamed to say so.'

'Yes, well, it's an interesting point of view, Jimmy,' I said.

But he hadn't finished. He took an enormous bite of his chicken drumstick and chewed for a moment, then said, 'It's all very well to talk about change, and modernisation as Robinson does. But if you throw away all your traditional values, what are you left with? Nothing, or worse than nothing. That's what's happening to this country, Michael; we've got to stop it happening in Grouchers. We must remember our true identity: we are English, first and last.' He paused, then added, 'When I say English, I mean British, of course. I mean, you live in Scotland, don't you?'

'We have quite a few Scottish members, Jimmy. And some Welsh ones.'

'Well, you see, that sort of thing is *perfectly* all right. But ... Patel ... I mean, really.'

I made a meaningless noise that might have been agreement or disagreement. As a matter of fact, a resolve was beginning to form within me. One day I would explain to the members of Grouchers just what being British really meant. They were unlikely to forgive me for pointing it out. My moment had not yet come, however.

'It's good to talk, Michael', Jimmy said. 'Clears the air, I always feel.'

'Absolutely.'

'Now then, how's the lovely Elizabeth?' he asked,

changing the subject. Before I could reply he called the waiter over, to get a further slice of tongue.

That afternoon I went home early. When I opened the door of the flat, it felt different inside: as if someone else was already there.

'Elizabeth?' I called, wondering whether she had returned home early. She might have done: her relationship with her mother was not always easy. 'Rupert?'

There was no answer. For a moment I thought I could hear the soft pad of feet, and imagined Rupert was coming to greet me. No wife, no dog appeared. The flat was empty. It did not feel empty.

I went and sat in the kitchen. I felt tired. I had gone out for a long walk the previous night. I couldn't remember where I had gone, only that it had been a starlit night and someone had been speaking to me. I had returned home at some ungodly hour and, too tired even to get into bed, had lain upon the bed fully dressed and slept until late: I had nearly been overdue for the meeting at Grouchers.

I was beginning to dislike the increasingly tricky and unrewarding job of membership secretary. A long time ago, when I had first joined the club, it had seemed like an ideal solution to the state of mind I had been in at the time. Grouchers was unchanging, rooted in its sense of itself, a place of tradition, of conservatism with a small 'c'. Now Peter Robinson, and no doubt others, wanted to change all that. I felt sure they would succeed, but what would their success mean?

Sometimes I wondered whether it was all worth it. There was obviously the most almighty row coming. I remembered with dread that, in a few weeks' time, there was a Grouchers golf tournament, the last of the autumn, and I would have to be present, along with Peter Robinson, David Martin and a number of others. That could turn out to be a very difficult few days, the way things were going.

But if I didn't keep my job at Grouchers, what would I do with my life? What would the purpose of my life be? I thought I remembered someone saying to me, very recently, '*I will find things for you to do that will change your life.*' It had been a woman's voice speaking, but not, as far as I could remember, Elizabeth's.

I sat at the kitchen table. A sense of purpose was what I needed. I knew that somewhere within me was the desire to achieve something; I just didn't know what it was yet. I stood up and went to get the A4 ruled pad that normally sat by the phone, and the pen beside it. Perhaps I ought to scribble down a few notes. I began to write.

A little later I looked at my watch and saw that it was nearly 6.30. I must have been sitting at the table for hours. God knows what I had been doing. I looked down at the scribbled lists of names in front of me. What was that about a sense of purpose? I felt confused, and heady, as if I were on the edge of some revelation. I decided I would have a shower to wake myself up and, if Elizabeth had not returned by then, I would go out and walk around for a bit, then meet her at the Italian restaurant as we had agreed.

Half an hour later I left the flat. After walking around for a while I turned into the road where the Italian restaurant was. As I rounded the corner a sudden gust of wind struck me, an updraught between two tall blocks of flats. A crumpled newspaper flew into the air and danced against an orange sky before falling back towards the ground. Then the wind dropped and I was inside the restaurant, smoothing down my hair and straightening my tie.

'Just you tonight, sir?' Alfredo fussed about me.

'No, my wife will be here soon,' I told him.

'In any case, your usual table.'

'Bring me a bottle of white wine and open it, Alfredo,' I told him. 'I will have a drink while I am waiting.'

'Ah, the beautiful ladies, the beautiful ladies – they keep us waiting, no?'

I waved Alfredo away. He came back quickly with an open bottle of Pinot Grigio and poured me a glass. I tasted it. It was chilled enough, so I nodded and Alfredo left me to myself. A silvery voice beside me said, 'May I sit down for a moment?'

I looked up. It was the girl from the train. Was that where I had last seen her? I wasn't sure. I stared at her in surprise, and yet somehow I was not really that astonished. What was her name? Something odd: Lamia, that was it. Lamia.

'I saw you come in here,' she told me, 'so I thought I would follow you and speak to you for a moment.'

This sounded so unlikely that I smiled. She smiled back and again I felt the intense sense of connection with her that I had felt before, as if I had known her for ever. I half stood up and gestured to her to be seated.

'Do sit down,' I said. 'How are you? Let me pour you a glass of wine.'

She was more beautiful than I had remembered, dark haired, pale olive skin and round dark eyes that were almost black. She was still wearing her dark green dress and ruby earrings. She had no coat, despite the chill of the evening outside. She pulled out the chair opposite me and sat down, and I filled her glass. She went on smiling as I did so, looking into my eyes with a disconcerting directness that I remembered from our previous meeting. She did not pick up her glass.

'How strange that we should meet again,' I said. 'You left rather suddenly on the train.'

'It is not strange,' she replied. 'There are things I need to tell you. It isn't chance that brings me here. There is work to be done. Don't you feel that yourself?'

I could not imagine what she meant. We had met only once, for a few minutes, on the train. I let her comment go unanswered, and instead asked, 'What are you doing in London? Have you found somewhere to live?'

She said, 'I am not far away now. We will talk again, soon enough.'

Another remark I found unsettling, and hard to follow. Should I ask her to stay to dinner? I couldn't see Elizabeth putting up with someone as cryptic as this. Then Lamia was standing up once more, and looking towards the doorway.

'Someone is coming,' she said. I followed her glance and saw Elizabeth in the entrance handing her coat to Alfredo.

'It's my wife Elizabeth,' I explained, 'we're having dinner together.' As I spoke Lamia glanced towards Elizabeth and I saw a peculiar expression on her face: longing, almost hunger. Then she started to move away.

'Won't you stay and have a drink with us?' I asked. Lamia shook her head and then turned away from me, weaving between the members of a small group who had just arrived and were seating themselves at a nearby table.

Then I could no longer see where she had gone and Elizabeth was occupying my attention, allowing Alfredo to pull her chair out for her and generally make a fuss.

'Hi, darling,' I said. 'Great to see you.' I kissed her on the cheek, and saw a look of surprise on her face as I did so. I suppose my normal greeting these days was often more in the way of a nod. I felt confused and wondered whether anyone had seen Lamia sitting at the table with me. It could only have been a few moments ago. Alfredo said nothing and neither did Elizabeth, so I took a sip from my glass and said, 'God, I've had the most absurd set of conversations at Grouchers. I've been longing to tell you.'

I thought I ought to make an effort to entertain Elizabeth. She was always exhausted after a few days of her mother's company. She looked as if she thought nothing was less likely to be amusing than anecdotes about Grouchers, but before she could say anything I picked up the menu and said, 'Let's choose something to eat, and then I'll tell you all about it.'

9

'Nothing I can't handle'

I would have thought I was more likely to laugh while reading a Great North Eastern Railway timetable than listening to Michael relating tales about Grouchers. But he did make me laugh: he gave imitations of Verey-Jones and Jimmy, another of the club bores I had met, that had me in stitches. As I laughed, a part of me was thinking: *Michael's such a good mimic, why have I never noticed that before?* Then another thought came in answer to the first: *Because we never laugh, we barely even talk.* We were laughing now, or at least I was, and Michael was smiling, that curious expression I had noticed recently in his eyes: something unfamiliar, something new.

Then he made me tell him about my stay with my mother, and although I say it myself I in turn gave a fairly good imitation of Charlie Summers, my mother's new-found love and dog-food salesman *extraordinaire*. I had finally met him, the evening before I came back home, and he was just as I had pictured him: sandy haired, clusters of broken veins on his cheeks, and watery blue eyes. He was clad in a dark blue blazer with a rich crop of dandruff on the shoulders and crested brass buttons, and a striped tie that suggested military origins without any precise regimental definition.

He wore very dirty brown suede shoes that peeped out from baggy corduroys. Rupert had a stomach upset after trying out the new dog food, and I had taken great pleasure in telling Mr Summers all about it.

Michael listened with enjoyment to this story, and I found we were sharing a second bottle of wine. By this time of the evening Michael would normally be looking at his watch and saying, 'Don't want to miss *News at Ten*, I think we ought to be getting back to the flat,' but now he didn't even look at his watch. He looked at me, all the time, and now and again a small smile crossed his face. Michael could really be quite good looking when he smiled. For most of our married life, he had had rather a dazed look, as if he had just been woken out of a deep sleep; or else it was a hollow look, like a house that is empty on the inside. I had learned to put up with it; I had known what I was getting into when we were married.

But now Michael was smiling at me, and I saw again something I had half noticed from time to time in recent weeks: he had lost some weight about the face. It made him look younger, and I was reminded of the photograph I had seen in Mrs McLeish's sitting room, of the young boy holding up a fish to the camera, his gaze full of charm and excitement.

'I went and had a cup of tea with Mrs McLeish,' I told him, 'while we were putting the big house to bed. I saw a photograph of you when you were a teenager, standing on a jetty by a lake. She said you were a very mischievous child, always up to something. You looked like it, in the picture. She said you used to be called Mikey.'

Michael sat back in his chair, then held his glass up in front of the candle and looked into it.

'Yes,' he said after a moment, 'some people used to call me Mikey, I remember now.'

'Mrs McLeish wouldn't tell me a thing about what you used to get up to when you were that age. She was frightfully discreet.'

'Well, perhaps one day I'll tell you,' said Michael. For some reason bringing the conversation round to Caorrun and Glen Gala made him fall silent again, and I wished I had not brought the subject up. But why should I not? What memories had I triggered: thoughts of his parents, perhaps?

A few minutes later he called for the bill and we walked back to the flat in silence. It was not, however, a grim silence, and as we turned the corner into our street Michael linked arms with me: another first. Inside we took our coats off. I suddenly remembered the sheets of paper that I had found lying on the kitchen table.

'Michael, I hope you don't mind, but I tidied away some ...'

Then I stopped speaking. I found that I was in Michael's arms and he was kissing me: at first tenderly, all over my face, and then more passionately. 'Michael, what's going on?' I said, or tried to say, but after a few more moments it was blindingly obvious what was going on, and I was lying across the bed in our bedroom half naked, with Michael first beside me, and then inside me. We made love from time to time during our marriage: had sexual relations anyway. When Michael took me to bed on those previous occasions, neither numerous nor memorable, his expression was always exactly the same, and one night I remembered where I had seen it before: when he was practising his golf swing on the driving range. This time could not have been more different, and when at last it was over, I found that I was in tears. I didn't really know why I was crying. Perhaps it was the sense of release I had felt, the sense of oneness, and the feeling that I had waited a very long time for a moment like this one.

'Darling, why couldn't it always have been like that?' I said to him, sniffing slightly into the duvet.

'You can call me Mikey, now,' he said, not answering my question. We were both naked and properly in bed now, our clothes scattered all over the bedroom floor. I rolled over and punched Michael lightly in the chest.

'Is *that* what you got up to when you were sixteen?'

He smiled and stroked my hair.

'I can't remember what I was like when I was sixteen.'

'You looked like one of those people who lives among the trees – a faun, I mean.'

'Ah, the people in the trees,' he said. 'I used to hear them sometimes.'

I wasn't quite sure what to make of this, but then he swung his legs over the side of the bed and stood up. He took his dressing gown from the hook on the door, and as he put it on I looked at him critically. He *was* thinner.

'I'm going to have a glass of whisky,' he said.

'After all that wine? Won't you have a splitting head in the morning?'

He looked at me and said, 'I'm afraid I have a splitting head often enough, anyway. The whisky will do more good than harm.'

He went back into the sitting room. I sat at my dressing table and put my face to bed, then I put on my nightdress and came and sat next to him on the sofa.

'Can't the doctor give you something to stop your headaches?' I asked.

'He has given me something, but I'm not sure it does me any good.'

Then, with a touch of his old self, he picked up the TV remote, flicked on *Newsnight*, and the conversation was over for the time being.

That night, while Michael slept quietly beside me, I thought things over for a long time. The more I thought, the less I understood. I slipped seamlessly into a dream without realising it. Mikey and I were standing by the rhododendrons that surrounded the house at Caorrun, and he had that curious half-smile on his face, the one I had seen for a moment in the restaurant.

'Forgotten but not gone,' he said, looking into my eyes.

Once, when my parents were still together, we went to stay with some relatives of my father who had a villa in Tuscany. We put the car on the train to Nice, where my father had some business (we later found out that the business was my father's newest squeeze, Marie-Claire Billancourt), and then drove on into Italy. I was about fifteen, I suppose, and it was my first holiday abroad. I knelt on the back seat looking out of the back window of the car, fascinated by every detail of this strange new landscape.

The thing I remember most about that journey was how the *autostrada* plunged into dark tunnels and then the next minute we were back in blinding sunlight, glimpsing fairy-tale towns that clung to the steep sides of hills above the soft blue of the sea.

I recalled this image as I lay in bed one morning a couple of days later. It was a Saturday, and I had the luxury of a lie-in as I waited for Michael to come back with the papers and fresh croissants from the bakery around the corner. My life was suddenly in blinding sunshine and everything was new and magical.

Years ago, when Michael had asked me to marry him, I suppose the question I had asked myself was not 'Do I love him?' but 'Have I the strength to stay with him?' If nothing else, ten years of marriage had demonstrated that at least I had commitment, although in my bleaker moments I thought it might just be inertia.

I heard Michael open the door of the flat and call out 'Darling, I'm back,' and I turned over lazily in bed and realised all at once how happy I was. With that realisation came another: a consciousness that Michael had always loved me, and just hadn't known how to show it. What had changed? He was showing it now, in every way. I didn't care, for the moment, why it had happened; I was just grateful that it had. He came into the bedroom with a breakfast tray and put it down carefully on the bed beside me.

I used to dread weekends; most of the time they were an endless desert to be crossed with only Michael for company. I used to look forward to Monday mornings, and the week-long escape to the office. Now suddenly it was the other way round. The column on the property market seemed a pointless waste of my life. The prices went up. The dreary little basement flats that you couldn't give away ten years earlier were now being sold for unimaginable amounts of money, and I had to explain why all this was a good thing that would go on for ever. I didn't believe any of it any more. The articles I wrote seemed increasingly to be part of a fantasy world; the reality was my life at home.

I was also beginning to think that I didn't really like my job. I certainly didn't like Celia, the woman I worked for.

And time spent in the office was time spent away from Michael. I knew that if I asked him, he would say that there was no need for me to work, that the money I earned made no difference. I tucked the thought away: it was a conversation we might have one day.

That night, as Michael lay asleep beside me, something woke me up. The curtains weren't fully drawn and there was enough light from the street to show me what had disturbed me. Michael was sound asleep, but his hands were moving. I sat up in bed and looked at him.

His hands fluttered like birds, moving so quickly I could scarcely follow them, making signs and shapes that I could not understand; yet the movements were peculiarly expressive. All the time the rest of Michael lay absolutely motionless. As I watched I thought there was something almost hypnotic in the movement of his hands, something beautiful that I could not quite understand. There was so much I did not understand about Michael. How could that be? I felt myself becoming drowsy, and then sank back into sleep. In my dreams I saw the shadows of running deer, and dancing hares, portrayed by hands that threw shadows against the wall of a cave in flickering firelight. It was only in the morning, when I was watching Michael knot his tie, that the memory of the birdlike movements of his hands came back to me.

The following weekend, Michael took me away on a long-planned (and long-dreaded) excursion to stay with one of his Grouchers acquaintances, Jimmy Bass. I remembered Jimmy from previous Grouchers parties and shoot weekends. He was one of those men who is always cast in the role of the group clown, who always ends up smiling sheepishly while others make jokes at his expense. Michael once told me that Jimmy Bass was known at Grouchers as 'Jimmy Bolognese', an unkind reference to the earlier Bass of the Basso family whose sterling work as pasta importers had laid the foundations of the Basso fortune. Michael had never found the nicknames funny, and Jimmy liked him for it.

At any rate, Jimmy was well off, and a bachelor. Michael said that Jimmy had never married because he knew any sensible wife would ban him from having lunch and dinner at Grouchers five days a week. The club was the centre of his world. Now it was his fiftieth birthday, and most of the club had been asked to attend a drinks party at his house in Suffolk. As a particular honour, we had been included in a smaller number of guests who were invited to stay the night. I had not been looking forward to the weekend, to put it mildly; now, with Michael in this new, affectionate frame of mind, it did not seem too bad a prospect after all.

Jimmy's house was a handsome eighteenth-century build-ing, with a central block fronted by a portico, and two small wings. It sat in grounds of a few acres, looking down towards a small village at the bottom of the valley. At the rear of the house was a large terrace, beyond which a marquee had been erected, where we were all to sit down to dinner later on.

Although we were well into autumn, it was an unusually warm and still evening, and before dinner the guests spilled out from the house with their drinks on to the terraced lawn. Jimmy was at the centre of a knot of guests, looking large and sleek in a maroon velvet smoking jacket. Michael and I stood together, waiting until we found someone we both wanted to talk to, like the Robinsons or the Martins.

Just then I caught sight of Anna Martin weaving her way

towards us. I turned to Michael and said, 'Oh, darling, there's Anna,' except that Michael wasn't there. Seconds ago I had felt his hand on the small of my back as he steered me gently to an empty patch of lawn where the crowd was not so thick. In fact I could have sworn that when I turned my head and caught sight of Anna, he had been only a foot away. Now, he was nowhere.

'Oh, Elizabeth, there you are,' said Anna, taking a pack of cigarettes out of her handbag and lighting one. 'Where's Michael? David is stuck in the house talking club politics. I couldn't bear it so I came looking for you.'

'I don't know,' I said 'He was here a second ago'.

Anna was looking over my shoulder and said, 'Well, he's at the far end of the lawn now. Talking to that dark-haired girl.'

I turned around and could see Michael some way off, talking to someone, but then a group of people moved between us and I lost sight of him.

'Come on, let's go and find out who his new girlfriend is,' said Anna in a malicious tone of voice.

Then suddenly Michael's hand was on my back again. I started violently and when I turned he was smiling and shaking drops of liquid from his left hand where my sudden movement had caused him to spill some of the wine he had been holding. He had given one glass to Anna; now he gave the second to me.

'Who were you talking to over there?' I asked.

'I was just getting you two a fresh drink,' he replied. I looked at Anna, but she simply shook her head. There was a puzzled look in her eyes.

One minute Michael had been fifty yards away. The next he had been standing right beside me. I could not see how he could have done it. I didn't think I had been looking at someone else. Michael's height, the stoop of his shoulders, the attitude of his head as he listened to the dark-haired girl were all unmistakable, at least to me. Yet I must have been looking at someone else.

'Let's go into the marquee,' said Michael. 'People are starting to sit down for dinner and we don't even know where our places are yet.'

The next morning after breakfast, when most of the other guests had either left or had retired to the drawing room to read the papers and doze, I dragged Michael outside with me and marched him around the garden. As soon as we were some distance from the house, I turned to him and began to speak, but he held up his hand. 'Listen,' he said. I heard a faint cheeping near by and suddenly two partridge whirred out of the rough grass beyond the path. Michael smiled.

'See how well they hid themselves. They were right there, and we could not see them.' Then he paused, waiting for me to speak. I hesitated for a moment. I was about to ask a question from which there was no going back. I felt like Pandora, opening the box; but I had to know the answer.

Without any preamble I said, 'Darling, what's Serendipozan? And why are you taking it?'

For a moment, Michael looked as if he might tell me to mind my own business. A chilly expression settled on his face and his grey eyes seemed to darken. But then he said, 'I'm not taking anything, darling.'

'But you were.'

He steered me towards a wooden bench and we sat down. 'Yes, I was.'

I wondered whether I was to be subjected to one of the famous Michael silences, but then he continued.

'When I was a child, I was considered a little odd.'

'Odd how?'

'Eccentric odd. I used to invent imaginary friends to play with. You were an only child, so I'm sure you understand.'

I took his hand. It felt cold.

'Yes, I do,' I said. 'So you used to invent imaginary friends. What sort of friends were they?'

'I can't remember the first ones,' said Michael, 'but later on I used to imagine I met people in the woods above Beinn Caorrun, people who must have died around ten thousand years ago. I used to hear their voices in my head; see them in my head. They told me things, showed me how to use powers I didn't know I had.'

'That *is* a bit different,' I said. 'My imaginary friends were mostly straight out of whatever girl's comic I was reading at the time. What powers?'

Michael shook his head. 'You wouldn't understand.'

'I might.'

'It sounds so strange now. Powers of concealment, of hunting without being seen. How to ward off evil with the branches and berries of the rowan tree.'

'Very imaginative of you, darling,' I said. 'Much more creative than dreaming about Black Beauty or being a Thunderbird.'

Michael looked at me. 'It wasn't imaginative, not as far as I was concerned. It was what they told me.'

There was a pause. I waited for him to answer my original question.

'Anyway,' he said, 'as I grew older it didn't seem appropriate for me to go wandering around telling everyone about the people in the woods. My parents were spooked by it. Mrs McLeish was always ready to listen, and she tried to teach me to be cautious about what I said and to whom I said it, but in the end they decided I had to have treatment.'

There was a silence. A pigeon fluttered down on to the lawn and started pecking at the grass. Far away I could hear car doors shutting as Jimmy's guests began to take their leave. I hoped no one would come and disturb us, as it would break Michael's train of thought.

'So what happened then?' I asked.

'It's a long story. It was felt I had behavioural problems. They tried various different things and eventually Alex Grant sent me to a man called Stephen Gunnerton, in Harley Street.'

Stephen Gunnerton. That name again.

'What does "behavioural problems" mean?'

Michael looked surprised by the question.

'I thought I'd explained. Hearing voices, that sort of thing. I wasn't normal, that was the point, and these days you have to be normal.'

His voice sounded bitter, but he was smiling as he said the words.

'Stephen put me on some stuff called Serendipozan. It was the very latest thing in neuroleptics. That's the proper name for the kind of drugs that modify behaviour. Serendipozan re-engineers your brain chemistry. It switches things off, and it switches things on, until you fit a programme designed by some clever Swiss scientist in Basel. It makes you normal, all right – so normal you can hardly remember your own name. But that doesn't matter, you see, because if you're normal, you're just like everyone else.'

I thought about this. There was a great deal I didn't understand, and a great deal that I wasn't being told. I concentrated on my next question.

'So, why did you stop taking it?'

Michael looked at me.

'Because of us; because we've been married for ten years and you must have been feeling as if you had married a zombie. The years have passed by, and we should have been having fun together, we should have had children. I don't know how you've stood it, but you have. The drug takes away one's spirit, one's individuality, one's enjoyment of life. And in the end it will probably kill the patient anyway. These things have side effects that include heart failure and Parkinson's. *Side effects?*'

He clenched his jaw as he spoke, almost grinding his teeth, and I could sense the sudden, tearing rage in him. Then he spoke more quietly.

'When I was on the stuff, Elizabeth, it was as if I was watching the world on an old black-and-white TV with a faulty aerial: now I'm off it, everything's High Definition, ten million pixels, Surround Sound. I feel part of the world again. I feel *myself* again.'

'And there are no side effects from coming off it?'

'None that I'm aware of. Nothing I can't handle.'

Which was it? I wondered. Aloud I said, 'Have you told anyone you're not taking the drug any more?'

Michael thought about that for a moment.

'No, but you're right, I ought to. I think I'll go and see Alex Grant.'

We sat for a while on the bench without talking, while the pale cold light of a late autumn morning grew around us, the scent of overripe apples and gentle decay wafting our from Jimmy's apple orchard near by. I waited to see whether Michael would say any more.

'They meant well, when they put me on those drugs,' he said finally. 'From their point of view, they probably felt they had no choice. But they took my life away from me. Now I feel as if I've been given it back. It's so important that I take this chance. I feel – I know – that there's a reason in all this, a purpose.'

He smiled again and stopped speaking. After a few moments more, we stood up and began to walk back to the house.

There was no one in the drawing room. We went upstairs to our bedroom and picked up our cases, which we had packed after breakfast. We were met on the landing by Jimmy's butler, Silvio. He took the bags from our hands and said, 'Allow me, Mr Gascoigne. I will put them in your car. Mr Bass is in the marquee, sir, if you want to say goodbye to him.'

A folded twenty-pound note changed hands. We went back downstairs and out across the lawn. There, in the huge tent, a scene of disarray greeted us. The caterers appeared to have cleared up some of the mess, but empty magnums of champagne and random glasses stood on tables here and there, and streamers of coloured paper from Party Poppers lay all over the floor. At the far end of the marquee a trestle table had been laid for a dozen or so people, and next to it was a side table groaning with cold leftovers from the night before: salads, poached salmon, cold chicken, cold lobster, plates of asparagus, bowls of strawberries and other unseasonable luxuries.

Jimmy was sitting on his own at the table. He looked

wrecked. His eyes were red and he had not shaved very well. He wore elephantine jeans and a generous V-necked pullover, with a large napkin tucked into the V. Everyone else who had been staying appeared to have gone. Jimmy waved a fork at us, bidding us to approach.

'Oh God,' said Michael. 'We're going to have to have lunch with him. We can't leave him on his own.'

'Come and join me,' said Jimmy, in a voice that sounded jollier than he looked. 'Loads of good things to eat. Have a glass of champagne. There's plenty left. Sit down here, next to me, Elizabeth. Michael will get you some lobster.'

There was no way out. We sat and lunched with Jimmy, although it was scarcely noon, the three of us sitting at one end of the long table amid the desolation and debris of the abandoned marquee. Jimmy seemed oblivious to the fact that, apart from us, every single one of his guests had abandoned him before Sunday lunch. Between mouthfuls of lobster he kept saying, 'I shouldn't say so myself, but not many people know how to entertain the way I do. Don't you think so, Elizabeth?'

It was painful.

'Yes, Jimmy,' I said. 'It was unforgettable.'

Neither Michael nor I was hungry, but we pecked away at some food and drank a glass of wine. Jimmy ate and talked, sometimes both at the same time. He said, 'Jolly good gathering of kindred spirits, don't you think, Michael?'

I removed a fleck of his lobster from my pullover.

'A very memorable evening,' agreed Michael. 'The party of the year, I should think.'

'The party of the year!' said Jimmy. 'Well, it is kind of you to say so. I think you are probably right. I will admit no expense was spared. Nothing but the best for my fellow members of Grouchers. Top champagne, top wines, top lobster straight from Billingsgate. Might as well spend it as let the taxman get it,' said Jimmy, smiling. Behind his smile I thought I could see him weighing up the cost against the grace conferred upon him by the presence of so many members of the club at his house.

As soon as we could, without being too obviously in a hurry, we stood up to go. Michael patted Jimmy briefly on the shoulder and murmured his thanks. I bent down and kissed him on the cheek, not ideal when the person you are kissing is still eating a chocolate profiterole.

'Thank you so much,' I said.

'It was my pleasure,' said Jimmy, beaming. As we left the marquee, and all its dreary litter of unwashed glasses, overturned chairs and empty bottles, we heard a noise behind us. It was our host standing up.

'I think it goes to show how important it is for us English to stick together,' he shouted. 'I mean us British, Michael. A night like last night ... the flower of English society ... the membership of Grouchers ...'

His voice trailed away as Michael and I left the tent.

10

He Shot out into the Street
and Disappeared

Monday was supposed to be a busy day. I was meant to be
organising a photo shoot of the interior of a new block of
flats in Belgravia: five million pounds for a two-bedroom
flat. In between phone calls I kept thinking about last
weekend. Michael – Mikey – had talked to me more openly
in the brief conversation we had held on Sunday morning
than he had in the whole of our marriage. Yet, open as he
had been, I did not feel he was telling me everything. For
every question he answered, more questions were raised.
For example, what did he mean by 'behavioural problems'?
And if the drug he had been taking had got rid of them, or
suppressed them, what would happen now that he was not
taking it any longer?

On the evidence so far, Mikey without Serendipozan was
infinitely more fun, more loving and more interesting to be
with than Michael with Serendipozan had been for the
entirety of our marriage. The changes in him had been
almost abrupt, taking place over days rather than weeks, as
far as I could tell, and suddenly our life together was
different. The sex was different, as well; very different. In
the past, when we went away together, the main activity
behind the bedroom door had been Michael complaining

that there was no trouser press, or shoe trees, or that there was the wrong sort of coat hanger in the wardrobe. On Saturday night – perhaps the effect of being in a strange bedroom, although a very comfortable one – I had felt very randy, and had drawn Michael towards me as soon as he climbed into bed. He too seemed to want to make up for years of relatively celibate existence, and as he entered me I saw on his face a smile that was part love, part triumph. The memory warmed me now, and with it came another thought.

For years I had been on the pill, both before and after our marriage. It had been a deliberate choice, although not one Michael and I had ever discussed. Then, for a whole lot of reasons, I had stopped taking it. There didn't seem to be any point: Michael and I made love together in recent years with an infrequency that was approaching extinction. Now all that had changed, and the idea struck me: what if I became pregnant? For some reason, the possibility no longer filled me with dread.

I realised I had to talk to someone. There was too much that was new in my life, too many new ideas and experiences going round and round. I gave up on the photo-shoot planning for a bit, and on an impulse I rang Mary Robinson and asked whether she could have lunch with me. I knew Mary wouldn't be busy, although she made a production out of looking in her diary and muttering about book club lunches and bridge classes. In the end I bullied her a little, and we agreed to meet at one o'clock in a small restaurant off Walton Street.

Mary was puzzled as to why I had made her cancel something in order to see me. After all, it was only two weeks since we had all been together in Scotland. When we had looked longingly at the menu and then both ordered salad and mineral water instead of the white wine and the veal escalope, or Thai grilled chicken, that we really wanted to order, I said, 'Mary, how did you think Michael was when we were all up at Caorrun?'

Mary looked startled for a moment and then said, 'I don't know: about the same. No, perhaps there was something: he seemed a bit more animated than usual.'

'That sounds awful.'

Mary blushed. She was a shy, straightforward sort of girl I had been at school with, and had met again a few years later, when she unexpectedly asked me to her wedding. Since then we had been firm friends.

'Well, you know what I mean. Michael's always been a quiet sort. He did get quite excited that evening when David Martin was teasing him. Or was David teasing Peter? I don't remember, but Michael practically jumped down his throat at one point. Anyway, he put David in his place, which has to be a good thing.'

'Mmm,' I said. There was a silence while Mary tried to decide whether she had just called my husband a crashing bore, and if so, what she ought to do about it.

'Mary,' I said. 'You must have told me, but how did you meet Michael? Was he your friend first, or Peter's?'

'Oh, Peter met him before we became engaged,' said Mary. 'Aren't we going to have a glass of wine with our lunch? Do let's.'

This was an obvious device to change the subject. I waited until the wine had been ordered and poured, and then returned to the attack.

'I mean, were they at school or university together? I'd

always imagined it was something like that but for some reason, I've never asked Michael about it.'

Mary fiddled with her fork.

'No, they weren't at school together.'

'So where did they meet?'

Mary looked up at me unhappily. I could see she didn't want to answer.

'Where?' I asked again. 'I mean, they weren't doing time together, were they? Your husband's the most respectable man in London. What's the big secret?'

'It isn't something Peter likes to talk about,' said Mary, after a moment. 'So of course, I don't. But you don't know either, which means Michael has never told you ...'

I just looked at her. I knew I could make Mary talk, and I did.

'Peter used to suffer from some sort of depression. Bipolar disorder was what the specialist called it. Peter used to have to attend a clinic, and before that he was briefly in hospital. He met Michael when they were both outpatients.'

Mary stopped speaking and looked at me. A huge blush suffused my face. I bit my lip to stop it trembling. My oldest friend had just told me that my husband and his oldest friend had met in a mental hospital, and I hadn't even known. Michael had spoken about taking pills for some sort of 'behavioural problems'; not about being in an institution. Mary, for whom kindness was as instinctive as breathing, put her hand out and covered mine as it lay on the table.

'You really didn't know, did you?'

'I feel so ashamed. I should have known,' I said.

'There's nothing to be ashamed of,' Mary replied. 'I told you, Peter doesn't like talking about it, either. Men are like that. They think mental illness can be cured with cold baths and long runs. They're ashamed when they shouldn't be. They think it's a black mark – that people will stop sending them briefs, or avoid them at the club, if they aren't "normal".'

She paused and then added, 'Stephen used to say that there is no such thing as normal, anyway. Not when it comes to the brain.'

'Who's Stephen?'

'Stephen Gunnerton. He's a psychiatrist, the consultant that Peter's doctor referred him to. He really helped Peter.'

That name again: I had heard Michael mention it last weekend, and had seen it written, again and again, on a sheet of paper in our sitting room.

Our salads arrived and the conversation stopped for a moment. Then I asked, 'Did this psychiatrist cure Peter?'

'Oh, absolutely,' she said. 'He's on some medication, but there are virtually no side effects, and he's miles better. He's been fine for years. Stephen must have helped Michael too, because Peter says Michael was very strange when he first met him. Now he's steady as a rock.'

We finished our lunch talking of other things, and then I went back to the office.

All that afternoon, and on the way home, I wondered what to do with the information Mary had given me. My first instinct was to ask Mikey to tell me more about it, but somehow my nerve failed me – darling, how come you never mentioned you used to be in a mental hospital? What sort of 'behavioural problems' did they put you in there for? I couldn't see myself saying that, or anything like it. My second instinct was to find out more. How could I not? If I just forgot about it I would know that there was always going to be a part of my husband that was secret from me, part of the story that had not yet been told. For ten years I had bottled up my own emotions and concentrated on having what I had once called a 'workable' marriage. What vast cynicism had welled up within me, when I had used those words, what inexcusable ignorance of life? I might as well put a line under those last ten years of marriage, because now, after the last few days, everything had changed. We either had to go forward, or we had to go back. We couldn't just stay as we were.

Michael wasn't in when I got home, which was unusual. I went into our bedroom and changed, then into the bathroom. Something prompted me to look in the medicine cupboard as I stood in front of the mirror, brushing my hair.

I found the packet almost immediately, tucked under a box of Nurofen. I remembered how it had fallen out of the cupboard when I was rummaging in it, just before I went up to Caorrun not quite three weeks before. Bathroom cupboards are full of mysterious bottles and packets: medicines picked up on holidays; pills prescribed for past ailments, imagined or real, unfinished and never thrown out; endless vitamin supplements and fish oils containing the secrets of eternal youth. At the time, I had been in a rush, but now I wanted another look. The label was faded, but I could make out the words 'Bridge of Gala Health Centre'. So our nice local GP at Caorrun, Alex Grant, had actually been prescribing the Serendipozan for Michael. I wondered how long it would be before he noticed Michael had not renewed his prescription. Perhaps he just sent them to Michael once a month without being asked.

I caught a movement in the mirror and jumped. Mikey was standing behind me.

'You gave me a shock,' I said. 'I didn't hear you come in. Where have you been?'

He looked at me – holding the packet of Serendipozan – and raised an eyebrow. I said nothing for a moment, and then, 'I was thinking of having a chuck-out. There's so much rubbish in these cupboards. Are you sure you don't want these any more?'

'I'm quite sure,' he said, taking the packet from my hand. He threw it in the waste bin beneath the basin. 'I've been out walking Rupert,' he added. 'Poor old boy looked rather bored. He'll sleep well tonight. We've been all the way to Hyde Park and back.'

'It must have taken you ages.'

'It did.'

Michael looked as if he, too, had benefited from the exercise. His cheeks had more colour than was usual and his hair was windswept, although it had been quite calm and windless when I came home. He put his arms around me in an embrace, then released me.

'I thought we might go to Rome this weekend. Can you get off work early on Friday; and Monday morning too? I hope so – I've looked on the internet and found a special offer at a very good hotel.'

I felt breathless.

'Rome? On Friday? This is very sudden. What about Rupert?'

'I've already arranged for Norma to come in and look after him.'

Norma was a neighbour, short of cash, who did flat-sitting and dog-walking for us from time to time.

'But Rome?' I knew I could get the time off: it would just be a matter of a few late evenings to make it up. That was the one good thing about my increasingly ghastly job.

'What made you decide to go to Rome?'

Michael looked at me and said, 'Don't you like surprises? I do.'

I remember our honeymoon. The official one, ten years ago, had consisted of a few damp days in a hotel in Ireland. It was by a links course and our days were punctuated by golf, which I could barely play, bad food, and sitting around in communal sitting rooms in a cheerless hotel, surrounded by perfect strangers and reading back issues of *Hello!* Magazine.

What I remembered most about our honeymoon night was the way Michael carefully unpacked his pyjamas and laid them out on his pillow. Then he unpacked a pair of slippers and put them on the carpet at precise right angles to the bed. Pyjamas, slippers? Where was the wild passion in pyjamas and slippers? The answer was: nowhere. We had been sleeping together for a couple of months, so there was no novelty to look forward to, except that now we were legal, as people used to say. Even so, I suppose I had been expecting at least some pretence of romance. I lay expectantly in bed while Michael brushed his teeth in the bathroom. Then I felt a sticky feeling against my legs and realised I had got into bed with the complimentary chocolate mint, which had slipped off the pillow without my noticing it and was now dissolving into a happy molten mass. Anyone but Michael would have roared with laughter at this. What Michael did was to ring Housekeeping and force them to come upstairs and remake the bed while we stood gazing blankly at each other wrapped in the hotel's towelling dressing gowns. Believe me, melted chocolate mints are a very effective passion-killer.

Those brief days in Rome were everything that first honeymoon should have been, and wasn't. We took the train out to Stansted at a very early hour, but it didn't matter, because we were going on holiday together: not golfing, not fishing, not stifling yawns trying to make conversation with some ghastly Grouchers wife.

The plane was on time, the luggage was not lost, there were no queues for taxis and the taxi driver was cheerful, the sky was blue and clear. As we drove into Rome from Ciampino airport, I thought, this could be what the rest of my life is going to be like: doing things together, having fun with Mikey. I leaned against him and pressed his arm.

We stayed in the Hassler, at the top of the Spanish Steps. Mikey had booked a suite, not just a room, and it contained a sitting room with a balcony, and a bathroom with a marble floor and gold tap fittings. Some special offer. We unpacked, then went down and sat on the terrace and stared out across the city, drinking a glass of wine. Next we wandered down the Spanish Steps, and along some side streets until we found a restaurant that suited our mood. After lunch, we walked and walked for miles, arriving back at the hotel footsore and happy. I lay and dozed on the bed until it was time to shower and get changed for dinner.

And that was how we spent our time in Rome, brief though it was. It seemed an endless daze of wine, and food, and happiness. We did all the sights, or as many as we could manage: the Colosseum, the Pantheon, St Peter's. We shopped in the Via Condotti, the Via Corso, the Via This and the Via That. Mikey bought me an eternity ring in a little jeweller's shop: a thick gold band studded with white diamonds and aquamarines. Every few minutes, it seemed, we stopped in a café: to take espresso, wine, or ice cream, regardless of the time of day, regardless of whether we had just lunched or dined. And how we lunched and dined: we ate our heads off, and then felt hungry immediately afterwards. When we weren't walking, we were in our room at the hotel, and Mikey made love to me: before breakfast, and in the golden hour before the first drink of the evening.

My mother, after her third or fourth glass of wine, had confided in me a few years earlier: 'Never allow a man to make love to you in the morning: their breath is disgusting, and you get a rash from their bristles. It's even worse at night: they roll off you and start to snore before you have a chance to say a word. The time to make love, darling, is what the French call *de cinq à sept*, a decent interval after lunch and with time to spare before going out for the evening. Then you can make it all as pretty and romantic as you like, and there's still time for a long bath and a stiff drink before dinner.'

I remember blushing to the roots of my hair; I was not married then, hardly even launched into the world of men, and this information, the only guidance my mother ever gave me about my sex life, seemed quite a lot to cope with at the time.

With Mikey, this advice now seemed redundant. Any time of day seemed like a good time for him to take me to bed, and I agreed. Our closeness wasn't just physical: we talked together as we had never talked before.

'What were you like as a child, really?' I asked, as we sat on the roof terrace on our last evening, watching the sky turn violet. 'Mrs McLeish obviously adored you but she's far too loyal to say a word out of place.'

Mikey said, 'I was a strange little boy, I suppose. I was left on my own a lot. My parents often went racing in the spring and summer, and then they would go abroad for the winter. They never took me abroad. We used to go to North Berwick, sometimes, but that was when I was very little.'

'Weren't you terribly lonely?' I asked.

'No, not at all. I always found someone to talk to, or play with. I was out on those hills a lot. I could run like a stag in those days.'

'And everyone called you Mikey,' I said. 'You sound as if you were like Mowgli in *The Jungle Book*.'

'Yes, brought up by the creatures and the people of the wood,' said Mikey warmly. 'It makes a nice story, doesn't it? But not everyone called me Mikey. Some of the children in Bridge of Gala called me "Mental Micky".'

'Oh, how horrible of them,' I said. My heart started racing. Mikey – on purpose or not – had given me another opportunity to ask him about his mental illness, about Serendipozan, and all the mysteries that now surrounded him.

'I told you I was rather an odd child,' said Mikey. 'And children are mostly horrible to each other in any case.'

He smiled at me, as if holding a deck of cards towards me like a conjuror: pick a card, any card, don't tell me what it is, I'll tell you. I drew a deep breath to ask him why he had really been prescribed Serendipozan, what darker truth might lie behind such bland terms as 'odd' and 'behavioural problems'. But as I did so, I realised how fragile this new happiness was; happiness that I now held in the palm of my hand, like a drop of quicksilver. How quickly it could slip through my fingers and fragment into a thousand droplets.

Instead of asking what I wanted to ask, a different question came out.

'Why did you decide to come to Rome so suddenly?'

'Do you wish we hadn't?' he replied, staring out at the view without turning his head to look at me. I could see that he was still smiling.

'Don't be a fool: you know how much I've loved every minute of it. What I meant was, why has it taken us ten years to do something like this? We've really been together, Mikey. Don't you think so?'

'You're asking me why we never did this before. Don't ask me, darling, just accept things as they are.'

'But how do I know they'll stay this way?'

He said nothing in reply to this, but a line appeared between his eyes.

'Mikey?'

'I like you calling me Mikey,' he said. But he still didn't answer my question.

We got home on Monday afternoon, and I decided I would go and freshen up, and then go straight into the office and put in a few hours, just to appear willing. But when we unlocked the door, Norma the dog minder was waiting for us with a grey face. She wouldn't look us in the eye.

'Hello, Norma,' I said, as we stepped into the hall and put our cases down.

'Where's Rupert?' Mikey asked, because Rupert, like many dogs, had the psychic power of knowing exactly when we would return from our rare trips away without him, and was always standing beside Norma wagging his tail as hard as he could when we came back.

'Oh, Mr Gascoigne ...' said Norma, and then burst into tears. We couldn't get any sense out of her, so I shepherded her into the kitchen and put the kettle on while she buried her head in her hands, unable to speak through muffled sobs that shook her narrow shoulders. I heard Mikey going from room to room calling for Rupert, and then I heard the front door bang as he went out to look up and down the street for him. He came back into the kitchen a short while later and shrugged, a bleak look on his face.

'What happened, Norma?' I asked, as gently as I could. She was still shaken, but had managed to calm down enough to sip some tea. 'Where's Rupert?'

'I don't know. He was so restless. I couldn't calm him down. Then, yesterday morning, when I opened the front door to pick up the newspaper, he shot out into the street and disappeared.'

After a while we managed to make sense of Norma's story. From the minute we left Rupert had seemed very anxious. That was quite customary, and it always took a while for Norma to calm him down, but this time she couldn't. Rupert kept going from room to room, looking for us. He slept the first night in his basket, which Norma moved into the spare bedroom so that he could be next to her. That was unusual: he was normally content to stay in the kitchen.

'Then, on Sunday morning, very early, he started to growl. He didn't leave his basket but he was growling with that awful low sound they make, you know, when they're really angry or frightened. I switched on the light and saw that his hackles were up.'

She looked at us with scared eyes.

'Of course, I started imagining that there was a burglar in the flat, and I didn't know what to do. They say these drug addicts will put a knife in you as soon as look at you. But I couldn't hear anything. It was very cold, too. The heating was on but it didn't seem to be working properly.

After a while I must have fallen asleep again. But I wasn't very happy, and neither was Rupert. I kept thinking I could hear someone padding about. I was very frightened.'

Despite Rupert's disappearance, I felt a little sympathy for Norma. She was in her sixties and not very robust. To have a dog growling beside you in the dark, while your fancy makes you interpret the small sounds of night as something more than they are, is not a comfortable thought.

'In the mofning I went around the flat. Of course, everything seemed to be in its place, and there was no sign of any disturbance or of anyone having been there except me. Then, when I got to your bedroom, I opened the door to take a quick look inside, just to make sure everything was all right.'

She looked at us, as if apologising for this invasion of privacy.

'Quite right, Norma,' I said. 'That was the right thing to do.'

'Rupert began whining,' she continued. 'Then he howled. It chilled me to hear it. Then there was a noise at the front door and I went to see what it was. I was frightened – I don't know why. When I opened the door I saw the newspaper lying there, and I bent down to pick it up. Rupert burst past me and ran out into the street. I couldn't stop him.'

Norma began to sob again.

That was all there was to it, really. By the time Norma had changed from her slippers and dressing gown into her clothes, Rupert was long gone. She walked and walked, she said, until she was fit to drop. Then she spent the afternoon phoning the police, the RSPCA, and every dog shelter in

London. Nothing: no sign of Rupert anywhere. Not then, and not now.

After a while we managed to get Norma out of the flat, although she kept apologising every five seconds as she went. It wasn't really her fault. I was devastated – I adored Rupert – but it was worse for Mikey. I could see that he was on the verge of tears. I had never seen him look so distressed.

'Poor Rupert,' he said. 'What harm did he do to anyone?'

That seemed an odd way to look at it. I just said, 'Perhaps he'll come back. They do that sometimes. They go walkabout and then come back.'

With a great effort Mikey smiled, and said he supposed that was possible.

'All the same, though, I'll just go out and look for him again. I can't bear the thought of him wandering about on his own. I'll get the car and drive about a bit. Would you mind not going into the office and staying here? Just in case he comes back?'

In the end it was nearly midnight when Mikey returned. I had made a dozen phone calls to some of the telephone numbers Norma had scribbled down, but no one had any news of Rupert; not the police, not the lost-dog centres. Mikey looked exhausted.

'Any news?' he asked me, but he knew the answer from my face before I spoke.

I poured him a very large whisky and water and we sat in the sitting room together. With an effort, Mikey said, 'Poor darling, what a rotten end to your holiday.'

I went across to him and kissed him.

'It was the best holiday I have ever had,' I said. 'I've been really, really happy.'

Mikey sipped his whisky and was silent for a moment.

'Have you noticed,' he asked, 'how happiness never seems to last?'

The *autostrada*, which had been travelling through Mediterranean landscapes of cypress trees and vineyards, plunged back into the blackness of the tunnels.

I I

I Smelled the Blood

When I was a child, I thought and spoke as a child.

My first memories are of waving goodbye to my parents as Mrs McLeish and I stood in the doorway of Caorrun Lodge, my parents' Bentley, laden with suitcases, disappearing down the drive. I don't have memories of them coming back from these endless trips: to Doncaster for the St Leger, to Newcastle for the Plate, to Newmarket for the 2000 Guineas, to Goodwood, to Ascot, to Deauville. I know that they must have been at home much more than memory suggests because it was talking to my mother that first got me into trouble.

When my parents were away I spent most of my free time wandering the hills behind the house, following the sheep and deer paths that led cunningly along their contours, finding other paths that ran through the tangled woods of the Forest of Gala. I walked up the sides of the burns that ran down from the distant slopes of Beinn Caorrun, and saw the silver salmon lying in the pools in the spring. Once I remember crossing a small burn and noticing, to my surprise, an old dog fox lying on the other bank, half in and half out of the water. I approached him carefully: he was still alive, but only just, his breath coming in shallow pants.

I looked at his flanks and chest – there was no blood, no sign of a wound. His ribs showed and his muzzle and coat were flecked with grey. It seemed as if he had come down to the burn for one last drink, and then had fallen on his side, unable to move, waiting patiently for death. It was not far away now.

The old hunter had survived, I thought, survived dogs, snares and the bullets of keepers and shepherds chasing him away from the spring lambs. He had hidden, and he had travelled the hills by his secret ways. Now he lay dying in a stream, with hill and sky around him, dying at his appointed time in a place of his own choosing.

On those long-ago excursions in the hills I talked to people too: the shepherds, the old stalker, Fraser; the occasional woodman cutting birch for charcoal. Then there were the others who, it seemed to me, I met in the darker clearings; who communicated with me in a different way, in the old language of gestures and signs that came before speech, so that their voices did not carry through the air but appeared directly inside my head. I told my mother about them one evening, as we sat in the nursery talking, because I hadn't seen her all day and didn't want to be read a story.

'Mummy,' I said. 'Who are the people who live in the wood?'

'What people, darling?' she asked. 'It's nearly time to put your light out. Get into bed.'

'They don't speak with their voices,' I explained. 'They speak with their hands. I see their voices in my head.'

My mother looked at me oddly. 'Darling, there are no people in the woods. Don't tell silly stories. Now get into bed.'

I hadn't expected my mother to say anything different:

grown-ups, I had already realised, didn't know very much about what went on in the world. All the same, as time went by, I became more interested in the people I met and what their voices told me, and sometimes, despite a natural caution that urged me to keep quiet, I found myself speaking to my mother about them. I told Mrs McLeish all this and more, and she never minded what I said; she never told me I was imagining things. My mother was different, though.

She took me 'to see somebody'.

The 'somebody' was a middle-aged, disapproving-looking lady in a set of consulting rooms in Edinburgh. We talked for a long time about the voices I saw in my head. It was a concept she had difficulty in grasping. I cannot remember that these first encounters with the world of psychiatry and medicine had any particular effect on my life. In those days the pharmacological treatment of mental illness was less all embracing than it is now. The rise of the giant drug companies was only just beginning, and the pharmacopoeia of antidepressants, antipsychotics and anti-anxiety pills, the whole chemical toolkit for dealing with modern life, was only just starting to roll off the production lines. There was still a lingering belief that if I confessed that all these stories about voices were just made up to get my parents' attention, then the whole problem would go away. Unfortunately, it did not.

The next such meeting was four years later, when I was twelve, after Fraser had found me in a gully far up the slopes of the mountain, gralloching a stag I had killed without his permission or even knowledge; above all, without a rifle. I had killed the stag with a knife stuck into the back of its neck. Before he took me to see my father, Fraser questioned me at length to try to find out how I had done it. I couldn't tell him, but I told my father. I told him how I had been taught to move without being seen, how a knife or a sharpened stick had worked well enough for hunters in the old days.

This time my father and mother both took me to see Alex Grant, and that was when they started to try to poison me. The first medicines they gave me – Alex and a specialist in Edinburgh, a different one this time – changed my life for ever. I could not believe that I was being made to ingest these pills that made me feel so awful. Yet such was my respect for my parents, my automatic obedience, my sense that if I did not take the pills then Alex Grant, with his, all-seeing eyes, would know, that it never occurred to me I had any choice but to keep taking the medicine. I have since read about these antipsychotic medicines. In one of the articles it said that symptoms similar to Parkinson's disease might be a possible side effect; in another, it even mentioned death. What was so terribly wrong with me that Parkinson's or death might be considered acceptable side effects? I didn't feel mad. My reality was not theirs, that was all. Years later, Stephen Gunnerton told me something. He was fond of the sound of his own voice, and as I was on such mega-doses of medication for much of the time, I was barely capable of interrupting him.

He said, 'You know, it's your bad luck that you are probably an evolutionary misstep, or sidestep. Your brain chemistry has reverted to that of the very earliest hunter-gatherers, before a social brain became the evolutionary path forward, as the climate forced early humans to huddle together for warmth and safety in caves, and learn to live together. You're the ghost in the machine, Michael.'

I stared at him without comprehension.

'There was a writer called Arthur Koestler. He advanced the theory, although he was not the first man to do so, that beneath the modern social brain there is an atavistic brain. He believed that this primitive brain still dictates our core behaviours, and if allowed to, urges us on to the destruction of ourselves and others. You might be rather a good example of his argument. In any case, I can't let you out into the community as you are. We need to reorganise your brain chemistry with a nice, powerful programme of neuroleptics.'

In my teenage years they changed the medication again, and sometimes relaxed it altogether until some incautious word or gesture would result in another trip to Dr Grant, and another prescription. Some of the pills gave me a feeling of crawling restlessness, as if insects were burrowing under my skin, and made me twitch constantly. They called that 'akathisia' and seemed rather proud of me when I exhibited the symptoms, as if it were proof that everything was going to plan. I didn't know what the plan was then. I know now: it was to replace my real identity with a new one.

At the age of sixteen I discovered the courage, or perhaps it was my instinct for survival, to throw the pills away. I stopped taking them and, after a while, it was as if I had crawled between the bars of some dark oubliette and somehow found my way back into the sunlight. I learned to dissimulate, to deceive. I didn't bother to pretend with Mrs McLeish, but when my parents were at home, I remembered to shuffle around the house with a dazed expression and to keep the pills on display in my bathroom, washing two a day down the loo in case they were counting.

Another effect of not taking the pills was that the vividness of my encounters with the people in the woods increased.

It really was fascinating. Their voices, their fluttering hands, made images in my head, and I began to understand what I might have to do in order to survive.

Then my mother died in her accident. That was bad enough, but five years later my father died in equally tragic circumstances. I became really ill. For a while I was beyond the help of any pills.

It was Mrs McLeish who called in Dr Grant, when she found me sitting in the kitchen a few weeks after my father's disappearance. I was naked. I couldn't speak and my mouth kept filling with saliva so that when I opened it to say, 'It's all right, Ellie, everything's all right, don't worry about me,' all that came out was spittle. She looked at me and shook her head, as if I were letting her down somehow, then called Dr Grant. I don't remember much about the months that followed. I ended up in a hospital with barred windows, somewhere in South London, and that's where I met Stephen Gunnerton.

Stephen put me on a drug called Serendipozan. I have been thinking about this drug, and the scientists who designed it, for a long time, and I keep wondering: what type of human being can conceive that a drug which obliterates the patient's identity so entirely is a cure for anything? This new drug stopped the voices, but it stopped a lot of other things as well. The worst side effect was not the loss of libido, though in due course that was bad enough – it was something Stephen called 'dysphoria'. What wonderful words they come up with: dysphoria meant a long descent into a bleak half-world, a constant inability to concentrate for more than a few minutes, a feeling of malaise as if one was about to go down with a bad bout of flu. From the first days of the new medication, I became separated from the world by an intangible curtain that filtered out light and meaning; that filtered out life itself.

Stephen Gunnerton was delighted with my progress.

'A few years ago, Michael, we would have had to institutionalise you permanently. Some of the methodology of the Fifties and Sixties was by modern standards, quite brutal: electroconvulsive shock treatment, even frontal lobotomy. Your life would have been spent mostly in a room like this one,' he waved his hands around my pastel-coloured cell, 'and probably in a straitjacket some of the time. A hundred years ago you would have been abandoned in what they used to call a house of correction. Schizophrenia simply wasn't understood in those days.'

I had already realised that Stephen Gunnerton liked nothing as much as a captive audience. I could scarcely frame a whole sentence in my mind at that point, let alone get the words out.

'We know a great deal more about it now,' said Stephen, 'thanks to major advances in antipsychotics. Serendipozan is really quite benign. It's all to do with brain chemistry. You have a genetic anomaly somewhere in your make-up. A gene has switched off the production of certain neurotransmitters instead of switching it on, and the circuitry in your brain – your synapses – isn't working like a normal person's should. But now we can deal with that.'

'Oh, good,' I tried to say, although it came out as 'Ooh goo'.

'What was that?' asked Stephen. 'Don't worry, your body will start to adjust to the new medication after a few months. The time will come when we might even be able to consider releasing you back into the community; with certain precautions, of course.'

I remember he was very tanned and told me he had just been to a conference in Bermuda convened by the Tertius Corporation, the makers of Serendipozan. A few months later I was indeed 'released back into the community', except that I didn't have a community to be released into, just an empty flat near Baker Street and the house in Glen Gala. I would have headed straight back to Scotland, except for two things: I had to report every other day to a social services case officer, and every week I had to go to Stephen's consulting rooms in Harley Street. The first thing that happened was that my social services officer left the job, and they never got around to replacing him. The second thing that happened was that I met Peter Robinson. Stephen introduced us when we were both attending his clinic as outpatients.

As a result of that meeting, Peter took an interest in me. I don't know what Stephen said to Peter exactly, or whether Peter just decided our shared experience of mental disorders was a good basis for a friendship. I doubt it. Whatever Peter had – some form of depression – I think it was relatively minor compared with what had happened to me. No, I believe it was something in Peter's make-up: he enjoyed control, he liked to intervene in other people's lives and have an influence on them.

First of all Peter made me join Grouchers, which at that time he was much more enthusiastic about than he is now. Then, he invited me to dinner. It was on the second invitation to his house that I met Elizabeth.

When I first met Elizabeth she made little impression on me. We sat next to each other at dinner and I thought she was one of those people who have to pigeonhole everyone they meet: who were your parents, where did you go to school, what do you do, how much money do you have? I did my best to cope with her questions but I know she found me difficult, because she eventually told me so. Then I met her a few days later in the street, and everything was different. A tall, fair-haired girl came and put her hand on my arm and said hello. I started in surprise. Then, by some miracle, I remembered who she was and addressed her by her name, and got it right. She was friendly, and Rupert liked her, and before I knew what was happening I had asked her to come and have a glass of wine. I don't know where I found the initiative to suggest such a thing. It was quite unlike me. But then we were sitting in a wine bar talking, and somehow nothing could have been easier or more natural.

After a few weeks we had drifted into some sort of a relationship. It was difficult to define what that relationship was: it was somewhere between friendship and love in my case; and friendship and indifference in Elizabeth's. The love I felt was, perhaps, not the same emotion that other people might describe with that word. Who can ever know what other people feel? I felt I needed her to be in my life, and as the weeks went on I felt my hold on her was slipping, that she had drifted towards me, into my life and into my bed, in a fit of absence of mind, and was about to wake up at any moment and leave me. As my grip on Elizabeth slackened, so did my desire not to lose her increase.

One evening, Elizabeth and I were sitting in a restaurant that we both liked, a small Italian place called Alfredo's that was close to my flat. We were talking in a desultory way and then I remembered I had something I needed to tell her.

'I'm afraid I've got to go up to Perthshire tomorrow for a few days.'

For a moment Elizabeth could not make the connection between me and Perthshire.

'Oh, why?' she asked. 'No, I remember. You've got a house up there, haven't you?'

'Yes, and some holiday cottages, and various bits of forestry. I need to keep an eye on it all from time to time.'

I could see that Elizabeth wanted to know more, but didn't like to ask.

'You've never really talked about that side of your life,' was what she said finally.

'Well, there's not much one can say. We have about thirty thousand acres of hill and forest, and a village. Most of the houses in the village are holiday lets now, because there aren't the jobs any more for the shepherds and the foresters that used to occupy the houses.'

Elizabeth looked surprised.

'Thirty thousand acres? But that's enormous!' she said.

'Not really; not in that part of the world. The only things that produce any income are the holiday lets and the tiny amount of money we make from letting the stalking. You ought to come and see it some time. It's wild country, but very beautiful. I think so, anyway.'

I date from that conversation a renewal of Elizabeth's interest in me. Her feelings for me did not change very much, but I could sense some calculation going on behind her eyes. She was on her way to thirty, and I didn't think there was much money in her family. Her father had abandoned his wife and daughter to their own devices some years before. Elizabeth had a job that she liked, but worked in an atmosphere of chronic insecurity, expecting to be fired at any moment, even though the dreaded dismissal never did arrive. I think from that point on, she began to think of me in a different way, and that was what gave me the courage to propose marriage to her. I don't think I could have done it if there hadn't been odd moments when she dropped her habit of making bright, amusing remarks about everything, and I discerned a softer, affectionate, rather lonely person underneath the armour.

A few months ago I realised that either my medication, or my marriage, had to go. The sense of detachment and depression that the Serendipozan gave me had never been a good basis for a relationship, and it was getting worse. Even in my numbed state of mind I could see that my relationship with Elizabeth was deteriorating. Worse than that, I could see that it hurt her. I realised through the fog that she, too, didn't want to lose me.

It took me a while to reach the decision to stop taking the Serendipozan. It wasn't that I didn't want to, although I thought I knew the risks involved. It was more the case that I found it difficult to think in a straight line about anything for more than a few moments. Even holding down the part-time job I had at Grouchers was almost beyond me, and I could never have coped with Beinn Caorrun without Mrs McLeish.

But I did stop. I stopped taking the medication, and when I did so I remember thinking to myself that it was rather a final step: I couldn't see myself voluntarily returning to the enslavement of the drug. All the same I didn't throw away the medicine. I used to hide it in a secret drawer in my dressing table. Then I moved it and kept it behind some bottles in the medicine cupboard. Perhaps I wanted Elizabeth to find it; I don't know.

At first nothing happened, and then, after a few weeks, the headaches began. They were sometimes so painful I could hardly stand it, but they were followed by periods of lucidity, of heightened perception, that I had not experienced in years. There were some odd hallucinatory effects as well, which was not unexpected, as I recalled having them on previous occasions when my condition had remained untreated.

Those anomalies were something I felt I had to put up with and just cope as best I could. The real change in me was worth anything, any inconvenience, any danger: the numbness in my emotions and in my brain that had so deadened my life with Elizabeth was slowly lifting. I felt like someone who had been saturated in anaesthetic from head to toe, inhabiting a body that was swollen and gro-tesque. Then, as the anaesthetic wore off, there was a faint tingling, and sensation slowly returned to limbs and brain. That is how it was with me: suddenly I woke up one morning and realised that ten years of life with Elizabeth had gone by in a chemical dream, and I needed to live the rest of whatever time I was granted with her to the full, while my sanity was still more or less intact; before whatever had overwhelmed me before resumed possession of my mind.

Maybe I was cured. It would be a scientific miracle, but miracles do happen. Meanwhile, life with Elizabeth was very good.

It was in this mood of optimism that I went to the travel agents we used in Baker Street, and managed to book a long weekend in Rome, as a surprise for Elizabeth. Then I thought that Rupert could do with a really good walk.

We walked through streets and squares towards Marble

Arch, and from there into Hyde Park. I took Rupert off his lead and he walked obediently at my heel. We wandered along avenues, and on paths, until we reached the Serpentine, and I stood on the bridge looking down at the water flowing beneath. Rupert sat beside me. I could see the colours of late autumn on the trees, occasional showers of dead leaves tumbling down even though the air was hardly stirring. I could see children playing on the far side of the water, and hear their shouts as they raced around a tall figure in a dark blue coat standing guard beside a pram. I could hear the sound of hoofs from a group of horses cantering along Rotten Row. I looked up and could see how the sky was turning from pale grey to a soft blue. Gently the still air began to stir. Beside us in the road was an empty polystyrene coffee cup, lying where someone had dropped it. Suddenly it began to roll in a circle. Rupert turned to watch it too, and then a sudden gust of wind lifted it from the ground and blew it away in a series of bounds. Rupert barked and chased after it, and I whistled for him to come back. He had caught up with the cup a hundred yards away, and had seized it in his mouth. Then he dropped it, and chased it again as it blew farther away.

I was about to go after him when a voice beside me said, not unexpectedly, 'You might at least say hello'.

I turned and saw the girl called Lamia, standing beside me, looking over the bridge at the water as I had done.

'I didn't know you were there,' I said.

'I'm nearly always somewhere close by.'

'I ought to go and get Rupert,' I said.

'Don't worry about your dog. You ought to be more grateful that I'm taking such an interest in you.'

She was paler than I remembered, and her dark eyes

seemed blacker. Her hair was tossed in the sudden wind. She gazed at me unsmilingly. This, I realised suddenly, was another of the anomalies that I would have to cope with.

'It's just I'm not used to being told off by one of my own hallucinations,' I explained.

She laughed; a cold, hard little sound.

'Oh, so you think I'm a hallucination? You'd like to think that, wouldn't you? Well, I can understand why you would jump to that conclusion. You're going mad again, you know. Try taking your little pills and see if that gets rid of me.'

I knew she must be a hallucination; what else could she be? Her voice was so familiar: it seemed to me as if Lamia was always whispering to me, whether I was awake or asleep.

'Circumstances have brought us together, Mikey, and together we must be,' said Lamia. She smiled for the first time, showing sharp white teeth. I wondered what age she was: she looked younger than Elizabeth, but there was something about her eyes that was very old indeed.

'What were the circumstances that brought us together?' I asked. 'You said our first meeting was random.'

'Oh, the circumstances were random. You happened to be passing and you caught my attention. That's how life works, you know. One likes to think everything is ordered and planned. Then something happens you couldn't have foreseen: like seeing your child being knocked down by a hit-and-run driver. Or being bitten by a venomous spider or struck down with an incurable illness. It's the randomness of things that makes life so entertaining.'

She looked me full in the face. She was very beautiful. As I knew she was only a hallucination, I saw no harm in going on with the conversation. After all, if that was the case, I was only talking to myself.

'And what made you interested in me? Why did you decide to come into *my* life?' I asked her.

'It was the smell of blood on your hands. And your madness; it makes you weak, you know, and vulnerable to me.'

I turned away in disgust at myself for carrying on this conversation. I would go and find Rupert, whom I could no longer see.

Lamia said behind me, 'You know there are things you must learn from me, Mikey.'

I shook my head. She wasn't there and I wasn't hearing her. She was an anomaly, like Mrs Patel had been, like the voices I used to hear in Glen Gala a lifetime ago. But her voice, silvery and irritating, persisted.

'You need to learn to do without those who love you, Mikey. You need to learn to do without love; to cope with loss. You don't have any real emotions, anyway. You're just a mimic. It's time you understood that.'

I walked off. A long way ahead, two or three black dogs were chasing each other, playing some complicated canine game on the grass. I hoped that one of them was Rupert. A few yards farther on, I risked a glance over my shoulder, knowing that by now the episode would be over, the delusion gone. But Lamia was still standing on the bridge. She saw my glance and gave a little wave. I walked on, and saw that one of the dogs *was* Rupert, thank God, and called him to me. As I knelt down to put him on his lead, I risked a further glance back at the bridge but it was empty. No one stood there giving me a mocking wave. No one had ever stood there, talking about blood or loss. I needed to become more robust about these episodes; recognise them for what they were and do my best to live with them.

Slowly I walked back to the flat. A holiday would do me good; it would do us both good. I needed my mind to be filled with new things. I needed to be with Elizabeth and enjoy the new intimacy that had sprung up between us. I smiled to myself. It was not impossible that things would turn out well after all.

When I returned to the flat and let myself in I saw that Elizabeth was back. Her coat was thrown across a chair and I could hear her moving about in the bathroom. Rupert padded off towards his basket for a well-deserved rest. I walked towards the bathroom door, about to say something, and then stopped. Elizabeth was standing by the washbasin, rummaging through the medicines. In her hand was the pale blue packet of Serendipozan. I tried to remember what it said on the label, and whether Alex Grant's name was on it.

Elizabeth raised her head and caught sight of my reflection in the mirror. She put her hand on her heart and gave a gasp.

'Oh, you gave me a shock. I didn't hear you come in. Where have you been?'

For a moment I said nothing, and just looked at her holding the packet. Thoughts raced across my mind. I should tell her a little bit more of what this was about, shouldn't I? But I couldn't tell her everything, not straight away. It would be too much. Then Elizabeth would start asking questions. I knew she would. She was inquisitive, intelligent and determined. Before I could think of what to say next she said, 'I was thinking of having a chuck-out. There's so much rubbish in these cupboards. Are you sure you don't want these any more?'

She looked at me, and I knew she was waiting for me to say something, to tell her more about the pills and why I took them. In that instant I knew she had already started to ask questions. Who she had been talking to, I did not know. There were a limited number of possibilities: Alex Grant, Stephen Gunnerton, Peter Robinson. Each of them knew a part of my story, but none of them knew all of it. Elizabeth had started asking questions, and once she had started she would keep going until she thought she had all the answers.

Clever girl.

I stepped forward and took the packet from her hands, hesitating only for an instant, before I said, 'Yes, I'm sure,' and threw the packet into the waste bin. Then we went next door and I told her about the trip to Rome, and for a while all thoughts of Serendipozan were banished.

12

Their Brains Are Not Like Ours

For a while Mikey was inconsolable about the loss of Rupert. I don't mean that he wept or tore his hair. He just looked ill, pale, almost gaunt. I tried to make him eat more, but his appetite had gone for the time being. I tried to cheer him up; and he did his best to be cheered up, but I wasn't convinced. I looked on the internet and found some pictures of scruffy but charming rescue dogs, which I showed to Mikey; all he did was shake his head.

None of this helped. It wasn't even as if he talked about Rupert very much; he just glanced from time to time at the empty basket in the corner of the kitchen, as if expecting to see Rupert raise his black head and thump his tail. The only thing Mikey actually said about Rupert was, 'I suppose he only had a year or so left anyway. He was nearly twelve.'

After a few days, however, his mood began to lift. I said something to that effect but didn't quite catch his reply, which sounded like, 'I'm learning to unlearn love.'

It sounded like nonsense, so I let it go.

Mikey's new warmth towards me remained the same. If anything, losing Rupert strengthened his need for me. He hugged me at night, almost clung to me, as if he needed reassurance that I had not vanished the way Rupert had done. When we awoke in the morning he sometimes looked at me with a mixture of surprise and relief that I was still there. It was rather touching; disturbing, too.

I remember lying in his arms one night, awakened by I don't know what, some small sound that brought me out of a deep sleep. As I listened to his soft breathing and felt his warmth next to me, I thought, *so this is what it's like to be married*, and felt a depth of affection and love that I would never have believed I was capable of before.

A few days after we arrived back from Rome, I sat in my office and did some research on the internet. It didn't take me long to find what I needed. I picked up the phone, and called Stephen Gunnerton. I wanted to know why Mikey had been treated by him, and what for. I simply didn't know how to ask Mikey any more questions about it, at least not yet. I needed some clues; some sense of what the changes in him were all about. The man I now lived with was so different to the man I had married, and perhaps the man I had married was different again from the man who had been sent, presumably by Alex Grant, to be treated by Stephen Gunnerton. Was it depression? Was it something that had gone away and might come back? Or was it, as I hoped, something that had been cured, a problem that had been dealt with, which meant I need never ask Mikey about it again?

I needed to know whether my new marriage was going to last.

It was a nightmare getting an appointment. His secretary kept saying things like, 'Mr Gunnerton will only see people who have been referred by their GP,' and it took several calls before she realised I wasn't going to go away, and was persuaded to take a note with my name through to the great man. That produced a result, and two days later I went to see him.

Stephen Gunnerton's consulting rooms were in Harley Street, only half a mile away from Helmsdale Mansions. From the outside the building looked like a private house, but there were two brass plates beside the brightly painted green door. When I pressed the bell I was let in by a buzzer, and then gave my name to a tough-looking woman behind a desk, who I supposed was the secretary. She greeted me without smiling, wrote my name in a book, and then stood up and showed me into a small waiting room, just large enough to accommodate a chair and a small table with a few magazines on it. I picked up a copy of *Country Life* and flicked through it without seeing it. For some reason my heart had started to beat rather fast, and the palms of my hands were damp. What on earth was I doing here? What was I going to say? The name of Stephen Gunnerton had acquired such resonance in my mind that I was almost dreading meeting him.

Then the entrance to the waiting room opened and a large, grey-haired man of about sixty put his head around the door.

'Mrs Gascoigne?'

I stood up, and he led me across the corridor into a much larger room. The walls were lined with bookshelves, and there were two leather armchairs set at an angle to each other, and a large old-fashioned partner's desk covered in papers. On a low mahogany table was a tray set with coffee cups and pots. Once we were inside, Stephen Gunnerton shut the door behind me and then turned and studied me for a moment. He was a portly man, with that smooth, well-fed look that some men acquire from living well, but without overdoing it. He was dressed in a dark blue wool suit, and wore a check shirt and a badly knotted bow tie. Spectacles hung on a cord around his neck. His face was thinner than the rest of him: sharp featured, with a beak of a nose, and close-set dark brown eyes. He looked exactly as I had imagined him. There was nothing especially sinister or frightening about him at all.

'Coffee, Mrs Gascoigne?' he asked, gesturing towards the tray.

'Thanks,' I said, 'just black.'

He busied himself pouring the coffee for a minute and then waved me towards one of the armchairs, before sitting down opposite me in the other.

I didn't know what to say. After sipping his coffee he looked at me over his cup and said, 'Medical ethics, Mrs Gascoigne, is a subject on which there is much confusion. One gets a constant flow of advice from the British Medical Association, which as you know is our trade union; from the Law Society; and from all sorts of well-informed and well-meaning people. The general idea is that we never speak about our patients except to our patients themselves, and even then we don't tell them much unless we have to.'

'I just wanted to ask ...' I began, but Stephen Gunnerton talked over me effortlessly. His voice was rich and rather treacly.

'I have a simple test, myself, or at least it ought to be simple. Am I acting in the best interests of my patient? That is the question we are meant to ask ourselves, but often it is a very difficult question to answer. Two different people might give two different answers, and then where might we be if we ended up in court?'

He put down his cup and saucer, finally giving me the opportunity to say something, but I had dried up.

'I remember your husband very well, Mrs Gascoigne. It was more than ten years ago since he was last in this room, but I remember him as clearly as if it were yesterday. I can't tell you details of his case, I'm afraid, or show you his file, or leave the file on my desk and pretend to leave the room for a minute. I don't know what you were expecting me to do?'

'I just . . .' I began, but he was off again.

'Let's talk generally, if we may. What do you understand by the term "schizophrenia"?'

I had a question of my own now.

'What is Serendipozan?'

Ah,' he said. 'We'll come to that, but we are getting ahead of ourselves. What do you think schizophrenia is?'

'Is that when you have a split personality? Like Jekyll and Hyde?'

Stephen Gunnerton sat back in his chair. He clearly wanted to lecture me, and if this was the only way he communicated with people like me, then I would have to join in the game.

'Yes, that is a common interpretation of the word, but it is rather more than that: schizophrenia is a generic term for a wide spectrum of conditions, from mild dissociative personality disorder through to extreme forms of psychosis. The question I was asking you was not a trick question: there are so many definitions of what schizophrenia is, or how the brain of a schizophrenic differs from that of a so-called "normal" person, that your answer might well be as good as any other.' He looked at me as he said this, in a way that made it clear his comment was not intended as a compliment to my intelligence. He steepled his fingers and went on with his lecture.

'When our remote ancestors lived in caves, a long time ago, perhaps sixty thousand years ago during the First and Second Ice Ages, humans had to learn to interact in a different way. They had to share shelter, warmth and food in order to survive, and to do this they had to develop a greater awareness of self, and a greater comprehension of others, and the intentions of others.'

I could not quite see what this had to do with Mikey, except that we were back to the Ice Age again. The words recalled to me the scene in the dining room at Beinn Caorrun.

'The brain evolved, and circumstances favoured brains that were genetically more capable of cognition. Humans developed gene sequences that helped the brain to grow in a certain way, forming synaptic connections that favoured the growth of the conscious mind. Today we call "normality" the brain at the evolutionary cliff edge: the optimal condition of the brain for the social environment it is in, not too little cognition and not too much.'

He paused to make sure I was following him. I wasn't sure that I was.

'Schizophrenics and geniuses have this in common: their brains are not like ours. Genetically they have grown in a different way and there are networks and synaptic connections and growths of neurons that we can only guess at. Synaptic connections that one would expect are simply not there. The brain chemistry may be different. It's like someone rewiring your house without telling you.'

Stephen Gunnerton smiled at me encouragingly.

'In practical terms a genius is someone who is fortunate enough to be able to control and articulate his different understanding of the world, and become a new Einstein or Isaac Newton. In schizophrenics, these networks mean their experience of the world can be dissimilar to ours, sometimes unimaginably so. They might externalise emotions and data so that their brain presents it to them as a separate person speaking to them from outside. They might actually see people who are not there, or hear voices telling them to do things. The classic schizophrenic condition is one in which the subject thinks he, and he alone, can hear messages coming to him from some unknown source, such as the secret service, or God. In extreme cases, the subject might even fragment into multiple identities, as you have suggested, although that is not common. At the same time schizophrenics are aware that they are not well, are not whole people, and this may lead, in very rare cases, to psychosis and violent acts against themselves or others.'

Gunnerton put on his glasses and stared at me for a moment, then took them off again. It was a piece of theatre designed to ensure that I listened carefully to what he said next.

'Many forms of schizophrenia include what we call "emotional blunting". This means there is no capacity for normal human emotions: love, friendship, ambition, desire. The more intelligent sufferers learn to replicate these emotions, just as some types of butterfly or lizard can alter their colours to match their surroundings. But they can't actually feel the same emotions that normal people do.'

He stopped speaking. I knew he was talking about Mikey. I also knew that if he was trying to tell me that Mikey did not really love me, then it was a lie. But which parts of the rest of what he had said were particular to Mikey, and which were not, I could not tell. Then he said something that I will remember for as long as I live.

'The truth is, Mrs Gascoigne, we don't really know everything about the structure of the brain. We know infinitely more than we did a generation ago. We can map electrical and electrochemical activity. We can use probes to stimulate different areas of the brain, and different functions. We can even guess, I think accurately, at where the seat of consciousness lies within the brain. But there is still so much of the brain that carries out functions we do not understand. We look at a map of the brain – picture a map of the London Underground if you like – and think we know what is going on. But now imagine other networks far below the main one, tunnels which interconnect with the tunnels we know of and then lead off, who knows where, into the darkness, perhaps linking up with other cities, and other realities. We just don't know. When I treat a schizophrenic I work on the assumption that he is experiencing a false reality which it is my duty to delete; but a small part of me asks, is his brain so different from mine that he is actually aware of a different reality to my own? Does he experience something as real as you are to me, sitting in that chair in front of me?'

'Is Mikey suffering from schizophrenia? Was he?'

Stephen Gunnerton shook his head and managed to glance at his watch at the same time.

'You asked me about Serendipozan just now,' he said.

'Yes, I did.'

'It's what we call a neuroleptic. Two hundred years ago, people who were mentally ill were often forced into a straitjacket or abandoned without further treatment. That phrase gives you some idea of the primitive approach to mental health, doesn't it?'

I shuddered.

'These new drugs operate on the theory that the genes of schizophrenics are affecting their brain chemistry. Serendipozan is the drug I usually recommend in these cases. Since I prescribed it for your husband, I have used it with great success in dozens of other cases. It has very few side effects: it can be somewhat depressive, but there is as yet no evidence that it damages the patient's long-term health. We are using chemical engineering to alter the brains and personalities of our patients, in order to help them lead fairly useful lives.'

So that's all right, then, I thought. Poor Mikey had been in a chemical prison of one sort or another for God knows how long, but he could still lead a 'fairly useful life', arranging golf matches for Grouchers.

'The important thing,' said Stephen Gunnerton, 'is that the patient should persist with the medication. Michael, I know, resisted the idea of medication until he realised that without it he would be institutionalised for the rest of his life. But it is a lifelong cure. Without the control of the neuroleptic, regression can be surprisingly fast. If I were related to, or in any way involved with, someone receiving this treatment, I would want to make sure that person kept taking his drugs. Early warning signs in people who abort their medication are personality change, erratic behaviour patterns, impulsiveness, mood swings. In those circumstances the patient must be encouraged to go back to taking the pills as soon as possible. Any other course of action is likely to have ...' He paused while he searched for the right words, '... extremely unfavourable consequences.' Stephen

Gunnerton looked at his watch again and said, 'I'm sorry to have to bring this to a close, but my next appointment is waiting.'

He stood up, and as he did so a light on the phone on his desk started blinking. He walked across, picked it up and spoke softly into it. The next thing I knew he was ushering me towards the door.

'I'm afraid I haven't been of much help, but I've said all I can.'

'I think it has been very useful,' I said, feeling I ought to say something. Then I was outside his room and, a moment later, back in the street, feeling as if I were coming up for air after being too long underwater.

That night I had to pretend to myself that there was no such person as Stephen Gunnerton, and no such drug as Serendipozan. Despite having taken time off during the day, I made a special effort to get home early enough to cook dinner. I knew Mikey would be late: arrangements for the Grouchers Golf Cup, the last golf tournament of the year, had to be finalised and Mikey had left home in the morning expecting a very trying day on the telephone talking to the club secretary at Muirfield, who was hosting the game, and to the manager of the Marine Hotel in North Berwick, where the Grouchers team were going to stay for three nights. In recent weeks Mikey had shown signs of becoming rather detached from his job at Grouchers. There were a lot of problems, he told me, and he was increasingly fed up with having to worry about it all. But the golf match at Muirfield was the equivalent, in the Grouchers calendar, of Royal Ascot or the Open.

I didn't want to cook Mikey anything too special as it

would make him ask me what the big occasion was, yet I ended up preparing a rather complicated spicy chicken dish, with lots of side dishes, so that when he came home he gave a low whistle as he smelled the aromas from the kitchen. He went in and looked at all the various pans simmering away and asked, 'What's the big occasion?'

'Oh, it started out being very simple and I just got carried away. It's all out of a cookbook, anyway.'

Mikey smiled and kissed me.

'Well, I wasn't that hungry a moment ago, but now I'm absolutely ravenous. Let's have a drink.'

I finished chopping up some coriander, and decided that everything would have to fend for itself for five minutes. In the sitting room, Mikey had poured himself a whisky, and handed me a glass of white wine.

'Something odd happened to me today,' he said.

Something odd happened to me today as well, I thought, only I don't know how to talk to you about it, darling.

'I went to see Mr Patel. I was fed up with arranging golf matches and dinners, and all the rest of it. By this stage, it's too late anyway – either it's going to work, or else all go horribly wrong. I no longer care. So I rang up Mr Patel, on impulse, and arranged to meet him.'

'Who on earth is Mr Patel?' I asked. Then I remembered. 'No, don't tell me, I've got it. So what happened?'

Mikey said, 'When I finally got to see him, I asked, "Mr Patel, why on earth do you want to join a club like Grouchers?"'

'What did he say?'

Mikey began to laugh.

'He said: 'But I don't *want* to join. I've nothing against the club, or its members. It's simply that I wouldn't use it.

I don't have the time.' He spends half his life in New York anyway. We both had to laugh. In fact, we couldn't stop laughing.'

Mikey was still laughing at the memory now.

'It's all Peter, of course. Control-freak Peter. He made Patel put his name forward for the club, and he won't let him withdraw.'

Tears were rolling down his cheeks.

'The whole situation is completely unnecessary; absolutely pointless. It sums up Grouchers perfectly.'

Michael would never have said that. This was Mikey speaking.

Over supper he calmed down, and concentrated on his food.

'Mmm,' he said, 'this is really delicious. Such a nice change from Italian.'

I said nothing, just smiled. Inside I was thinking: all that laughing, is that normal, or is it because he's off his drugs? I shook my head; of course it was normal to laugh. It wasn't normal *not* to laugh; Michael had scarcely laughed at all.

'Penny for them?' said Mikey.

'Oh, just wool-gathering,' I said, looking at my plate as I chased a bit of chicken around the rim with my fork.

'You tell me your thoughts, I'll tell you mine?'

I looked at him, and now he had that curious smile on his face I had seen once or twice before. It was a smile I found rather unsettling, as if he were looking right through me, seeing my thoughts as clearly as if they were written on a page.

'I was wondering what you were going to do about Mr Patel. Will you talk to Peter about it?'

'Is that what you were thinking? Truly? Well, I suppose

I will have to, although I know that Peter will tell me to mind my own business. You know what he's like.'

'I don't know that I've ever seen that side of him.'

'Yes, well, he can become very fixated on things. You probably don't know this, but Peter used to suffer from depression.'

I froze. Did Mikey know, somehow, that I had been to see Stephen Gunnerton behind his back?

'No! Really?' I said, as naturally as I could.

'Yes, really,' said Mikey, smiling at me again. 'This was many years ago, before you and I met. I don't know what they did to cure it, but one result is that Peter can be more than a little obsessive about things. He gets very stuck on an idea, and it is very difficult to unstick him. So it all depends how he takes it. I might get away with it, but I am rather expecting a lecture about it all being a point of principle.'

We talked about other things then moved back next door, where I sat reading my book. About ten o'clock, Mikey suddenly stood up and said, 'I'm going out for a walk. I won't sleep if I don't stretch my legs, get some fresh air. There are too many thoughts buzzing around in my head, what with Muirfield, and Mr Patel. Don't wait up for me, I'll take my keys.'

I looked at him in surprise.

'Do you want me to come with you?'

'No, darling, you know how you hate walking. I won't be too long.'

In a moment he had grabbed his coat and scarf, and I heard the front door shut. I waited up for a while, but then sleep got the better of me. I put myself to bed and lay there, thinking about Stephen Gunnerton, and then about vast networks of tunnels, getting on the tube at Baker Street and somehow travelling forever downwards, through unknown tunnels and silent stations where silent people stood on the platforms like ghosts, and then downwards again, into the darkness.

I awoke with a start as I felt Mikey's cold body slip into bed beside me. I looked at the bedside clock and saw that it was three in the morning.

A couple of days later I rang Peter Robinson and persuaded him to meet me at his chambers near Lincoln's Inn.

'It's not about that Patel thing, is it? Michael isn't trying to use you to soften me up? Because—'

'No, Peter, it has nothing to do with Grouchers. I would never interfere. I just need half an hour of your time. Please.'

We agreed a time and a while later I knocked on the door of my editor's office. I half opened it and said, through the gap, 'Celia, I'm just popping out for three-quarters of an hour, something's come up. I'll work late, I promise. Do you need me for anything in the next hour?'

Celia looked up from a series of photos she was studying.

'No, dear, you just go off and enjoy yourself. We're getting quite used to managing without you.'

I'd heard Celia use that sarcastic tone with others from time to time. It was not pleasant, and most of the people she'd spoken to like that were no longer with us. The familiar sense of dread that Celia produced in me stayed with me until I got off the bus in Holborn. As I walked down towards Peter's chambers I thought: if she fires me, she fires me. Mikey will look after me. I realised, not for the first time, how much things had turned around. I wanted to spend more time with Mikey now, not less.

Peter Robinson didn't keep me waiting. He was a tall, thin, intense-looking man, and while I was fond of him in a way, because Mary was such a good friend, I still had reservations about him. To start with, he was always sweating: people who perspire a lot shouldn't wear dark blue shirts, and there were dark crescents under each armpit, even though it was a cool day.

He took some papers off a chair and invited me to sit down.

'Peter,' I said, 'it's very good of you to see me. It's about—'

'It's about Michael, I know. I rang Mary and asked her what you could possibly want to see me about in my chambers.'

'You're right. It is about Michael,' I agreed.

'Stephen Gunnerton won't tell you a thing. You're much better off talking to someone like me. I've known Michael for quite a while. Stephen Gunnerton won't even see you.'

I did not waste time disagreeing. Instead, I asked, 'Peter, exactly how *long* have you known Michael?'

'Quite some time.' He rubbed his nose and then put a forefinger briefly into an ear and twirled it around. I don't think he was conscious of doing it. 'I suppose I met him a few months before Mary and I got married. He came out of nowhere. No family, no friends that I've ever met. I don't know where he went to school, and I don't think that he went to university. He just turned up, aged twenty-something, and his past is a complete mystery to me. Do you know anything about his past?'

'Not really,' I admitted. 'Just bits and pieces about his childhood at Glen Gala.'

'It's inconceivable to me,' said Peter, having found some-thing in his ear and transferred it to a handkerchief beneath the desk, 'that a man can leave so little trace in the world. He must have friends and relations, but I've never met any.' Peter sighed.

'And you met him where?' I asked. Peter looked at me sharply.

'We both know where I met him, and why I was there, because I know that Mary told you. I had some very minor problems I needed to sort out, and they were sorted out very satisfactorily. But we're not here to discuss me. Your husband's condition was more complex. Do you know what it was?'

'Maybe,' I said, but Peter wasn't interested. Here was another man who liked an audience, without the slightest interest in anything I might have to say.

'He was schizophrenic,' said Peter. 'Still is, I imagine, except that the medication keeps it under control. But you probably wanted to ask me about Michael's very bizarre behaviour that night at Beinn Caorrun? When that vulgar man David Martin was there?'

I hadn't especially wanted to ask that question, but it was as good a starting point as any, so I sat and listened, nodding respectfully when appropriate.

'All that stuff about genes and DNA that Michael started spouting took me by surprise. In fact, I was rather interested in what he said, and subsequently took the trouble to read up about it. This idea that Britishness is an invented concept, that a lot of our DNA comes from hunter-gatherers who moved up from the Pyrenees – it's an interesting concept and I believe it is very much at the sharp edge of modern genetic archaeology. Michael's obviously been reading some of the popular science on the subject. But that's not the important thing.'

'Oh,' I said, 'so what's the important thing?'

'What's important,' said Peter, 'is his motivation. He's obsessed by issues of identity. That's what makes him do it. As a former schizophrenic, he wants to locate himself in some structure, some form of logic that gives him a sense of self. A sense of self is what schizophrenics don't have, it's what sets them apart from people like you and me, Elizabeth. So Michael is, I hope, quite cured and able to live a more or less normal life and hold down a job, even if it is a bit of a non-job compared to that of most men of his age and intellect. It's just that he obsesses a little about certain things, and this whole "who are the British?" notion is one of them. Quite harmless; nothing sinister in it. Certainly nothing for you to worry about. As long as he keeps taking his medication, that is. I'm surprised in a way that you don't appear to have ever asked him about it. Still, that's your business.'

'Oh, good,' I said. 'That's a relief.'

'I hope that was helpful,' said Peter. He had found something in his nose now, but couldn't quite bring himself to fish it out while I was still sitting there.

'Yes, absolutely. Thank you so much.'

I stood up to go.

'When are we going to see you both?' asked Peter, all smiles now that the ordeal of having to talk to me was nearly over.

'Soon, I hope.'

'I'll get Mary to look in the diary,' he said. 'We're quite busy at the moment but I'm sure we can fix something up in a month or two.'

'Are you going to the Grouchers golf tournament?' I asked.

'Of course,' he said, his eyes glinting. 'It will be a very big occasion.'

13

Rule Britannia!

Elizabeth cooked the most delicious dinner, but if it was intended to distract me from recent events, it did not succeed. I could smell Stephen Gunnerton on her, hear his oily tones echoed in her voice. Just to make sure, while Elizabeth was putting things away in the kitchen, I went into the sitting room, where I had seen her handbag, and reached into it. I pulled out her mobile. I supposed Stephen would not have changed his telephone number in the last ten years. I scrolled down through the recently dialled numbers, and there it was. I smiled to myself.

Clever girl, I thought once again.

I had given her Stephen Gunnerton's name, and I had told her about Alex Grant. It was curious, how I seemed to be pointing Elizabeth at my own past like a loaded gun. What Stephen might have told Elizabeth, I did not know. Not much, probably, but that would only compel her to ask further questions. When she picked up that packet of Serendipozan, it was like watching a stone being thrown into a pool, and the ripples were still widening out across the surface. It was stupid of me not to have hidden the packet from her. I had managed to conceal my medication for ten years, and it was only when I had stopped taking it that I grew careless and left it in the medicine cabinet in the bathroom, where she was bound to find it.

Perhaps I had wanted her to find it. Perhaps I wanted to talk to her about my past. But once the talking started, where would it end? I could not tell her the whole story, but Elizabeth was Elizabeth. She would know if I was holding back, and then she would want to know what I was holding back.

That could lead to difficulties.

It was ironic, wasn't it? A few months ago, while I was still on medication, our relationship had been so cool and distant that if I had appeared at breakfast with two heads, Elizabeth would not have taken much notice. Since I had stopped taking the drug and its poison had started to withdraw from my system, our marriage had changed so much for the better. Now Elizabeth cared for me more than she ever had before. I knew that. I could see it in her glance, feel it in her embrace, hear it in her voice. And because she cared, she was asking questions. Because she was asking questions, I was going to have to do something. I didn't want to hide anything from Elizabeth; at the same time, a part of me knew that, if I told her everything, she might not be able to bear it. Then there was another question: what is more important, love, or survival? I thought I would soon find out.

At about ten o'clock, with these thoughts going around in my head, I knew I had to talk to someone. I made an excuse about needing some fresh air, and stood up to go out. I could see the worry in Elizabeth's eyes as she smiled and told me not to be late.

I walked to the bridge across the Serpentine and, as the

divine wind flowed around me, I found the girl, leaning over the parapet beside me and studying the dark water.

'Did you make my dog run away?' I asked her. She turned and laughed, studying my face in the lamplight with her black eyes. In the dark she no longer seemed young, or attractive: her shadowed face was all hollows and eye sockets.

'We're not here to talk about dogs, are we?' she said. 'But if we are, then that bitch you live with is asking questions. And you don't know what to do.'

'Please don't talk about Elizabeth like that,' I said, 'or I will have to go.'

'Oh, I'm sorry. I don't know where you think you can go that I can't find you. Perhaps you would like me to come home with you now? I know the way, as I am sure you realise. Perhaps we could go and see your darling wife together?'

I looked at the girl as she spoke.

'What is your name?'

She seemed surprised, and turned away from me to look down at the black water.

'I don't have a name. I don't need one,' she said, after a moment.

'I thought you said you were called Lamia.'

'That is what I am, not who I am. But you came here because you needed to talk to someone who understands what *you* are. I am your only friend, you should listen to me. You have a choice, don't you? You must decide whether you will follow your own nature, or go back to the drugs. You know this. You have always known this. The people who poisoned you and took away your life will do it all over again if you let them.'

We stood together in silence for a while. I don't know for how long, but her silences gave me more comfort than her words. She knew everything, she understood everything, and she would never be far away from me now. After a time she left. I did not see her go. Then I walked slowly through the empty streets back home.

The Grouchers golf team flew to Edinburgh and were then decanted into a coach and driven down to North Berwick. I drove up, because there were one or two things I wanted to do while I was in that part of the world that might make it more convenient for me to have my own transport. I had to leave early in the morning in order to get to the Marine Hotel before everyone else and make sure, as far as I could, that all the arrangements were in order.

'Will you be all right?' I asked as I said goodbye to Elizabeth.

'Of course I will be,' she answered. 'When have I not been? You have a lovely time with all your Grouchers golfers, and remember not to tell me anything about it when you come back.'

She smiled as she said this, and we embraced. She looked better than I ever remembered, glowing with life. I felt her warmth, smelled her fragrance, and wondered when I would next hold her against me.

'Take care of yourself, darling,' she whispered, as I released her.

'It's only a game of golf,' I said. We both knew she wasn't thinking about golf.

It took me about seven hours to get up to North Berwick, but I managed to arrive ahead of everybody else. There was to be a day at Muirfield, playing the Honourable Company of Edinburgh Golfers, a bye day when people could play golf at other local links courses around North Berwick, and then a match against a northern team, the Borderers, at Gullane. On the way up I had used the hands-free mobile to ring my opposite numbers at the other clubs involved, and as far as I could see, it would all work out on the day. While I was at it, I made one or two other arrangements as well.

This golf trip was the most important event in the Grouchers calendar, even though the golf team never won a single match it played. This was not an isolated occurrence, or a symptom of any particular weakness at golf among the Grouchers faithful. Most members played regularly, as they played backgammon, bridge, snooker and real tennis. In all of these sports, no matter whom we played, whether we were up against White's Club, or the Conservative Club in Dorking, Grouchers teams were invariably beaten. Despite an unbroken string of defeats stretching back at least to the Second World War, morale among Grouchers members remained high. Team talks were a regular feature of these events. Tactics were discussed, and every move of the opposing team was second-guessed and triple-guessed. The war gaming that went on in the bar at Grouchers before any competitive match was second to none. It never made any difference.

Nevertheless it was, for everyone concerned – except perhaps the organisers – a huge honour to be involved in one of these golf matches. Every event was heavily oversubscribed, and there was considerable acrimony and accusations of favouritism from those who, for reasons of space, could not be included in the tour. The sense of belonging to an elite group, therefore, was almost over-whelming, the *esprit de corps* a shining example of what discipline and commitment can achieve. Nor was defeat always by a wide margin; often the contest was close enough to allow members to reflect afterwards, over their triple Gordon's and tonic, on what might have been.

I was conscious that this might be one of the last events I organised for Grouchers. I sensed that my time with the club might be coming to an end, so I wanted it to be looked back on as a success; it would please me to be able to imagine members saying, 'Michael Gascoigne? He'll be a hard act to follow.'

The Marine Hotel looks out across the West Links towards the Firth of Forth. The hotel itself is a rather grand relic that fell on hard times and has since been rescued and smartened up. Golfers stay there, and families come for bucket-and-spade holidays, although as a beach resort North Berwick is a quiet and dignified town, rather than a fish-and-chips, cockles-and-winkles sort of place. Visitors arriving there might imagine they have slipped, without quite knowing how, into the understated charm of a seaside town in the 1970s.

Beyond the West Links are the Cowton Rocks, flanked by Broad Sands to the west and North Berwick beach to the east. Out to sea are Fidra and Craigleith, two small islands, and the even smaller Lamb. To the south and east are the guano-covered terraces of the Bass Rock, where thousands of gannets, guillemots, puffins and shags line the rocks and scream at the visitors who come in boats to see them. My parents brought me here as a small child from time to time, as a change from the Fife coast on the far side of the Firth. Those were the days before the voices started, my brief age of innocence. I remember those holidays vividly, although in truth they were a long time ago, before my relationship with my parents became strained and we stopped going away together.

In those days we would take adjoining rooms at the Marine Hotel: my parents in a suite, my nanny and I in adjoining smaller rooms on the same floor. My father would golf at one of the many links courses, and my mother would take me out in a hired fishing boat, hand-lining for mackerel or cod. In the evenings we would walk on Broad Sands together, and I would look for hermit crabs in the spume of the ebbing tide. My father would stroll ahead of us, puffing on a cigar, wreathing us in clouds of fragrant smoke that mingled oddly with the smells of the beach.

It was this memory that first drew me back to North Berwick a few years ago, and persuaded me to try to organise a golf tour so far away from our normal haunts. The choice proved popular with the members. When I went to bed after our first dinner that night, I felt a rare sense of peacefulness as I listened, for a moment, to the sigh of waves on the beaches beyond.

The next morning after breakfast I cornered David Martin and said, 'David, I've got a spot of bother, can you help me out?'

David was our star player and team captain. He was clad in plus-fours, with yellow stockings, and a red jersey with a pair of crossed golf clubs emblazoned on it. Perhaps owing to an air of pre-match tension, our first night had been relatively sober. Even David had limited his consumption of drink the night before, and now he looked fresh and ready for action.

'What can I do for you, old boy?'

'Something has come up – a legal problem at Beinn Caorrun. I have to run into Edinburgh to see the lawyers for a few hours. I'm terribly sorry, but it simply can't wait. Can you find someone to cover for me?'

The last time I had played golf with David was when he had been staying with us at Beinn Caorrun and I had been out of sorts. I had played as badly as I ever had that day, so when I said I couldn't take part today I thought David looked rather relieved.

'Don't worry. I'll find someone to play your round for you. You go and sort out your troubles. We'll see you at dinner tonight.'

'I hope so,' I said. 'Good luck.'

David nodded and sauntered off, whistling between his teeth. Twenty minutes later I was in the car and heading towards the Edinburgh bypass.

I did get back in time for dinner that night. It was a subdued affair. The defeat by the Honourable Company of Edinburgh Golfers, notwithstanding their reputation and the fact that they were playing on their home course, or that they had never even come close to being beaten by Grouchers, still seemed to have taken the Grouchers golf team by surprise. So the fact that I had hardly any appetite for food and drink did not attract attention, and I was not the only person to make an excuse and go off to bed early.

The next morning dawned bright and breezy. It was our bye day, and I went off with David Martin and two others to play a round at Gullane. My game was quite respectable, for once, and David was in an affable mood as we left the course.

'We'll beat those buggers tomorrow if we can keep our form from today,' he said.

We were back at the hotel by three and I decided to change and take a walk along the beach. By the time I got down there dusk was approaching, but it was a fine evening, and the tide had just turned and was starting to come in. I walked across the now deserted links and found myself on Cowton Rocks. Beyond, the rocks ran out in jagged lines into the sea. These were the Hummel Ridges, and when the tide came in they were covered. Now I was struck by the presence of a tall, thin figure standing on the ridges, the incoming tide lapping around his bare legs and feet.

It was Peter Robinson. He was still wearing his golfing clothes: a jersey, and plus-fours rolled up above the knee. His socks and shoes had been left somewhere, I hoped for his sake above the tideline. He was looking down at a rock pool at his feet. To get back to land he would have to wade through this pool, or jump off the ridges into the sea and risk breaking a leg or at least turning an ankle on the hidden rocks. I scrambled along the slippery ridges, beginning to get quite damp myself in the spray, and said, 'Peter? Hadn't you better come back? The tide's coming in quite fast now.'

He did not move. He was staring down into the rock pool. A wave crashed against the rocks and from where I was standing, it looked as if the spray must have soaked him from the waist down, but still he did not move or even flinch. As I got closer I could make out, even in the fading light, how white and strained his face appeared, his mouth set in a rictus that was a grotesque mockery of a smile.

'Peter!' I called again. 'You must come ashore ... you'll be swept off the rocks.'

I heard him mumble something but could not make out the words. The light was fading fast now, and the rocks on which I stood were intermittently covered in seawater, which floated the seaweed, making it difficult to progress any farther. I managed another couple of steps and called out, 'Peter, come towards me.'

Another, bigger wave crashed against the rocks behind him, making him stagger forward under the impact of the water, and I saw a look of terror on his face as he put a foot into the rock pool. He must be soaked from head to toe, I thought. He pulled his foot out of the pool and stepped back.

'Peter, come to me,' I shouted at him once more.

'I can't,' he wailed.

'Why not?'

'There's a lobster in that pool.'

A lobster?

'Oh, for God's sake,' I muttered and, edging forward, I arrived at the pool and looked into its clear water. I thought I saw the antennae of a small lobster waving but as I came close, whatever it was edged into a crevice out of sight.

'It's gone now,' I said to Peter. He looked at me like a great baby on the verge of tears.

'You're just saying that,' he said accusingly.

I stepped into the pool and said, 'Look, it's quite safe,' then reached out and took him by the hand. At first he resisted but then he allowed me to pull him gently forward. I could feel a shudder run through his body as we crossed the pool, but once we were past the lobster – real or imagined – his resistance vanished. Together we made our way back awkwardly to the safety of Cowton Rocks. Peter found his shoes, but did not put them on as by now they were the only dry item of clothing he had. The lights of the Marine Hotel were ahead of us as we crossed the links. Peter turned to me then, and said in a voice that was almost normal, 'Thank God it was you that found me.'

'Thank God it was anyone. Why were you standing there?'

Peter did not answer directly. 'Because you understand. You've been ill too, only you weren't fool enough to stop taking your medication. I had to stop, the drugs were making me feel so lousy. I haven't taken anything for weeks. But I could have died out there, if you hadn't come along.'

Suddenly he sat down on the short grass and began to weep.

'The lobster looked so big. I thought it would eat me.'

I put my hand on his shoulder. If this was happening to Peter after a couple of weeks off the pills, what on earth was happening to me? But I knew. I knew what was happening to me, and I no longer cared.

Peter straightened up, and then got to his feet.

'They re-engineer us with these drugs,' he said, as we walked slowly back to the hotel. 'That's what Stephen Gunnerton told me when I went to see him, when you and I first met. I was on the edge of serious mental illness at the time. My career was at risk and so was my relationship with Mary. I'd simply lost my ability to cope. Stephen told me the drugs would deal with all of that and, in a way, he was right. I'm one of the best human rights barristers in London now, I have a happy marriage, and life would be wonderful if I didn't feel like crap half the time. So life is a trade-off. I will go back on my medication when I get back to my room. But it's all so unfair. Don't you ever think that?'

I was silent for a second, thinking about what he had said. It was all about choices, after all. We could choose to accept the chemicals that allowed us to float through the world like ghosts, or we could revert to whatever we had been intended to be.

'We always have a choice, Peter,' I said.

'No, we don't,' he said. 'Not if we want to survive.'

Peter must have started on his medication straight away, and it must have gone to work on him quickly because the next morning he was his normal, intense, overbearing self. We played our match with the Borderers, and lost, but not by as much as the year before. It was generally agreed we were making progress, rather than that the other team was getting worse.

That evening was the formal dinner that always marked the end of these trips. I had arranged a private room, and David and I had agreed a menu and a wine list. It was black tie, of course, as all Grouchers formal dinners were, and it started out as a very convivial evening. I was sitting at one end of the table, flanked by Peter Robinson and Edward Macy, another lawyer. At the other end was David Martin. As the evening progressed, I could not help becoming aware that, with the golf behind us, the group of people around the table was dividing into two camps. Peter Robinson's set was one, and mostly at my end of the table; David Martin's was the other. The conversation became even more polarised until I almost wished I had split everyone up on to two tables.

As the pudding plates were cleared away, I saw Peter rise

to his feet and clink his glass with a knife. This was *lèse-majesté*. It was accepted convention that only the captain, in this case David Martin, made a speech on a golf night, and his main job was to toast, first the team for being such sporting losers, and then the membership secretary for organising it all. I saw David give Peter a murderous look, but once Peter was on his feet he was unstoppable. It was what he did for a living, after all.

'Gentlemen,' he said, 'having so many of the club's leading members here is too good an opportunity to miss, and I want to say just a very few words before giving way to our excellent captain, David Martin.'

He had sufficient force of personality to command silence, at least for a time.

'Today is another example of what a wonderful institution Grouchers is.' He paused long enough for someone to say, 'Hear, hear,' but nobody did. 'And as in all institutions,' said Peter, looking around over the top of his spectacles, 'it is our ability to change and adapt that is our best guarantee for the future. Some of you may have been wondering why I have been so active in promoting the candidacy of a particular gentleman I would like to see become a member of the club.'

At this there were cries of 'Sooty!' and a bread roll was thrown but landed nowhere near Peter. It would have required a lot of courage, or alcohol, to throw a roll *directly* at Peter when he was in barrister mode. He held his hand up for silence, and got it.

'I am aware that this action has caused discomfort to some members and for this, I apologise unreservedly. The last thing I want to do is upset anybody. But I also think Mr Patel is a gentleman, and would be an asset to any club he joined.' This time his neighbour Edward Macy said, 'Hear, hear,' although he said it quietly. 'That in itself is not the point. I am pursuing the matter because I believe that, if we cannot adapt to the modern world, and if we cannot show ourselves to be free from ancient and unseemly prejudices, I fear we will no longer be a club worth belonging to. So this has become a matter of principle for me and some other gentlemen sitting here tonight. I repeat that I am sorry for any discomfort I have caused, but I urge you to reflect on what I have said. This is about the future of Grouchers, not about an individual candidate. We must change and modernise. We must discard attitudes that are now out of date. That is the way forward for Grouchers.'

With that he sat down to a deathly silence. After a moment, David Martin broke it by drawling, 'Thank *you*, dear boy, for giving me the chance to say a few words. Are you quite sure you have finished? Don't want to give us a potted history of the tribes of Uganda? [Laughter from one end of the table; silence at the other.] No? Then I'll give a little speech of my own.'

To my relief David did not continue with his leaden sarcasm, but instead simply made the traditional golfing-dinner speech. It was mercifully short, and he earned a brief round of applause as he sat down, but between the two of them, they had killed off the evening and now the two camps were barely speaking to each other.

A bar had been set up at the other end of the room, and David Martin and his friends gathered around it, clutching large whisky and sodas; Peter and one or two of his friends remained at the table, drinking glasses of port. I longed to go to bed, to get away from these people, but it was still too early to disappear.

'Where were you the first day?' asked Edward Macy, pushing the port decanter in my direction. I passed it straight on to a neighbour. I was beyond alcohol now.

'I had to pop into Edinburgh on some business,' I said.

'Oh yes, you're from this part of the world, aren't you?'

'Perthshire,' I said briefly.

'My wife thought she saw you filling up your car at the Milnathort service station on the M90, coming back from Perth. We live part of the time in Fife, you know. We're almost neighbours.'

'Are we?' I replied. 'Well, she must have mistaken me for someone else.' At that moment the group at the bar burst into song:

> *Rule, Britannia*
> *Britannia rules the waves*
> *For Britons never, never, never shall be slaves.*

There was a lot of laughter and back-slapping. Peter Robinson gave the men around the bar his most supercilious look. David Martin raised a brimming beaker of whisky and soda to him in an ironic toast.

Who did they all think they were, these people? I wondered. When they sang their ridiculous song about Britons, what did they mean? Small fractions of their genetic make-up might be Saxon, perhaps even Viking or Norman. A larger part of the blood that flowed through their veins contained the genes of the Ordovicians, the Silures, the Catevallauni, the Iceni or the Brigantes: one or other of the ancient Belgic tribes that had been here when the Romans came. But mostly their DNA came from the real Britons: aboriginal inhabitants of the islands, the people who were here before the Celts, hunter-gatherers from the Atlantic coast of France and Spain, an ancient people who had been invaded, enslaved, raped, colonised, murdered, persecuted by almost everyone who had taken the time to land on our shores. Britons in that sense had always been slaves, ruled by one elite after another – by Roman governors; by Saxon and then Viking warlords; Norman barons; Dutch Orangemen; German princes; and now by the political classes of the present age.

Members of Grouchers needed to know who they really were. It was my duty to tell them, and I would find an opportunity to do so. It would be my gift to them before I finally severed my association with the club. The Extraordinary General Meeting, held to debate the candidacy of Mr Patel, was in a few days' time. I would be there, if my luck held out.

I could not tell them tonight. It needed thought and preparation, and all of a sudden I was weary to death. It had been a busy three days, and I was exhausted. I made an excuse to my neighbours and left.

As I lie in my bed I can hear the waves singing on the beach again. The tide is in, but now the sound of the waves gives me no peace. In the crash and music of the surf I think I can hear the Lamia, calling to me. She howls for me as she once howled in the ruins of Babylon. She is wandering on the beach somewhere, a demon of the night with whom I am somehow joined. She is no delusion: I wish she were. The Lamia is enraptured with me now. She is a creature that needs blood, and I have begun to feed her.

I understand my purpose now, to become what I was born to become, to hunt and to kill. I have already done such things as will ensure I never know peace again, that I in turn will now be hunted for ever. Like the old fox I once saw on the hill, I must find my secret ways if I am to avoid the bullets and the snares. All I wanted to do was recover my identity, to escape from the prison of my medication, to know love, to experience again what human emotions feel like, to know the love of another person, and to survive. For a few weeks I was on the cusp, between the life of the chemical ghost that I was, and whatever I am now becoming. In that short time, I have been happy. That is to say, I believe that I have been happy. I believe I have understood what it must be like to be human: to be loved, and to love another person.

It is no longer safe for Elizabeth to be with me now. The thought that I must separate myself from her hurts me more deeply than I could ever have imagined. That is what the Lamia warned me: that I must learn to separate myself from the things I love.

'You cannot really feel love,' she told me. 'You have no real emotions.'

But I have. I am two people: human; and whatever else I must become. But I do have emotions. I remember what love is.

Stephen Gunnerton once told me that I might be a genetic anomaly, the result of some ancient interbreeding between our species and another manlike species. An extra gene has been added or else a gene is missing, producing what Stephen called 'schizotypy', a predisposition to psychosis, an abnormality of the brain. My brain has grown in a different way. My reality is different to other people's: as a child I saw people among the trees at Glen Gala that no one else could see, and their voices were in my head. As I grew from childhood to adolescence, and from adolescence to manhood, they showed me the choices I had to make if I was to survive. Now I don't just hear voices no one else can hear: I see things that no one else can see. For me they are as real as Elizabeth, or Verey-Jones, or the man next door. The Lamia is real enough.

My nature is what I was born with. I am an evolutionary step behind, or an evolutionary step ahead, of the human race. It doesn't matter which, only that I am out of step and so will not be allowed to roam freely, undrugged and unrestrained. A thousand years ago I might have been accepted as someone touched with divine madness, like a shaman. Now I will be thought of as a rogue, a predator: a bear or a wolf that has developed a taste for human flesh, and has to be hunted down. No drugs can cure me now. No drugs can undo the things I have done. Nothing except my own death can prevent me from doing the things I am going to do.

I am desperate to see Elizabeth again, if only I can keep the Lamia from her. I cannot bear the idea that we will never meet, and never speak, again. I want her to know how much I have loved her; I want her to understand, as far as she is capable of understanding, what my story is. I know how dangerous it is for us to meet, dangerous for me, and dangerous for her. But I will find a way. I must find a way.

14

While the Cat's Away

As soon as Mikey drove off in the Range Rover, with his golf clubs on the back seat, and his evening clothes still in the bag from the dry cleaners hanging from a grab handle, I burst into tears.

I couldn't explain why I did that. There was something so touching about the way Mikey looked as he said goodbye. He hugged me for a moment and I felt the current pass between us. As soon as he had gone I thought, *Supposing I never see him again?*

I don't know why I thought that, either.

I managed to calm myself down and then sat down by the phone and looked through the old address book that lay beside it on the table. After a while I found the number I wanted and dialled it.

'Bridge of Gala Health Centre,' said a voice.

'It's Elizabeth Gascoigne calling for Dr Alex Grant, please,' I said, expecting to be told he was away, or out on a call, or in surgery. To my surprise I was put through almost straight away. Although we had rarely met since he turned up unexpectedly on the day of my wedding, his voice was familiar and full of warmth.

'Elizabeth,' he said. 'Good morning. How nice to hear

from you. I didn't know you were in Glen Gala. What can I do for you?'

'I'm not calling from Glen Gala, Alex,' I told him. 'I'm in London. I'm ringing you about Mikey – about Michael. Please don't hang up or start telling me about medical ethics like that other man. Please listen to me for just a minute.'

There was a pause and then Alex Grant said, 'Is Michael ill? Don't worry, I'm listening.'

'Michael has stopped taking his Serendipozan. I think he's been off it for quite a while now. I saw him throw a packet away and I didn't think much about it until I went to see Stephen Gunnerton.'

'You went to see Stephen Gunnerton?' said Alex Grant in a surprised voice. 'You did well to get an appointment with him. I'm a GP and even I had to use all my ingenuity to get him on the phone, on the rare occasions I had to speak to him. I don't suppose he told you much, did he?'

'Not really. It was what he didn't tell me that's made me so worried.'

There was a long silence at the other end.

'Hello, are you still there?'

'Yes, I'm here. Wait a moment.'

There was a rustling noise in the background, and then Alex Grant said, 'Elizabeth, I've got Michael's file in front of me now. I don't really need it because I have known Michael since he was a boy. He was born with an illness. You know that.'

'He's schizophrenic, isn't he?' I whispered.

Alex Grant said gently, 'We can call it that if you like. We both know what you mean. Has he never said anything about his condition?'

'He just said that he used to have behavioural problems.'

'Behavioural problems? Has his behaviour altered in any way recently?'

Then I described how Michael had changed, and as I talked about him I found myself calling him Mikey, even though I had promised myself that name would remain private between Mikey and me. I described how much more outgoing and alive he had become in the last few weeks, and how much our relationship had improved. Alex Grant listened and then said, 'We haven't seen all that much of you since you got married. You don't come up to Beinn Caorrun frequently, do you? And when you do, we don't often meet. Have you ever wondered why?'

'Well, no, but I don't quite see what—'

'Michael is wary of me, Elizabeth. For him, I'm the man who has been prescribing him drugs ever since he can remember, who used to go up to see his parents and recommend that they consider putting him in a secure institution, a decision that, regrettably, they never made.'

'Put him in an institution?' I said indignantly. 'Whatever for? Just for hearing voices? For being a bit eccentric?'

Alex Grant did not answer me at once. He was clearly a man who thought before he spoke, not a type I was terribly familiar with.

'I tried to persuade John Gascoigne to have his son sectioned,' he said.

Sectioned? It must have been the stress, but for a moment I really thought he meant cutting poor Mikey into slices like a Swiss roll, and the backs of my eyes began to prickle. Then it dawned on me what he meant.

'You mean put away?'

'I mean detained in a mental health establishment for his own safety, and the safety of others, until a proper diagnosis could be made under controlled conditions. Then a decision could be taken as to whether it was safe to release him back into the community. Don't misunderstand me: I feel deeply, deeply sorry for Michael. I also felt sorry, and very concerned, for his parents at the time. It would have been much better for him to have been born with some more obvious physical defect which everyone could see, and understand. Very few people really do understand what is wrong with someone like Michael. I'm not an expert in this myself. I'm not a psychiatrist. But I do think Michael, for a very long time, has been a great danger both to himself and others. The Serendipozan was prescribed to keep those aspects of his personality subdued and under control.'

This was ridiculous.

'Michael is the kindest, gentlest man on the planet,' I said with some heat. 'He wouldn't harm anyone.'

'People like Michael develop enormous skills to conceal how different they are. They can be very manipulative, very controlling, even charming. But their nature never changes. It can't. They are almost without any form of social brain.'

I could think of nothing to say. This was getting worse and worse. After years of insipid marriage to someone who barely spoke, I had now rediscovered my husband and fallen in love with him. Now all these hints were being dropped that he was quite different to the man I knew. What was I meant to think? That he was a monster?

'Can you come up to Glen Gala?' said Alex Grant, in a different voice. 'I mean now, today?'

'I don't know,' I said 'I'm supposed to be in the office in a quarter of an hour and I'm late already. I'll probably get the sack if I don't turn up. What's the urgency?'

'How long did you say he has been off the Serendipozan?'

'I don't know, but it must be a month or two at least.'

'That's why it's urgent,' said Alex Grant. 'He will be regressing straight back to where he came from, clinically and psychologically. You might be in considerable danger. I might be. Stephen Gunnerton might be. A perfect stranger in the street might be. I'll check our records to see when he last reordered his prescription, but if he's been off it for more than a month, it is not good news.' I heard him say 'I'm coming,' and then he put his hand over the phone for a moment. Then he was back.

'I'm sorry, I have a patient waiting. Elizabeth, I think it is vital that you come and see me. There are things I can tell you about Michael that I think you need to know. In fact, I think it is essential. It's quite out of the question to have that kind of conversation over the phone. In any case, when I've told you the full story, I need you to be there with me because I'm going to ask you to help me fill in a form under Section Four of the Mental Health Act. That will allow us to detain Michael for seventy-two hours, so that we can make a proper assessment of his condition and his medication requirements. We must get him back on Serendipozan, to stabilise the situation. If he is as safe as you say, then he will be released at the end of that period, and no one will be more delighted than I will be – except perhaps you,' he added, as an afterthought. 'Will you come?'

I had to say yes. I just had to; how could I not after that?

'But I'm not promising to sign anything,' I said.

'You don't have to. But you *will* want to, when you've heard what I have to say. It's probably not realistic that you get here today. Could you be at Beinn Caorrun tomorrow morning around ten, at the lodge?'

'I suppose I could get the shuttle up to Edinburgh and hire a car.'

'That's an excellent plan. One other thought, Elizabeth.'

'Yes?'

'If you've got a friend – a girlfriend, I mean, someone you can really trust, then try to bring her with you. I'm thinking it would be good for you to have some support tomorrow.'

We hung up. For a long time I sat gazing at nothing in particular. I wondered whether I was the one who had gone mad. My darling, gentle Mikey – how could he harm anyone? Who could possibly believe that, once they had met him?

Then I remembered Michael at Beinn Caorrun that night, not so long ago, when the Martins and the Robinsons had been staying and Michael had snarled, '*Just listen*' or something like that. It wasn't the words: it had been the voice, the expression, as if a wolf was sitting next to us at the table. I remembered how frightened I had been as I lay beside him in bed that night – frightened of what, I did not know, except the strangeness of it all.

A great calmness overtook me. I reached for the phone and rang the office, and asked to be put through to Celia.

'Yes?' she said, when she came on the line. There was no 'How are you?' or 'Is everything all right?'

'Celia, I know you won't be happy about this but I need two days off, today and tomorrow. I've got a real problem and I have to deal with it.'

'And I've got a real problem, too, darling. I'm paying someone to do a job and they are never there to do it.'

'Please, Celia. You know I wouldn't ask if it wasn't an emergency.'

'Take two days off,' said Celia. 'In fact, take the next two hundred days off and start looking for another job.'

She hung up. I wasn't certain whether I'd just been fired. Probably not – even Celia knew that you couldn't just dismiss people over the phone. But I felt fairly sure she would be on the line to the ghastly little man called Lionel in Human Resources, to make sure that my dismissal proceedings were put in motion.

The next call was to Mary Robinson. Again I got hold of her straight away – at least it was a good day for making phone calls – and I told her I wanted her to come up to Beinn Caorrun with me.

'Oh, how nice. Were you thinking about spring some time? I'll get the diary. Peter's already bought next year's. Isn't that organised of him?'

'No, I don't mean next year, Mary. I mean today. And don't say you can't come, because I know Peter's up in North Berwick playing golf with Michael.'

There was a silence, then Mary said, 'But Elizabeth, that is quite out of the question. I'm giving a book club lunch here, tomorrow. It's my turn. I couldn't possibly miss it.'

She sounded very firm, so I replied, 'Mary, do you remember we talked about Mikey – Michael's illness?'

'Yes, of course I do. Then you went to see Peter without telling me.'

'I'm really sorry, I know I should have said something. But Michael's illness has come back. I've just finished having the most horrible phone call with his doctor. He wants me to go up to see him. He said I should bring a friend I could trust. Mary, I'm dreading it.'

I dried up. I simply couldn't speak any more. Then Mary

said, in a quite different voice, 'Of course I'll come, darling. When do we go?'

After that a sort of fever of truancy overtook us both. Mary got on the phone to her book club friends, cancelling the lunch, no doubt enjoying being very mysterious about why. I checked flight times and in the end we decided we would fly up to Edinburgh late that afternoon, stop in an airport hotel, and then rent a car and drive up to Glen Gala first thing the next morning.

We agreed, too, on a cover story in case either of our husbands rang home – we were off on a shopping trip to Bath. Not that either Peter or Mikey rang home much when they were away, but no one ever asks questions about a shopping trip, at least until the credit card statement comes in.

I had finished packing and was waiting for the doorbell to ring. Mary was due any moment, and then we were going to take a taxi to Paddington and get the Heathrow Express. Instead the phone rang. I hesitated for a moment, then picked it up. It was my mother.

'Mummy,' I said, 'I've got to be quick, I'm just dashing out of the door.'

My mother ignored this.

'Charlie's left me,' she wailed. 'He's disappeared.'

I couldn't get her off the phone. Charlie Summers, the dog food salesman, had suddenly absconded, owing six months on the house he had rented in Stanton St Mary and not insubstantial sums at the village shop and the Stanton Arms. Other unpaid debts were emerging with every day that passed. Then I heard a yapping in the background.

'What on earth's that?'

The doorbell rang.

'It's our dog, darling. We bought a dog, the sweetest little chihuahua you ever saw. He's called Ned and he—'

'Mummy, I must go, there's someone at the door.'

'You never have any time for me, you're so self-absorbed.'

I said goodbye and hung up firmly, but gently. I knew quite well the next time we spoke my mother would accuse me of slamming the phone down on her.

Mary and I travelled out to Heathrow and got the shuttle up to Edinburgh. There we picked up a small car and then put ourselves up in the airport hotel I had booked that morning. We kept firmly off the subject of our husbands and the evening had a superficial jollity to it. We drank rather a lot of white wine and I felt a little unsteady going to bed. Once my bedroom door closed behind me, I was stone cold sober in a moment. What on earth was I going to be told in the morning?

I lay awake half the night, or so it seemed. In body I was in a small, anonymous hotel room; in spirit I was already in Glen Gala, watching the dark trees waving in the wind, picturing the grim bulk of Beinn Caorrun Lodge. I had rung Mrs McLeish a few hours ago, to warn her we were coming up. There had been no reply; my only unsuccessful phone call of the day. Then I had rung Donald the stalker. He was in, but did not know where Mrs McLeish was.

'I'm away myself in the morning to help a friend with the hind-stalking up in Aberdeenshire for a couple of weeks. He's been giving me a hand here, so I owe him one.'

It sounded as if Beinn Caorrun would be deserted when we got there. Perhaps that would be a good thing: my meeting with Alex Grant would go unreported and I could decide for myself when, or if, I would tell Mikey about it. At last I fell into a shallow doze. Almost as soon as I had closed my eyes, it seemed, the telephone was ringing. It was my wake-up call.

Mary ate her two pieces of toast and a bowl of fruit that looked as if it had come straight from the tin. I sipped my coffee, but could barely swallow. I felt sick with apprehension. Then we were scraping the ice off the windshield of the hire car and, all too soon, were crossing the Forth Road Bridge and heading up the M90 towards Perth.

The roads were not busy but I seemed to have miscalculated all the same and it was already a few minutes after ten when we turned off the A9 up the narrow, single-track road that leads though Glen Gala. It was winter now, rather than late autumn, and the sky was a pale blue, feathered with high white cloud. In the hollows frost lingered; it had been a cold night.

'Isn't everything looking beautiful in this sunshine,' exclaimed Mary brightly as we came towards the two white stones that marked the entrance to the Beinn Caorrun estate. I drove around the next bend and then slammed my brakes on, narrowly avoiding a car that was parked in the middle of the track.

It was a dark blue Land Rover Defender. The legend 'Bridge of Gala Health Centre' was stencilled in white lettering on the tailgate, beside the spare wheel. It sat squarely in the middle of the track and there was no possibility of edging past it as the trees on either side hemmed in too close. Overhead their canopy almost hid the sky, and the track itself was covered in pine needles so that it looked like part of the forest floor. The door on the driver's side of the Land Rover was open.

'The driver can't be far away,' suggested Mary. I gave

two light taps on the horn but wished I hadn't: the sound echoed loudly through the trees. Then I remembered where I had seen the car before.

'That's Alex Grant's Land Rover,' I said to Mary. 'Why on earth has he parked it here?' We both got out. The silence of early winter was absolute. The woods were still: only the faintest of breezes rustled the tops of the trees, bringing down the occasional shower of needles. No birds sang. The chill in the air very quickly got into our bones as we stood staring at the vehicle, which looked as if it had just been cleaned and polished that morning. I could hear a ticking sound, as if the Land Rover's engine was still cooling down.

'Alex?' I called, nervously. 'Dr Grant?'

I felt that the trees around me were listening, but in their dark silences there were no clues about what had happened here. There was something about the empty car, parked in the middle of the track, the driver's door still open: it didn't add up. Then Mary, who had walked a few steps farther, said, 'Oh.' Then frantically, 'Elizabeth, come and see. This isn't right; this isn't right at all.'

At the edge of the track, beyond the driver's door, lay something that the door itself had hidden from me. It was a man's shoe, a brown suede boot, and it was lying upside down among the pine cones. We both backed away from it instinctively. Why would a man stop his car in the middle of the track, and then lose a shoe, and not come back for it?

'Alex?' I shouted again.

'Don't,' said Mary. 'Someone might hear you.'

I turned to tell her not to be an idiot, that I was shouting precisely because I wanted someone to hear me, when the force of what she had just said struck me. She was one step ahead of me. I was trying to reconstruct a bizarre series of events that had ended up with a man hopping around on one leg in the middle of a wood because he had lost his shoe. Mary had gone to the next level of the riddle. Alex Grant hadn't come back for his shoe because he hadn't been able to. He hadn't been able to because someone had taken him from the car. Someone who didn't much care whether Alex Grant had his shoes on or not. Another unwelcome thought crowded in on the last. As I remembered him, Alex Grant, although into his sixties, had been a big man. Whatever had happened here, he had been unable to resist. I suddenly realised I was thinking about Alex Grant in the past tense.

I began to shake uncontrollably.

'We ought to tell someone about this,' said Mary, 'as soon as possible.'

'Let's get back down to the main road,' I said. 'Let's go to the health centre at the Bridge of Gala. Just in case Alex is there.'

'And if he's not?'

We both knew he wouldn't be.

'Then we'll have to tell someone. The police, maybe. You drive. I don't think I can.'

We got back in the car and Mary started reversing back down the track to the junction with the road. It was impossible to turn here. She reversed very slowly and carefully, and I could hardly stop myself from screaming at her to go faster. At any moment I expected someone – or something – to come rushing at us from the darkness of the trees. Thankfully nothing did, and a moment later, although it seemed like a lifetime, Mary was driving us back down the road. A quarter of an hour later we were at the health centre.

No, said the receptionist, Dr Grant wasn't in just now, he had gone up Glen Gala.

'That's why I'm here,' I said. 'I'm Elizabeth Gascoigne from Beinn Caorrun Lodge. Dr Grant was coming to meet me. We found his Land Rover on the Beinn Caorrun track but he wasn't in it. We shouted for him but he didn't come.'

Maybe his car had broken down, suggested the receptionist. Maybe he had decided to walk back.

'The only sensible way back down is the road we just drove along. He wasn't on it.'

'Tell her about the shoe,' suggested Mary. So I told her. The shoe did for the receptionist what it had done for us, and within moments she had gone next door to tell one of the other doctors. There was a short conference and then I heard somebody calling the Tayside Police.

It was a very long day. The police turned up in two squad cars, and then followed us up to the turn-off for Beinn Caorrun. I didn't want to leave the road, so told them to go on up the driveway on their own. A policeman stayed with us while the rest of them went along the track. After about half an hour, a policeman came out of the woods on foot and approached our car. He leaned down to the window and said, 'We need you two ladies to come with me for a moment, just to confirm the scene is as you first saw it. We need to know if anything's been disturbed, if someone's been back.'

With some reluctance we drove slowly back up the drive, and found the two police cars nose to tail behind the Land Rover. Yellow tape had been criss-crossed around the trees.

We both looked at the scene carefully. The dark blue vehicle's door was still open, and the shoe was exactly where we had seen it. 'No, nothing's changed.'

'We're treating this as a potential crime scene until we know better,' said the officer who had walked in front of our car as we drove up the track. 'One of our lads has been up to the big house and he's just radioed in to say it's all locked up. There doesn't seem to be anyone there.'

I handed him the house keys. 'Go and see for yourself,' I said. 'It ought to be empty, but you never know. Do you mind? I couldn't face going there myself. There's no alarm or anything.'

The officer walked around the edge of the scene and up towards the Lodge. Another policeman came over and said, 'Let's go down to the station at Perth and have a nice cup of tea until we can find out a bit more about what's going on here.'

It sounded like a suggestion, but it wasn't.

The waiting seemed interminable. After we had been at the station in Perth for an hour, a plainclothes policeman came and introduced himself to us. He was a tall, sandy-haired man, with pale blue eyes and a pale complexion, and he looked as if he knew his job. We were sitting in a small waiting room, with not much in the way of distraction, and Mary had begun to talk anxiously about getting back to London.

'I'm Detective Sergeant Ferguson,' he said. 'Can you tell me why you two ladies were up in Glen Gala?'

I explained about the meeting with Dr Grant. I was careful not to say too much about why I was meeting him, but I couldn't avoid saying that I was worried about my husband's health.

'And where is your husband just now?' asked Ferguson.

'He's playing golf down in North Berwick with Mary's husband Peter, and a whole lot of other people.'

The policeman took down details of where the members of Grouchers were staying, but otherwise did not seem inclined to ask further questions about Mikey, which came as something of a relief, for lots of reasons.

'Have they come across any trace of Alex Grant yet?' I asked.

'Well, if you mean have we found him, I'm afraid the answer is not yet. We've got a big search team lined up to start tomorrow, but today we've only had the officers we could muster at short notice, and the Forest of Gala is awful thick and awful big. I don't really want to tell you much more at the moment. You might be required as witnesses.'

'Then can we go back to London?' Mary said.

'The duty sergeant's got all your details, I believe?' replied Ferguson. 'Then we won't detain you any further. We may need to be in touch, depending on how things develop in the next day or so. It's likely we'll copy the file to the National Missing Persons Bureau at Scotland Yard, and they may contact you as well.'

'Please tell us as soon as there is any news,' I said.

Ferguson didn't smile. 'It depends what the news is. You will be hearing from us, or from our colleagues in London, as soon as we are in a position to tell you anything.'

Mary and I drove back to Edinburgh Airport in silence. As we approached the rental return parking, I said, 'Mary, I'm so sorry I've involved you in all this.'

She didn't say anything, but parked the car in its slot. We both got out and took our overnight bags from the back seat. As we walked towards the rental office, Mary suddenly said, 'Do you know more about this than you're telling me, Elizabeth?'

We both stopped and stared at each other.

'I swear to God I don't,' I said. 'That's why we went up – to find out from Alex Grant whatever it was he wanted to tell me about Mikey. Now I might never know.'

We returned the keys and papers and then went to the terminal and sat in the departure lounge. Just before we were called for boarding, Mary, who had not spoken for almost half an hour, asked me: 'What do you think happened up there?'

What did I think? I was trying as hard as I could not to think. I was trying to shut my brain down, to deprive it of the power of rational thought, of putting two and two together. I knew Mikey and Peter were together at North Berwick playing golf. That was what I knew. I knew that Mikey had been there all day, playing a round with three other men, never out of anyone's sight for a moment. I knew I would ring him tonight, probably tomorrow morning now because it would be late when we got back, and he would be cheerful, and tell jokes about the other golfers.

I knew Alex Grant had asked me to meet him because there was something awful about Mikey he felt he had to tell me. I knew that whatever it was, some chance had prevented me from hearing it, and now I might never learn what he had to say. I shook my head.

'I don't know, Mary. I don't want to know.'

*

I don't know, I said to myself a thousand times as the plane taxied down the runway and took off. I looked out of the window as we flew south, the dark clouds below reflecting the glow of a waxing moon, and said to myself: *I don't know I don't know I don't know I don't know I don't know I don't know I don't know I don't know.*

As I lay awake in bed at Helmsdale Mansions, my heart said to me, *But you do know. You do.*

15

Her Black Gaze Made Me Shudder
in My Sleep

Mary had offered to put me up at her house that night, but I wanted to be at home in case Mikey came back from North Berwick, or rang me. He did neither. I don't know why I expected that he would. For some reason that I did not want to articulate to myself, I could not raise the courage to call him at the Marine Hotel and tell him about Alex Grant.

The next morning I was half awake and wondering whether I shouldn't be getting ready for work when the doorbell rang. I put on a dressing gown and went to the door. Outside was a courier, in motorbike leathers. He handed me a black plastic bag, and a document pack, and asked me to sign for them, which I did without thinking. I went back into the flat and looked at what he had given me. The black plastic bag was a bin liner, containing all my personal belongings from my desk at work. The document pack required more effort: first to open it, then to understand its contents. It was from my employers, and it took me a moment or two to decode the legal jargon, but 'stay at home until we find a legal way of firing you' was what it came down to. I scribbled, 'Don't worry, I resign' across the face of the letter, signed and dated it, and then dropped it on the kitchen table to deal with later. Then I trailed off to the bathroom to have a shower.

Today was Mikey's last day at North Berwick and he would be home some time tomorrow. Between now and then I needed to understand what was going on. I needed to work out what I would say to him, after he had come through the door and poured himself his whisky, and asked me how things were. I'd tell him about losing my job, of course, or giving it up, but I didn't think that would worry him much. Then what would I say? How about something like, 'Oh, by the way, Mikey, Alex Grant asked me to go up and see him so he could tell me more about your mental condition. Only the funny thing is, Dr Grant seems to have disappeared.'

I couldn't really see how the conversation would work. I made myself a cup of coffee and then did something I hadn't done for three years. I went to a drawer where I knew there was a packet of cigarettes from the last time I had given them up, and found that I had three left. They were very stale, but I lit one all the same and smoked it.

Another thought struck me. Supposing the door opened and Mikey came in but it wasn't the Mikey I knew and loved? What if it were some other version of Mikey that came into the flat, something that looked like him, but wasn't him at all? What if he was dangerous? That was what Alex Grant had implied. I could hear his voice in my head, as clearly as when he had spoken to me over the telephone not quite forty-eight hours earlier: 'You might be in danger. I might be. Stephen Gunnerton might be.'

Why us three? Because we all knew different aspects of Mikey and joining up those jigsaw pieces might reveal a very different picture to the one I held in my mind or, these days, in my heart. Something had happened to Alex Grant, hadn't it? If he were safe and sound, then where was he? Why hadn't he rung in to say: *I went for a walk and got lost. I saw something in the wood and went to look for it. It's OK. I'm back at home now.* There were too many questions, and no answers at all.

I didn't know what to do with myself. I was beginning to feel I would go mad, sitting alone in the flat, waiting for something to happen. Then something did happen: the doorbell rang again. I went to the door thinking, it's another courier, it's a letter from Celia begging me to come back. But it wasn't a courier. A young dark-haired man in a dark blue suit stood there, holding up some ID. He was thin, and quite short, and had a sharp-featured face like a fox.

'Detective Sergeant Henshaw, Mrs Gascoigne, from the National Missing Persons Bureau at Scotland Yard. Can I come in for a moment?'

I felt sick. What was he going to tell me?

'Is it about Alex Grant?' I asked, opening the door to allow him in.

'In a way, yes, Mrs Gascoigne. I'm here to help my colleagues in the Tayside Police. They've faxed down this form they want you to sign, as soon as possible. I'd better explain.'

I took him into the kitchen and, in order to get some semblance of mental balance back, fussed about making two mugs of Nescafé, which I don't think either of us wanted.

'It's a consent form, Mrs Gascoigne, to say you consent to the police applying to the court to get possession of your husband's medical records.'

My heart almost stopped and for a moment I couldn't breathe. Then I managed to ask, 'Why do you need to see those? What have they got to do with Dr Grant?'

'Because we're led to believe,' said DS Henshaw, 'that Dr Grant was going to meet you to discuss the contents of those records. We wondered if there was any material in there that might ...' He paused, searching for the right phrase, '... shed any light on Dr Grant's disappearance.'

'Why don't you just ask my husband?' I said. 'I can tell you where he is, and has been for the last three days. He's staying at the Marine Hotel in North Berwick, playing golf.'

'We don't think that it would be appropriate to interview your husband at the moment, Mrs Gascoigne. It would be very helpful if you could just sign the consent form. The longer Dr Grant is missing, the more concerned we become, and my colleagues in Perth believe access to the documents in question may be helpful. I really can't tell you any more at the moment.'

'Is my husband a suspect?'

DS Henshaw looked at me for a moment, and then said, 'We're not aware that any crime has been committed at present. This is a missing person enquiry, and we are exploring any and every line of enquiry that might help us find him.'

He pushed the consent form across and finally I signed it.

'Won't this take days, if you've got to go to court?'

The detective smiled. 'No, it will be done as soon as the fax gets to Perth. There is a judge standing by and they'll have the order by noon today.'

After the policeman left I sat staring at nothing for a while. The sick feeling didn't go away. I stood up and walked around the flat, picking up bits of paper from Mikey's desk, not exactly snooping, just picking them up and putting them down again. I laid out his post for him. I looked at the books on his bookshelf, which had titles such as: *Improve Your Golf in Six Easy Lessons*, *Make Your Tricks – Some Hints for Contract Bridge Players* and, a more scholarly work, *A History of Emmanuel Groucher's Club for Gentlemen* by Alwyn Verey-Jones. This last was a slim, privately printed volume, with gold lettering on a dark blue binding. There were no books about genes, or DNA, or schizophrenia, or Serendipozan. This was the minimalist collection of a man with few interests outside golf, fishing or card games.

I checked the bathroom cabinet: there were no more packets of Serendipozan hidden in there, just lots of Nurofen. I was about to start going through Mikey's suit pockets when I managed to stop myself. This was becoming ridiculous. I had to do something, but I wanted to be on my own. In the end I went and wandered around Harvey Nichols for two or three hours, without actually buying anything. If nothing else, it tired me out. I made myself some soup for an early supper, watched TV and was in bed by nine.

In my sleep I dreamed of Mikey. He was walking along a beach. Small waves subsided gently on the sand. There was a full moon, almost as bright as daylight. Out to sea were three small rocky islands. I followed Mikey's footprints, which were so fresh that they were still filling with seawater as I passed. Then I noticed he was not alone. A dark-haired girl in a long green dress walked beside him. She was not touching him or holding his arm, but their heads were close together, as if they must be talking, in a way that somehow told me their relationship was of long standing, even intimate. As I followed them I saw that the dark-haired girl was so light she left no footprints in the sand, not even the slightest indentation. I opened my mouth to say something but she must have heard my thoughts before I could even speak. She turned and stared at me and her black gaze made me shudder in my sleep. Then the sound of the telephone awoke me.

I rolled over in bed, and managed to find the light switch without quite knocking the bedside lamp over. I saw that it was half past three in the morning. I picked up the phone and said, 'Hello?'

There was no answer, not even the sound of breathing.

'Hello?' I said again, then, 'Mikey, is that you?', for I imagined that in the background I could hear the sound of waves rolling gently on to a beach. Perhaps it was just static.

'Mikey, if that's you, please speak to me. *Please*.'

There was still no reply. Then, just when I had persuaded myself that it must have been a misdial, or a false call generated by some computer in Bangalore, I heard the unmistakable click of the phone at the other end being put down.

After that, there was no further possibility of sleep. I got out of bed, put my dressing gown on, and switched on all the lights in the flat. I made myself a cup of tea, and then listened to a fascinating programme on the BBC World Service about female circumcision among certain Congolese tribes; and then to a very interesting item on *Farming Today* about biofuel farming. I kept my mobile beside me in case somebody broke down the front door with an axe. Only when daylight came did I feel it was safe to fall asleep, and I dozed on the sitting-room sofa for three or four hours.

*

I awoke again, unrefreshed, at about ten in the morning. I felt rather ashamed I had been so upset by a silent phone call. Lots of people got them, and didn't make a fuss. But it had not been just the phone call; that awful, vivid dream had disturbed me as well. I ran a hot bath and lay in it for a while until I began to feel human again. Then I dressed, and had some coffee and toast. Gradually the unease that lingered in me began to fade. I checked my watch. It was about seven hours' drive down from North Berwick, and if Mikey left about nine or ten he should be home by five at the latest.

For a few minutes I thought again about Mikey's return. Why should I be fearful of it? He was my husband. I either believed in him or I did not. All he had been doing for three days was playing golf at North Berwick. Now it was time to welcome him home.

I decided I would make a fuss of him, and went out and bought armloads of food with which I restocked the fridge. I started leafing through recipe books until I found something I thought he would like. The distraction kept me from thinking about Mikey, at least not at every moment.

Then, because it wasn't Magda the cleaner's day, I did a bit of hoovering and dusted my way around the sitting room. Anything to keep busy. When I had finished cleaning I went and sat in the study, switched on the laptop and Googled. I consulted various sites on schizophrenia. It was a mistake. Either I couldn't understand a word on the web page, or they were simply too depressing. I found one site called 'Schizophrenia.com' which appeared to be used by sufferers. On one page I read a text about how schizophrenics used to be thought of as possessed. The article concluded: 'There may be cases of divine chastisement or demonic influence, but most of the time demons can be ruled out.'

Well, that was good news, anyway.

At six I tried Mikey's mobile, which was probably turned off. It was. He had never discovered voicemail. At a quarter to seven I realised he would probably have looked in at Grouchers on the way home so I rang Nigel, the night porter. No, Mr Gascoigne wasn't in, and wasn't expected, as far as he knew. At 7.30 it suddenly occurred to me that the Marine Hotel might remember when he had left. He had checked out at 6.30 a.m., I was told, before the other gentlemen were up, because they had all asked where he was, and seemed a bit put out to find he had gone. I took dinner out of the oven and put it in the warmer. At eight o'clock I rang the Robinsons.

'Peter's in the bath,' said Mary, when I rang. Her voice sounded guarded, almost defensive. 'Can I get him to ring you?'

'Michael isn't back,' I explained. 'I just wondered if Peter might know where he is, or when he will be home.'

'It's best if Peter speaks to you himself,' said Mary. I couldn't understand why she was being so cold. Then she asked, 'Has there been any news about Dr Grant?'

'Not so far,' I said.

'Well, let me know if you hear anything.'

I sat by the phone and waited for half an hour, and at last it rang again. When Peter spoke, he too sounded guarded.

'Yes, Elizabeth, how are you? What can I do for you?'

'I just wondered if you knew where Mikey ... where Michael might be. He hasn't turned up here and I haven't heard from him. I'm just a bit worried.'

'Well, I don't know. He left the hotel very early, without saying a word to anyone.'

I digested this.

'Well, he's not here, Peter,' I said. 'I'm not really sure what to do. It seems a bit dramatic to ring the police.'

There was another silence and then Peter said, 'Elizabeth, Mary has told me about your trip to Beinn Caorrun. I must say, I find myself wishing you had not involved Mary in this. I don't know what's going on, exactly, but there is something you ought to know. The first day's golf match ... Michael wasn't there. He made some excuse to David about an urgent meeting in Edinburgh and then took off. No one saw him again until that evening.'

'The first day – you mean the day before yesterday?'

'That's right,' said Peter. 'The day the two of you were in Glen Gala.'

Somehow I managed to bring the conversation to an end and then sat down, my legs almost folding underneath me.

Mikey had not been in North Berwick the day we were supposed to meet Alex Grant.

Mikey could have been anywhere. Peter said he had been away the whole day.

Mikey could have been in Glen Gala. It was only two hours' drive from there.

Mikey could have—

I tried to pull myself together but it was difficult. I kept feeling as if I had fallen into a parallel world where everything was the opposite of what it should be. I went and opened the wine I had put in the fridge, poured a glass and took a deep gulp. It tasted of nothing. If only Mikey would ring.

I checked my watch. It was just past nine. The phone rang.

'Darling,' said my mother, 'I suppose at this time of night you might have five minutes to spare for me? Or is that too much to ask?'

'Mikey's disappeared,' I said.

'Mikey? Oh, *Michael*. Well, that's exactly what Charlie Summers has done, as I was trying to tell you the other day. Do you know, he told me he was off to collect a delivery of dog food from Southampton, then simply walked out of my life.'

My mother began to weep. I had never seen her shed a tear, since my father had left her; after that it had been all stiff upper lip, and not showing any emotion in front of the children or what she called 'the servants' (our housekeeper, who got the sack the same week).

'Why Southampton?' I said, because I couldn't bear the anguish in my mother's voice. I realised she was crying for a wasted, loveless life, abandoned by her husband, preyed on by a series of middle-aged charmers of varying ability and moderate personal qualities. Despite my own predicament, I suddenly felt very sorry for her. At least it took my mind away from the growing nightmare in my own life.

'Because it's shipped in from Japan,' she said, recovering herself. 'I thought I had told you that. It's specially made up in Osaka to an old Japanese formula. That's why it's been such a huge success.'

She started to sniff again. I could just picture Charlie Summers buying the cheapest mass-produced dog food that he could find at the local cash-and-carry, and then relabelling it at dead of night in his workshop. Japanese dog food, indeed!

'He owes so much money,' she said. 'He even borrowed two hundred pounds from me. Poor Mrs Johnson at the shop is owed God knows how much. I don't know how she'll cope. Do you think I should pay Charlie's debts? I feel responsible in some way. People might not have given him so much credit if they hadn't known I had taken him under my wing, so to speak.'

My mother could barely afford to keep a roof over her own head, let alone pay some conman's debts.

'Well, he is Henry Newark's cousin,' 'I said carefully. 'Perhaps Henry might feel he has to do something about it?'

My mother was pleased with this suggestion. Undoubtedly she had thought of it herself, but she wanted someone else to say it.

'You're right. I believe Charlie was a second cousin of Henry's, but it's still family, isn't it? I shouldn't interfere, really.' Then my mother asked, 'What did you mean, Michael's disappeared?'

I told her Mikey had failed to appear after leaving North Berwick.

'Well, darling, men are like that. They never tell you what they're doing. Your father never did. I expect you had supper waiting as well?'

I admitted that I had.

'He'll turn up tomorrow with some feeble excuse, don't you worry. At least Michael would never run away.'

Then we were back to Charlie. It was half an hour before I put the phone down. I was still debating whether to phone the police when the police rang me.

It was DS Henshaw. He sounded tired. Could he have a word with Mr Gascoigne, please?

'He's not here,' I said. I heard a rustle as the detective looked at his notes. 'But you were expecting him?'

'Yes, hours ago. Should I be telling someone about this?'

'Well, you've just told me,' said DS Henshaw, reasonably. 'We're looking for him anyway. So if we find him, you'll be the first to know. I just want to say one thing, Mrs Gascoigne, and I want you to pay very close attention. Have you got your mobile handy?'

I told him to hang on while I went and got it.

'What's the number?' he asked, so I gave it to him. Then he told me to key in the number he read out to me.

'If Mr Gascoigne should turn up,' said DS Henshaw, 'no matter what time, no matter where you are when you see him, call this number. Don't stop to say "Hello". Don't make him a sandwich, or pour him a drink, at least not until you've called this number. When the call is picked up, it will show it's connected on the screen. Then hang up. You don't need to say a thing. We'll know he's with you, and we'll know where you are, whether you are in your flat or in the middle of Scotland. We're tracking the number on a computer and will be able to pinpoint your location to within a few metres at any time.'

He cleared his throat. 'That's all you have to do. Have you got that, Mrs Gascoigne? Can you promise me you'll dial that number when you next see Mr Gascoigne, and as soon as you see him?'

I didn't understand, and said so.

'It's best if we keep this simple, Mrs Gascoigne,' said DS Henshaw. 'We believe Mr Gascoigne may be a risk to you, to himself, or to others. This is simply a sensible precaution. Please do one last thing for me, Mrs Gascoigne?'

'Yes,' I whispered.

'Make sure your mobile is fully charged.'

There were no phone calls, no disturbances of any sort during the night, but I slept little. I was grieving for Mikey. I lay awake for hours reviewing our life together, and reproaching myself. How could I have been so blind, so unsympathetic? How could I not have understood what had been going on? The moment I discovered that Michael had once been treated for a mental illness was the worst in my life. My own husband, whom I had promised to love and cherish (I don't think I ever said obey), had been shrouded in the mists of some powerful drug, and I didn't know anything about it.

Of course I had noticed something; I had just decided that that was what Michael was like, and I had to put up with it. It had never been a passionate romance. It was what it was.

I hated myself now as I thought about my complacency. I might have helped, if I had known. Even if I hadn't helped, I might have understood, and with understanding there might have been more affection, more closeness. Now, all too briefly, we had known and loved each other as we should always have done. I was trapped in my own unforgiving and new-found perception. The fault was all mine, the self-centred, ignorant, *oh well, let's just make the most of what we've got* attitude: that was all me.

Michael had loved me, just as Mikey now did, only Michel hadn't known how to show it. He hadn't been able to show it. The drugs had masked so much of Michael's true self that little was visible to the casual observer of the real person underneath.

251

That was what I had been: the casual observer.

A week ago I would have said we had the perfect marriage, reinvented out of nowhere, rescued by Mikey, free from the cobwebs of his medication. Now I was being warned that, when I saw Mikey, I had to call for help. What would happen when I did? Black-clad men swinging through the windows on ropes? What the hell was going on? I had to find someone who could tell me, and I thought I knew who that might be.

The next morning I was on Stephen Gunnerton's doorstep at half past eight. I wasn't sure whether anyone would be there that early, but when I pressed the bell it was Stephen Gunnerton's voice that spoke down the intercom.

'Who's there?' he said.

'It's Elizabeth Gascoigne, Mr Gunnerton. I don't have an appointment, but please will you see me for a few moments? It's urgent.'

'Are you alone?' said the voice suspiciously. A whining above my head distracted me and I looked up to see what I had not noticed on my last visit: a small CCTV camera fixed to the wall above the door frame. It panned the street and then pointed itself down at me again.

'I'm on my own,' I told the intercom.

'Look around the street again. Anyone you recognise?'

But the street was still quite empty. A few figures were walking quickly through the dark morning, faces averted from a keen wind that had begun to blow. 'I'm absolutely on my own,' I repeated, 'and it's important. Can I come in for a moment, please?'

There was a buzz and then the sound of an electrically operated lock. I pushed the door open and went inside. It shut behind me with a loud click. The reception desk was empty. I wondered whether I should wait, but then Stephen Gunnerton appeared in the corridor and waved to me.

'Come on, come on,' he said, 'I haven't got much time. Where's your husband?'

'I don't know,' I replied. 'He went to Scotland on a golf trip and hasn't come back. He should have been home yesterday.'

We went into the consulting room I had been in a few days before. A large black suitcase stood in the middle of the room. Stephen Gunnerton was staring at me and I noticed that there were beads of sweat on his forehead. His charcoal suit was immaculate, his grey silk tie was carefully knotted against a cream silk shirt, and yet he gave the impression of nothing so much as a forest animal in full flight.

'What do you want?' he asked. As he spoke, he walked across to a double-fronted bookcase and opened the central section, to reveal some decanters and glasses. He poured himself a large neat whisky, while he waited for my reply.

'I want you to tell me everything you didn't tell me when I came here the other day. There's no point in worrying about your stupid medical ethics any more, is there?'

'I won't offer you a whisky,' he said. 'It's probably a bit early for you. A bit early for me, too; steadies the nerves, though. I don't know everything. Some of it is speculation. But it's in the public domain now, or soon will be.'

He took a gulp from his glass.

'Michael was referred to me years ago by his GP, Dr Grant. Dr Grant thought that his patient was exhibiting classic symptoms of an acute form of psychosis. He also thought, but couldn't prove, that Michael had killed his own mother a few years earlier. Faked a boating accident, I believe.'

I expelled all the breath in my body in a gasp, as if someone had punched me in the pit of the stomach.

'Michael was an interesting patient. He had developed a complex delusional construct that was quite unique in my clinical experience. Not because it was bizarre – they're always bizarre. People hear God talking to them. They hear their dead ancestors telling them to do things. They invent detailed fantastical explanations to justify themselves. Sometimes their delusions are complicated by drugs like cannabis. Not in this case. What made Michael different, on the rare occasions when he spoke for any length of time, was the *absolute* sense of conviction he conveyed when he spoke.'

He sipped some more whisky, and grimaced.

'He believed that, since childhood, he had been able to communicate with the spirits of ancient hunter-gatherers who had roamed the hills and woods of Glen Gala long ago. Michael's conviction that he was communicating with people none of the rest of us could see was classic delusional stuff; it was the detail that was so unusual. He said that they taught him forgotten magic; primitive enchantments, using the berries and branches of the rowan tree, herbs, other things now forgotten by modern man. He told me that they taught him the art of concealment, how to stalk larger and more dangerous animals than he and kill them before they knew he was there. They taught him he had to learn how to survive at all costs.'

'He told me they spoke to him by gesture,' I said. 'Sometimes when he is asleep I've seen his hands twitching and fluttering – it really does look like some kind of sign language.'

'Yes, that was one of his fantasies,' Stephen Gunnerton said. 'He believed – he'd read somewhere, I suspect – that sign language preceded speech in human development, and that the evolution of the vocal cord is – in evolutionary terms – a recent development. I am afraid he was probably rationalising the trembling that was starting in his own hands. That's an early symptom of a condition rather like Parkinson's disease. It's almost certainly a side effect of some of the drug treatments he was on before he came to me.'

He sipped again, and coughed, then put his whisky tumbler down on his desk. He had drunk two inches in about the same number of minutes.

'I'm not used to this stuff,' he said apologetically. 'Anyway, Michael's delusional construct was classic. Alex Grant was quite right. It was a metaphor for concealing his own illness, for learning to hide his true nature from others, in order to survive. When I first met him he was intense, vivid in his language, unexpected in his movements. It was sometimes very disquieting, being with him. I thought he was potentially the most dangerous individual I had ever treated. For a year he was kept in a maximum-security institution in South London, and I visited him twice a week. Eventually, NICE approved Serendipozan just as I was wondering what the next step would be. It seemed an ideal solution. We started treating him, and he responded. We were able to move him to a medium-security institution, and then the time came when we could think about returning him to the community. That is now best practice: to provide a patient with a good safety network in the form of a case officer from social services, and then to continue to see them as an outpatient until we can tell whether their condition is stable or not.'

Stephen Gunnerton then unnerved me by going to the window and looking out into the street for a moment. He came back and said, 'It all worked. It all so nearly worked. Michael responded to treatment, he calmed down and became less volatile; lethargic and dull, in fact, but that was a small price to pay. After a while we let him back into the community, and he came to the clinic as an outpatient, as good as gold, never missing an appointment. Where it went wrong was that after six months the case officer assigned to Michael resigned, and they never got around to replacing him. I didn't find this out until a few days ago. When you told me you knew nothing about Michael's condition, I realised you should have done. He should have been receiving visits from someone. Obviously you knew nothing about that.'

I shook my head. The words condemned me too. Stephen Gunnerton looked at his watch. 'I must go,' he said. 'I'm catching the Eurostar to Paris in an hour.'

'That's it?'

'That's it,' he said. 'I could go on if I had the time, but you wouldn't learn much more. I don't even really know *what* Michael is. I know that, underneath the drugs, there is a great deal of intelligence that he tried to conceal from me, and from others who tried to help him. I don't think I ever really understood him. I will tell you one thing I used to think, sometimes, when he was talking to me, when he was going on about how the old people had taught him how to hunt, how he could hide himself from anyone and run for days in pursuit of his prey. You don't want to know the detail. It isn't pleasant to recall, not at the moment.'

I stared at him. 'What was the one thing you were going to tell me?'

'I found myself wondering: *what if it is all true? What if his world is no less real than ours?*'

Then Stephen Gunnerton began to make shooing gestures with his arms, as if I were a hen or a sheep.

'You must go,' he said. 'So must I. Michael will come looking for me soon, Mrs Gascoigne. He might be on his way here now. He thinks I'm his enemy, someone who tried to take his life away from him. Maybe he thinks you're his enemy, too. I don't plan to let Michael Gascoigne find me. I don't know what happened to Alex Grant and I don't want to find out the hard way. Yes, the police have been here, a little man called Henshaw. Thank God, he seems competent. Maybe they'll find Michael first, but I'm not taking any chances. Goodbye, Mrs Gascoigne, and good luck.'

16

He Could Run for Days in
Pursuit of His Prey

I left Stephen Gunnerton's clinic, and I walked and walked. At first I headed towards home but then I realised there was no point. I didn't have a home. There was a flat I still had the keys to, but I didn't have a home. A home was somewhere you came back to, and somebody else was there doing the crossword, or writing out golf team lists for his club, and usually a home had a dog in it, which lifted its black head and thumped its tail when you came in. I didn't have a home, I didn't have a dog, and I didn't have a husband.

There was someone out there who used to be my husband, who used to say in a dull grey voice, 'Looks like the sun might come out later,' when he knew and I knew that I was just off to work for nine hours in a crowded open-plan office that barely let in any light at all. How bad had that really been? It had seemed as if it had been bad, painfully bad sometimes, but all the time I was grinding my teeth at the monotony of his conversation, or the even greater monotony of no conversation at all, I hadn't known what this would feel like, this fractured reality, and I felt as if I were standing on the edge of a terrible abyss.

I wondered how long it would be before the police caught him. Not long, I supposed, with their devices for tracking mobile phones, and their CCTVs on every corner: some-where Mikey would emerge from whichever shadows he had wrapped himself in and then they would have him. They couldn't lock him away in jail. He would be put in a 'secure institution'. Perhaps after a few years they would rebuild my beloved Mikey, re-engineer him with more drugs, shatter the bad parts of his brain, the bits they didn't understand, with more powerful chemicals. Then they might eventually hand him back to me, my very own bespoke grey zombie unable to feed himself.

Suddenly I felt very tired, very cold and very alone. I reached into my bag and pulled out my mobile. It was after one o'clock. I had been in some sort of a trance for the last few hours and now I was God knows where, somewhere in Fulham probably, without the slightest recollection of how I had got here. I looked at the phone and saw that I had a missed call, from a few minutes ago. I hadn't heard the phone ring, but it must have done. It was from Mary Robinson. I didn't really want to speak to Mary at the moment, but then I realised I needed some form of human contact or I would start to go mad myself.

'Elizabeth,' said Mary's voice. 'I rang your office and they said you were away from your desk. I rang twice and I rang your mobile twice. Where are you?'

'I'm not at work,' I explained. 'I'm just wandering about, trying to think things through.'

'Well, get over here as fast as you can,' said Mary. 'Peter and the club secretary are here, and they want to see you.'

The last thing I wanted to do was talk to Peter or that dreadful old man Verey-Jones, whom I had met once or twice at Grouchers functions I had been unable to excuse myself from. But before I could think of a reason not to go, Mary said, 'They've seen Michael.'

'What? Where? What was he doing?'

Mary wouldn't tell me and just repeated that I should get over there as soon as possible. By some miracle of divine intervention, an empty taxi came along a few minutes later, probably the only taxi to go along that road in weeks. I flagged it down and gave the driver Mary's address.

On the way I tried to think where they could possibly have seen Mikey. Did that mean he was in custody? By the time the taxi reached Peter and Mary's, I was nearly frantic. I paid the driver off, overtipped in my hurry, went up the steps of the terraced house where the Robinsons lived and pressed the bell. Mary must have been watching out for me because she opened the door so suddenly I almost fell on my face on the doormat.

'They're in the drawing room,' was all she said, but as she led me down the corridor she took my hand and gave it a squeeze. When we entered the drawing room, Peter Robinson and Alwyn Verey-Jones were sitting side by side on the sofa, looking uncomfortable. Peter's forehead gleamed with perspiration, but the rest of his face was pale, almost grey. The room looked as it always did – smart, clean and lifeless. Copies of *Country Life, Homes & Gardens* and *The World of Interiors* were neatly laid out on the low glass table in front of the sofa. When I came in, Peter sprang to his feet.

'Ah, Elizabeth,' he said, turning slightly to indicate the brittle figure of Verey-Jones. 'You know our secretary, of course?'

'We've met,' I said, and tried to smile, but my lips were too stiff; my whole face felt frozen.

'I'll make some tea,' said Mary, disappearing out of the door.

'We've seen Michael,' said Peter.

'So I heard,' I said, trying to keep my voice from shaking. 'Have the police got him? Do you know where he is now?'

'If they have,' said Verey-Jones, 'we haven't been informed; as for where he is now, I have not the slightest idea. But I *can* tell you where he was,' he added with an air of triumph. 'Two hours ago he was in the morning room at Grouchers at our Extraordinary General Meeting.'

For a moment there was some confusion as Peter Robinson and Alwyn Verey-Jones talked over each other. I knew a meeting had been planned for a while, to discuss an amendment to the club's constitution: it had arisen from the candidacy of Mr Patel. Michael had told Peter Robinson that Mr Patel no longer wanted to be proposed as a member of the club; had never, in fact, contemplated joining it and would never use it if he did become a member. Mikey told me that Peter Robinson wouldn't hear of withdrawing his candidate: 'The wheels have been set in motion,' he said, 'and besides, it's a matter of principle. It's Patel's human rights we are talking about here, not to mention the future of Grouchers. I'll pay his subscription myself, if I have to.'

The proposed amendment to the club's constitution simply said, 'Any candidate who can find six supporters who have themselves been members of the club for five years, and who have known the candidate for at least that number of years, may be elected, provided in the opinion of members he is a gentleman ...' So far so good. The sting was in the tail, in the last few words that Peter Robinson wanted to add: 'and without reference to race, nationality, colour or religious creed.'

It was this suggestion that was dividing Grouchers, like a sword thrust into its ample breast, and which had caused the EGM to be called. Many members, Mikey had told me, believed that whichever way the vote went future historians of Grouchers would look back and say that this meeting and this resolution, carried or not, would mark the beginning of the end for the club.

'Various speeches were made from the floor,' said Peter. 'I made one myself, as a matter of fact. I wanted people to understand how important it is for Grouchers to evolve, and adapt to the modern world. I am rather proud of the effect it had on members.'

From the sofa Verey-Jones said, in a dry voice, 'It was certainly memorable for its length.'

Peter was too distracted to allow this to annoy him. At this point Mary must have come back into the room because I found I was clutching a mug of tea. I went over to an armchair, sat down and sipped the tea gratefully.

'David Martin had just taken the floor,' said Peter shakily. 'The morning room was full. Every member who could walk, crawl or be carried was in that room. I don't suppose it has ever been so full. I even saw James, the day porter, lurking somewhere in the background. No one told him off; after all his job is on the line if the club is wound up.'

'And mine,' added Verey-Jones, 'not that I matter in the least.'

'There was a commotion near the door,' said Peter, 'and then Michael appeared. He had no difficulty getting to the front of the room where the chairman and committee members were sitting because people made way for him. There was something bizarre about his appearance, although at first it didn't quite register. Then I realised he was wearing the sort of clothes he wears when we go out stalking at Beinn Caorrun.'

'Not the standard of dress we expect from our members,' said Verey-Jones.

Peter Robinson looked at the secretary in annoyance, and then continued: 'There was a stain down the front of Michael's shirt. I thought it was fruit juice at first. He had a carrier bag in his hand—'

'He had brought it to the office just before going away on the golf tour,' interrupted Verey-Jones, 'so he must have been planning what he did next for a while.'

Peter Robinson said: 'He put the bag down on the table in front of Andrew Farrell and said something like, "Apologies, Chairman, may I just break in and say a few words?" Andrew nodded. Then we all realised that it wasn't fruit juice; it was fresh blood running down the front of Michael's shirt. Michael saw Andrew staring at the stains, looked down at himself, and then he smiled and said, "Don't worry, Chairman, it's not mine." His voice was chilling.'

Peter shuddered and his face looked drawn. I was glad I was sitting down. I felt faint. Then Peter stopped. He sat and mopped his forehead with a handkerchief and swallowed a few times, but was still unable to speak.

Verey-Jones said, 'Michael pulled out an armful of cotton wool buds and plastic bags from his carrier bag. He told everyone that the little cotton buds were for swabbing the inside of the cheek. He asked everyone to use the cotton buds to absorb some saliva, then put them back in the plastic bag and write their name on the tag. Michael said he would send the whole lot off to a genetics lab in Oxford for DNA testing. He said, "It will be fascinating. I expect to find that we all have significant proportions of DNA found in post-Pyrenean Mesolithic hunter-gatherers. I think it will put this debate we're having today into perspective." Then he stopped for a moment, and added, "Unfortunately, I am not aware of a DNA test that will reveal whether we are gentlemen or not, but no doubt that will come."'

Verey-Jones chuckled and said, 'I liked that. A DNA test for gentlemen. I thought that was terribly funny in the circumstances.'

'Get a grip on yourself, Alwyn,' said Peter. 'Remember what we are talking about here.'

'What happened then?' I asked. Peter continued with the story.

'Michael was just trying to get people to form an orderly line so that he could DNA-test them – and there was something so intimidating about him I almost wonder if he mightn't have succeeded – when there was a commotion.'

Peter looked away from me then, and I saw how hollowed out his eye sockets seemed, and I knew that something awful had happened.

'There was a lot of shouting from the back of the room, around the doorway. Then somebody said that Carlos, the wine steward, had found a body in the wine cellar behind the 2005 Burgundies. There was a great rush to the exits. I don't know where people thought they were going. That was the last I saw of Michael.'

'What do you mean? Where did he go? Whose body did they find?' I said, gasping each sentence out. I felt too breathless to talk properly, and my head was swimming.

'He just vanished,' said Peter. 'He must have slipped away. No one saw him go. I didn't, Alwyn didn't, and we were both almost next to him. But then there was complete chaos for a few moments until Andrew Farrell remembered he had once been a major general, and took charge.'

'Whose body?' I asked again.

'I'm going to have to let the police tell you that,' said Peter Robinson sadly. 'They know you're here, of course. They need a statement from you and it's important from an evidential point of view that I don't say too much.'

'Oh, Peter,' I said. 'Please tell me.'

He shook his head.

'I'm afraid I mustn't. The police want to take a statement from you uncontaminated by anything I might say. They should be here any moment; we were asked to phone them whenever we had got in touch with you.'

He went and sat on the sofa, before jumping to his feet again.

'Remember, Elizabeth, whatever Michael may or may not have done, we must remember his basic human rights.'

I sat in an office at New Scotland Yard with Detective Sergeant Henshaw and another officer, watching a video file on a wide-screen laptop. The policeman at the computer said, 'Here, I'll run it again. You have to keep your eyes open, it's all a bit quick.'

The film was a grainy black and white. People walked backwards and forwards with the jerky movements of extras in a Charlie Chaplin movie, the footage on fast forward. The film had been recorded somewhere where there were a lot of people hurrying about: an airport; no, a railway station. It was the concourse of a large, modern, busy station. If it was in London, I could not tell which terminal it was. There was a soundless section of visual static, as the camera lost focus for a moment, or something else happened to stop it filming, then the picture came back and I could see a large black suitcase standing on its own in the middle of the picture. A large black suitcase I had seen before.

'Oh God,' I breathed.

'Recognised somebody that time?' asked the laptop operator.

'No, but I might have seen the suitcase before. Can we go through it again?'

'Slow it down if you can, Charlie,' said Sergeant Henshaw. Charlie opened up a window on the screen and adjusted some controls, then ran the clip again.

Stephen Gunnerton walked slowly into the picture, wheeling his case behind him. He stopped immediately below the camera and looked up. Charlie paused the film clip.

'Recognise him?' asked Sergeant Henshaw

'Of course. It's Stephen Gunnerton.'

'We think he's looking up at the departures board there. Now watch carefully.'

A man walked in front of Stephen Gunnerton, hurrying, his head down, carrying a briefcase. A dark-haired girl came and stood near by for a moment, looking up too, perhaps also checking the departures board. Then she moved out of the picture to the right. Then there was a jolt, as if the camera had lurched, and someone was standing next to Stephen Gunnerton, very close to him. He was wearing a grey fleece and camouflage trousers. I couldn't understand where he had come from. He put his arm around the consultant's shoulders, as if greeting an old friend and they walked away from the suitcase. The camera went blank for a second, and then came back online. There was no sign of the two men.

'Recognise that other chap?' asked Henshaw.

'Yes,' I said in a dull voice.

'Take your time. Have another look.'

I let them run the clip once more, but I didn't need to see Mikey again. I didn't want to. Charlie closed the video clip and turned in his chair to face me. I had been sitting looking over his shoulder, and DS Henshaw had been standing looking over mine. Now the sergeant pulled up a chair and sat beside Charlie, opposite me. It was a nice, cosy circle.

'We'll get a proper statement in a minute in the interview room. Just a couple of quick questions, so that we can all get our bearings. When did you last see Stephen Gunnerton?'

'Early this morning.'

'Right. We can go into the details of that for the benefit of the tape in a moment or so. When did you last see your husband, Mrs Gascoigne?'

I started to weep.

'Three nights ago. I told you last time.'

'I just wanted to be sure you hadn't seen him since.'

'No – no – I would have told you.'

I was brought a cup of tea. I had to go to the loo to tidy myself up and mop up my face. Then I went into the interview room with both officers, and Charlie unsealed a fresh cassette tape and put it in the machine. For half an hour we went through my interview with Stephen Gunnerton. They weren't very interested in what he had told me about Mikey's psychiatric history; they wanted to know what Stephen Gunnerton's demeanour had been like, and why he had been packing to go abroad. I told them that he seemed to be afraid.

Charlie switched off the tape and then DS Henshaw said, 'He was right to be afraid, Mrs Gascoigne. We don't know exactly what happened there at St Pancras station. We can see Mr Gascoigne suddenly in shot standing next to Stephen

267

Gunnerton, and we have no idea why the camera didn't pick him up earlier. Then the wretched thing goes on the blink for a few seconds and, by the time we get the picture back, they've both disappeared.'

'What happened, then?' I asked. 'Why am I here?'

DS Henshaw didn't answer my question for a moment. Instead, he said, 'We are lucky that British Transport Security didn't simply blow up the suitcase. After all, something that size could have been a large bomb. But an officer had the wit to look at the address label and thought he'd ring us first. Not many terrorists have a Harley Street address.'

'Why am I here, Inspector?' I repeated.

'We want to interview Mr Gascoigne in connection with the murder of Stephen Gunnerton. They found him in the cellar of Grouchers Club. You don't need to know the details, but he was dead. I'm sorry, Mrs Gascoigne, but a lot of violence had been used by whoever murdered him.'

I was sitting down, of course, but all the same my vision blurred, then dwindled to a vanishing speck of light, and I fainted.

I spent that night in a hotel the police found for me. They didn't want me to be alone in the flat. They weren't too concerned about my safety in itself; after all, in their minds I was the wife of a murderer, possibly the wife of a serial killer. As far as they were concerned, I might well have known about Mikey all along, and just kept the good news to myself. But they did want to keep me alive as a potential witness. DS Henshaw said, in a kindly tone, 'Mr Gascoigne does seem to have a way with CCTV cameras. That clip you saw was the only bit of footage we've found so far with an image of him on it. We're a little worried he might find

268

some clever way of slipping past us if we simply put a couple of officers in a car to keep an eye on your flat.'

'Mikey would never harm me,' I said.

DS Henshaw looked thoughtful, but then added, 'And how Mr Gascoigne got Stephen Gunnerton into that club of his is beyond me. Of course, we're just speculating at this stage. Mr Gascoigne may have had nothing to do with it. But he was the last person to be seen with Mr Gunnerton at St Pancras, and then there they both are, on the scene at the club. Mr Gascoigne arrives in that big room, covered in blood, according to witnesses, and then the next thing someone finds the body in the cellar. And your husband does his vanishing act again.'

I found myself saying, 'Every single member of Grouchers and nearly all the staff were in that morning room for the meeting; even the porter. Peter Robinson said so. You could have brought an elephant into the club that morning, and no one would have noticed.'

'Your husband would have known that, wouldn't he?' asked Henshaw in a gentler voice. I nodded in my misery.

'Well, we'll keep looking for him,' he said. 'There's a lot of us and only one of him. We'll find him soon, today we hope. Then we'll have to see.'

'You won't hurt him?' I asked. DS Henshaw looked offended.

'We'll do our job as professionally as we can, as always. I'll look in tomorrow morning and let you know what's going on. You're safe here, Mrs Gascoigne.'

I wanted to scream at him then, to tell him once more that Mikey would never hurt me. But then I thought: I don't really know what Mikey will or won't do; not any more. In my mind a grainy film clip replayed itself in a loop: first he wasn't anywhere, then he was, his arm around Stephen Gunnerton's shoulders. First he wasn't anywhere, and then he was there.

The next morning went by without any sign of Sergeant Henshaw. I wanted to leave the hotel and go for a walk to clear my head, but the police officer outside the door wouldn't let me – even breakfast had to be brought up on a tray. After drinking a cup of tea I lay on my bed and dozed. I was tired beyond all knowledge after the events of the last few days. I shut my eyes and tried drifting off into sleep, but in the end just lay there, half waking, half sleeping, while the world turned on its axis. I wanted everything to be the way it had been only a few days ago, when Mikey and I had embraced each other on the doorstep of our flat.

At noon DS Henshaw reappeared. He seemed tired and there were dark circles under his eyes. I looked at him as he came into the room, my whole expression a question mark. He shook his head even though I had not spoken.

'Nothing,' he said, 'nothing anywhere. No sign of Mr Gascoigne and, come to that, no sign of Dr Grant. We've rather given up hope of ever seeing Dr Grant again, especially now we've been told that Mr Gascoigne was away from North Berwick for a whole day. It's only just over two hours up the road to Glen Gala, isn't it?'

He pulled out the chair from writing desk and sat on it.

'The thing is, Mrs Gascoigne, we're really worried now. We have had one very violent killing. We've got one missing person, connected through your husband with the person who was murdered. I know that, at this point, Mr Gunnerton was murdered by a person or persons unknown, but I think you know why we're very anxious to interview Mr Gascoigne and – if possible – eliminate him from our enquiries.'

I said nothing. There was a long silence, while Sergeant Henshaw looked at the floor, as if he could see clues in the pattern of the carpet. Then he raised his head and said, 'I've read Mr Gascoigne's medical files, Mrs Gascoigne. I'm no psychiatrist but it seems to me that he has a very strong emotional connection with that place of yours up in Scotland – what's it called?'

'Beinn Caorrun,' I said.

'Perhaps he'll feel safer up there than down in the city, if he can get back without being picked up.'

He can run for days, I repeated to myself, remembering what Stephen Gunnerton had said, *he can hide from anyone.*

'Perhaps – this is only a thought, Mrs Gascoigne – perhaps if he knew you were there waiting for him, that emotional connection would be even stronger. It might be irresistible. He might feel compelled to show himself to you, to talk to you.'

I stared at Sergeant Henshaw in horror but he was unabashed. He looked me straight in the eye without blinking.

'You know what I'm saying, Mrs Gascoigne,' he went on. 'Your husband may be a very sick, very dangerous man. We have to take him into care, somehow, for his own protection, as well as that of other people. We have to do it soon. Once something like this starts, it doesn't stop until there have been more deaths.'

'You can't ask me to go up there on my own,' I whispered. 'You can't.'

'You wouldn't be on your own,' said Sergeant Henshaw. 'Of course not. There are officers, not beat constables, but very special people who know everything there is to know about lying up and waiting without being seen. We'd get them in by night; they'd dig themselves in and watch the house. When we're all set, you go up north to your place, you go into the house, and you wait. Mr Gascoigne comes. His instincts bring him. Maybe, most likely, we will intercept him before he gets anywhere near the house. If he does get as far as the house, talk to him and hit the send button on your phone. We'll be there within minutes – seconds even. What's the mobile signal like up there?'

'Mikey let them put a mast up last summer. It's strong.' Then I said, 'You just want me to be a sacrificial goat, don't you? You want me to be the bait to trap my own husband. I won't do it. I couldn't.'

Sergeant Henshaw stood up. 'We can't make you do it. It's your choice. Think about the other choices for a moment, though. You can't stay here for ever, in this hotel room. At some point we will have to decide what to do with you: whether to put you in a witness protection programme or let you go back to your flat and wait: for Mr Gascoigne to turn up there, perhaps, if we can't find him. Think about it. I'm going to make a few calls. I'll be back in a couple of hours. Please see if you can bring yourself to do this. It's our best option.'

Then he was gone and I was left staring at the door as it shut behind him. I thought for a long time without getting past what I had known as soon as Sergeant Henshaw had first spoken.

If I went to Beinn Caorrun, Mikey would come.

17

Forgotten but Not Gone

The air in front of the trees was shimmering and it seemed to me as if a man was walking out of the forest towards me. I did not know how he had got there, or how he had walked past the watchers without them doing anything about it. I did not understand why the air was shimmering: it was not hot, but nearly Christmas and very cold. The ground was like iron and there was a sprinkling of snow that even the direct rays of the sun could not shift. In London the Christmas illuminations had been on in Regent's Street for weeks, and all the shop windows were full of upmarket elves, Santa's sleighs, tinsel and artificial snow. The first Christmas we were married, I had given him a huge glossy picture book entitled *Best Golf Courses of England, Scotland, and Ireland*, and he had given me his heart, and he said to me—

WAKE UP!

The rental car had drifted over the centre line of the road and there was a huge foghorn blast from an articulated truck that was barrelling down the southbound lane of the A9 towards me; I wrenched the wheel and the small car shuddered in the slipstream of the huge vehicle I had so nearly collided with. I pulled over into the next layby and sat for a moment with my hands on the steering wheel, trying to control the shaking. Wouldn't it have been for the best if I had not woken out of my daydream for another second or two? Then I wouldn't have to explain to Mikey, if he came, why I was betraying him for his own good, and I wouldn't have to spend the rest of my life waiting for him to come, if he didn't come this time.

After a while, I switched the engine back on and drove to the turning off the A9 and up Glen Gala another two miles, without managing to kill myself.

As I drove up the narrow road that led up the glen, for the first time I understood what drew Mikey to this place. Although it was already the afternoon, hoar frost still clung to the branches of the trees, and at the road edges the puddles had turned to ice. The sky above was a pale, remote blue. The air was so cold it almost glittered, and I both saw and felt the silent, deadly beauty of this valley. Perhaps my senses were heightened by the increasing amounts of adrenalin my body was manufacturing as I drew closer to Beinn Caorrun. I knew that the police were not far away, and that no harm would come to me. That had nothing to do with my decision to come here in the end, my answer to the London detective's question; I had come here because I wanted to see Mikey again. I wanted to ask him what was going on; to look him in the eye and see whether I still knew who he really was. I couldn't bear the thought I might never see him again.

Now came the two white stones that marked the entrance to the drive up to the lodge, and for a while I drove through the dark forest, wondering whether, at each bend, I might meet an abandoned blue Land Rover with the door open; see a man's shoe lying upside down by the side of the track.

274

There was nothing in my way. I saw no one among the trees. Everything was quiet.

When I came out of the forest and on to the gravel sweep among the rhododendrons at the front of Beinn Caorrun, it had a sad, almost abandoned look to it. I knew Mrs McLeish would not have opened the place up because Mrs McLeish was not there. At first we had worried that she, too, had gone missing. Then she left a message on my answerphone in London, to say that she had gone to stay with her cousin in Troon for a while. There was no mention of when she might be back, or who was looking after things while she was away, or how I could get in touch with her. In all the years of my marriage to Mikey, Mrs McLeish had never been away from Beinn Caorrun for more than a day or two, as far as I could recall.

I opened the car door, half wondering whether Mikey would suddenly emerge from the trees. What would happen if he did? Would the police rise up from camouflaged hiding places? Sergeant Henshaw said it was much better that I knew nothing about that side of things.

I looked up. The sun was lower in the sky now, and I needed to unpack and warm up the house before it got dark. I had brought my warmest clothes from London. In Perth I had stopped at Tesco and bought three days' supply of groceries. I thought that if Mikey were able to come to Beinn Caorrun, he would have come by then. I carried my suitcase and the carrier bags into the house, lit a fire in the drawing room and switched the water heaters on. I had bought a blow heater for our bedroom, something Mikey would not approve of, but I thought I might die of hypo-thermia without it. It took me over an hour to unpack and open up the house and by then the light was beginning to fade. I put the kettle on and went upstairs to draw the curtains of our bedroom. I switched lights on everywhere: on the landing, in our bedroom, in the guest rooms. I didn't want any corner of the house to be dark when night came. On my way back from the bedroom, I suddenly noticed that there was something different about the landing. Someone had put a linen press against one wall, and then I remembered that Mrs McLeish had said she would get Donald to bring this old piece of furniture in from the barn, to give her more storage space. There was an odd resonance about the landing with the linen press in it, and it reminded me of an image seen long ago, since forgotten. I stood for a moment, trying to catch the elusive memory, then dismissed it from my mind.

The kettle was whistling downstairs, so I went towards the kitchen to take it off the gas. As I walked through the kitchen door, the whistling stopped.

I saw Mikey, his back to me, pouring the boiling water into the teapot.

'Oh, there you are,' he said without turning around, as if he were not wanted for questioning in connection with the murder of one man and the disappearance of another. 'I wondered where you had got to.'

I pulled out a chair and sat down before my legs gave way. My heart was hammering in my chest.

'I was drawing the curtains in the bedroom,' I said faintly.

'And you've put a blow heater on,' he said, turning around now and smiling at me. 'I can hear it from here.'

He looked older and even thinner than I remembered him. His face was drawn and his hair seemed to have more grey in it, though how was that possible after only a few days? He had not shaved. His clothes were the same clothes he wore for stalking: a dark grey fleece open at the neck, a plaid shirt underneath, army camouflage trousers tucked into thick socks, and walking boots. He stirred the tea in the pot for a moment and then went and took two mugs from a cupboard, and opened the fridge to find the long life milk I had just put in there. He made two mugs of tea for us and then came and sat opposite me at the kitchen table. Some fresh-cut branches with berries still on them lay on the table – rowan branches, I imagined.

Mikey said, 'The police sent you, I suppose?'

I didn't answer for a moment, then said, 'Mikey, how did you get here? What's going on? I've been so worried about you.'

He sipped his tea without answering, and looked at me over the rim of the mug with his grey eyes. His face seemed remote now, the smile gone. Grey eyes, grey hair, grey fleece: there was something ghostlike about Mikey; yet he was real and substantial enough. I wanted to hug him before he vanished again. There was no trace of the man I had married now, nothing in this man that recalled Michael Gascoigne. This was Mikey, and something other than Mikey, as if he were still changing, receding from my grasp, and my understanding.

'You still love me, Elizabeth. Don't you?' he asked.

'You know I do. That's why I'm here. It wasn't the police ... it wasn't *just* the police. Darling, wouldn't it be better if I called them and you just waited here for them? Then we could sort this whole thing out. I just want you to be better.'

'Better?' he said, smiling again. 'I *am* better, better than I've felt for years. You said you wanted to know what's going on. I'll tell you, because I trust you, and there have been too many secrets between us. I want you to know as much as I can tell you. I won't tell you about how. I will tell you about why. Come outside into the garden with me for a moment, while there's still daylight. There's something I want to show you. It will help you understand.'

He stood up and wandered out of the kitchen to the front door. I followed him; I had to.

We went outside. I slipped the mobile from my pocket and checked the signal. It showed three bars: good enough. I should have rung the police. They had told me to ring them before I said a word to Mikey, but I didn't want to ring them just yet. I needed to understand. I followed Mikey across the lawns and we stopped at the entrance to a little path between giant rhododendrons.

The sun was just beginning to dip below the ridge over which the Falls of Gala tumbled, but there was still enough light to see. It was very cold, and I shivered and wrapped my arms around myself.

Mikey turned and said to me, 'They've probably told you by now that I killed my mother?'

I stared at him, my mouth open.

'When I was still too young to know better, I told her things I shouldn't have. Where I went when I roamed these hills as a child, who I met, what they said to me. I trusted her, as children trust their mothers, but she went to Alex Grant and told him about me, and what I had been saying. Alex came to see me and we sat in the drawing room – Alex, my parents and me – and he started asking me questions. I was very angry, but I didn't let it show. I waited. I waited for years. They poisoned me with medicines, until I learned to throw away the pills that Alex Grant had prescribed for me, and pretend I had taken them. Then one day my mother and I decided to go trout-fishing on the loch. I rowed the boat; she fished. I came back to shore; she didn't.'

Mikey turned his back on me and began to force a way through the rhododendrons. I didn't want to go in there with him, not after this, not at any price, but he turned and looked at me with his grey eyes and said, 'Come on, you want to know, and I want to show you something. There should be no more secrets between us, darling.' I followed him as though he were pulling me on a string.

'Alex Grant wasn't fooled. His instincts were good. One or two incidents had occurred in the glen, which he quite correctly decided I had something to do with.' I shuddered. Mikey gave me a kind, remote glance. 'You're cold, darling,' he said. 'Don't worry. I won't be much longer. Alex knew that either I wasn't taking the medication he had prescribed, or it wasn't working. He came out here again one winter's day, and asked to see my father. They went into the drawing room. I stood outside the drawing-room door, but they never heard or saw me. I can be quiet when I want to be. I heard Alex ask my father for his consent to have me put in a mental hospital. My father said he'd think about it, and let him know. Then he came to the door and called for me, and we stood outside the drawing room and he asked me, "Is it true?"'

Mikey paused and looked up at the sky, smiling at some memory that had crossed his mind. He looked down again, down at me, and then down at the long, bleached grass that grew in the little clearing we now stood in, surrounded by a tangle of giant *Ponticum* and tree rhododendrons. Mikey scuffed the grass with his foot.

'Before Alex was gone I had made my plan. My father stood in the drive, waving Alex off, just as he did for any visitor who made the journey out to Beinn Caorrun, and as he walked back to the house, I shot him with the estate rifle. In those days gunrooms were never locked. All I had to do was go in and get the rifle and the ammunition clip, and chamber a round. It wasn't what you might call a sporting shot, at less than fifty yards, but it did the job. A .275 high-velocity bullet will drop an eighteen-stone stag at a hundred and fifty yards just like that, and this was only a thirteen-stone man.'

Mikey scuffed the grass some more, parting it to show what lay beneath.

'I dragged him in here and bled him out and gralloched him, to give him the same rites of departure as he had taught me to give a stag. Then I hid the rifle on the hill. I was not sure what to do next, but then the weather turned and a blizzard blew in. I waited for a few hours and then rang the police and told them my father had gone missing, hind-stalking on the hill.'

I was fascinated by Mikey's right boot. As he continued to dig at the ground with his foot I could see brown bits of wood; no, not wood, something else, a ribcage perhaps, and the long thigh bone of a large animal: a thirteen-stone animal.

'On his gravestone, when he was finally declared legally dead, I had engraved the words "*Gone but Not Forgotten*". Everyone thought it was rather touching, if not very original. But as you see,' said Mikey, poking the old bones beneath the rhododendrons, 'he is forgotten, but not gone.' He looked at me with that curious new smile of his.

'They looked everywhere – every yard of the mountains between here and God knows where. But they never searched these rhododendrons, right in front of the house.'

I started to back away from Mikey, then stopped and said, 'And Alex Grant, where is he?'

'He's gone.'

'Where is his body?'

'He doesn't need it now.'

I kept edging away from Mikey, but didn't take my eyes from him.

'Don't worry, darling, don't be afraid,' he said softly. He followed me slowly, as if he were conscious that any sudden movement would panic me into a run.

'And Stephen Gunnerton?'

Mikey stopped and frowned.

'Yes, the psychiatrist. He was my jailer, my tormentor. After my father went missing I became very depressed. I couldn't look after myself for a while, and the day after the funeral, despite everything, Alex Grant managed to get some sort of legal order to have me put in a hospital. I was too unwell to resist. Even Ellie wouldn't help me. I suppose I was pretty far gone by that stage. That's where I met Stephen Gunnerton. Between them, Alex and Stephen knew a lot about me by the time I got out of there. What they didn't know, they guessed. No one ever accused me of any crime. There was no body, no evidence and no obvious motive. But they wouldn't allow me my freedom until they had done a very thorough job of poisoning me with their drugs.'

We were on the lawn now, and the sun had dipped below the ridges. Frost had started to form upon the lawn.

'She told me it would be best if I dealt with Alex and Stephen,' said Mikey.

'Who told you?' I asked, bewildered.

'Lamia. The Lamia.'

'Who *is* that?' I asked, looking around me as if this Lamia were about to appear. It was absurd, because I knew that everything was going on in Mikey's head, and nothing and no one would appear, except the police, as soon as I had a chance to use my mobile. I didn't dare do it in front of Mikey. Maybe he would consider it a final act of betrayal and deal with me as he seemed to have dealt with everyone else. I looked into his eyes, trying to understand how much of what was behind them was still human.

'Oh. She's usually about somewhere. She's never far away.'

I turned then and ran into the house, slamming the front door behind me and locking it. Then I ran up to our bedroom and locked that door too. I took out my mobile phone. On the screen it said 'Searching for Network'. The signal had, inexplicably, disappeared. I pressed it anyway. Nothing happened.

I turned off the blow heater so I could hear better, and stood and listened. The house was absolutely silent. No creaking floorboards, no slamming doors, nothing except the distant rumble of the Falls of Gala. A wind sighed through the trees, and wrapped itself around the house, rattling the window frames. All was silent again. Then someone spoke right outside the door and I almost jumped with shock. A girl's voice, clear and silver as moonlight: 'Let's go in and see her, shall we?'

Mikey's voice replied, 'No, Lamia. Leave her alone. I don't want any harm to come to her.'

I was fascinated. Mikey was speaking to himself in two quite different voices. It made every hair on my arms stand on end, as if a wave of static had passed through me. The silver voice laughed.

'What are you? Her guardian angel?'

Mikey's voice said: 'She's bearing my child. Get your hand off the doorknob.'

I started with shock. How could he know? I wasn't even sure myself yet. I was late by a few days but it had happened before. As soon as he spoke, though, I knew the truth of what he said.

I was still clutching the mobile, and I saw that first a single then a double bar had appeared. I was picking up a signal. I pressed send, and kept pressing it again and again, while I had the chance.

The girl's voice said, 'Don't wave your stupid rowan branches in front of me. You think that will stop me? The trees have no power in winter. You must give her to me like the others.'

Then there was a hissing noise, louder than a steam engine, like a huge serpent coiled outside the door. I began to scream. The hissing stopped and then there was a single soft blow on the door, but its force was such that the oak cracked from top to bottom and it seemed to me as if the whole house shook. I went on screaming, or perhaps it wasn't me now that was making the noise, but it was a wailing that came from somewhere outside. The room pulsated with light, blue and white, and I realised I was hearing the sirens of several police cars as they pulled up outside. I backed towards the window and risked taking my eyes off the door for a second to look out. Men were spilling out of the cars, and torch beams searched everywhere. More powerful lanterns shone out of the woods around the house. I waited.

Then there was shouting and the thunder of many foot-steps on the stairs and on the landing outside. Somebody hammered on the door and shouted, 'Police!' I didn't move. It might be another of Mikey's voices. Another man called, 'Mrs Gascoigne, are you in there?' and I recognised the voice of Sergeant Henshaw. I made myself cross the room and unlock the door. DS Henshaw stood there, with two armed officers wearing flak jackets and helmets with torches strapped to them.

'Where is he?' asked the sergeant. 'Which way did he go?' I shook my head. I could not speak.

18

It's about Survival,
Not Love

The night I last saw Elizabeth was the night I last saw the Lamia. She stood there on the landing, as familiar to me as a dream I'd had many times, but I refused her what she wanted from me. I would not let her pass. Perhaps there was something cathartic about that act of resistance, because I have not seen her since. Maybe she was a hallucination, after all, just like the others, and not some ghost or demon. Maybe she was the price I had to pay for not taking my medication and reclaiming my life.

She was more real to me than any of the other delusions I had experienced: her black gaze, her clear voice, seemed beyond my own invention. She was real, persistent, terrifying. In the end, though, perhaps she was just what Stephen Gunnerton used to call a 'command hallucination'. When I defied the Lamia that night in Beinn Caorrun, maybe it was some aspect of my inner self I was confronting, and Elizabeth was spared. That night I had been Elizabeth's guardian angel, my one and only act of goodness. I remember the dark-haired girl turning on me and hissing at me like a cobra: indeed, for a moment her green dress seemed to wrap itself around her and flow into a serpent's form. Then she was gone, and I was outside the house, moving silently past the unseeing network of watchers, out into the Forest of Gala.

For years I have known, been warned by some instinct, that the day might come when I would need hiding places: bank accounts under different names, cash in the accounts, a bolthole somewhere. Long ago I prepared for flight and hiding. Now I live in an anonymous block of flats in the southern suburbs of Glasgow. They will not find me, not for the time being at least. Since Stephen Gunnerton, I have not killed, at least not as far as I can remember. There are gaps in my life I cannot account for: moments when I rediscover myself, miles from the flat where I live, covered in mud and bits of branches, as if I have been hunting in the hills and woods. I'm not always clear about these gaps. But, so far, I haven't found myself covered in anyone's blood; the blood on me has not been human, as far as I know.

I don't know what the future holds for me. There is no future, only the present; a dark, flowing river. I am content to go wherever it takes me.

I have not seen, or tried to see, Elizabeth. She has my child now. It would have been born in August. I know it is a boy. He carries my DNA, and Elizabeth's too. It will be interesting to see which of us he takes after.

One day I will go and see him; perhaps I will take him away with me when he is old enough.

If what I am is evil, is it really all a matter of brain chemistry, as Stephen Gunnerton and Alex Grant once believed? How comfortable that idea is: that everything wrong with the human race is the result of some malfunction, some microscopic chemical change in our brains, some evolutionary wrong turning in our genetic code. The Gunnerton view of the world was that all the evil that exists is already within us, locked inside in our skulls, and can be cured by finding the right pill. Perhaps that is more acceptable than any alternative: for example, that good and evil are principles in a Manichaean universe, locked in an eternal struggle in which the entire human race only has a walk-on part.

I prefer another view: that evil – and good, for that matter – can also come from beyond ourselves, hurtling in at random from some outside darkness, like meteorites from distant galaxies with spores and viruses locked inside them, bringing life itself to our dead planet. In that view, the Lamia is no delusion, but a creature of the night. In that view, my life changed when she entered my world.

I cannot afford these speculations. All I want to do now is survive. There should be room for no other thought in my mind.

And yet my mind will not do as it is told. Over and over again it recurs to an image, distant yet sharp and clear, as if seen through the wrong end of a telescope. I am in Ireland again, and I am standing in front of the house Elizabeth and I once stayed in. I can feel the soft air stirring as a breeze bends the tops of the trees, I can see their colours turning from green to russet, the horse chestnuts already a vivid red, the limes turning yellow and brown. I can feel the gravel under the thin soles of my shoes, and I look up at the house in front of me. Its creeper-covered walls make the house look as though the woods around it are embracing it, taking it back into themselves. Its windows are dark and unlit. I am inside the house now, moving soundlessly up the great staircase. I walk towards the bedroom we shared, in that last year when Elizabeth and I shared a life together. I see the pictures on the wall. I bend down and I see a smaller picture. It is just as I remember it. There is a figure there, shadowed but distinct. It is no blemish in the canvas, no accident of the painter's brush. It is a picture of a girl, on a landing.

Epilogue

A year has gone by since that dark night at Beinn Caorrun.

There are two schools of thought about Mikey. There is my school of thought, which is that he is alive and out there, somewhere. There is the official school of thought, subscribed to by the police and the family solicitor, that Mikey is probably dead, at the bottom of a gully somewhere in the hills around Glen Gala. They still haven't found his body – nor that of Alex Grant. On the other hand, the police haven't said they've closed the file. They haven't said much to me at all. They want to interview Mikey in connection with the murder of his father, of Stephen Gunnerton (bled out and gralloched like a stag, in the wine cellar at Grouchers, as Peter Robinson kindly told me), and in connection with the disappearance of Alex Grant. I suspect there are other incidents they want to talk to Mikey about as well, but I don't really know, and don't want to know.

The months went past after that night and no one saw any sign of Mikey. There were no cash withdrawals from his account, no traces that he still existed anywhere in this world. The family solicitor, who was also Michael's trustee and executor, wrote to me asking whether I wanted to start the long process of having Mikey declared legally dead. I wrote back saying that I thought it was too soon. The solicitor makes me an allowance from the estate which is quite generous and, even though I am unemployed and probably unemployable, I am not badly off. My wants are few. I might start doing some freelancing, more for the interest than the money, just to prove to myself that I am still alive. But not just yet.

What do I really think about Mikey? I think that he is a very clever man, much cleverer than I had ever realised. I think that if he wanted to disappear he could, and has done so. I think that if he wanted to create a new identity he could. I think that if he wanted to set up new bank accounts in another name he probably did so. When his solicitor and I went through the inventories for Beinn Caorrun all his mother's jewellery had disappeared. I had never actually seen it apart from my engagement ring, and a diamond necklace which I still have, but as far as I could see from the inventory, it was a very substantial collection. Mikey's pair of Holland & Holland shotguns had also disappeared, and so had a collection of first editions belonging to his father. I suspect Mikey has turned all these things into cash.

I also think Mikey has the ability to become whoever he wants to become. He has no identity, perhaps no humanity, left that we would recognise. He was changing so fast when I last saw him. When I remember the voice of the girl on the landing outside my bedroom door, I still shudder at the perfect quality of Mikey's mimicry. If I had not known it was only Mikey out there, I would have been utterly convinced by that strange, cold voice.

I don't know whether I want to see Mikey again. I still

love them, both Michael and Mikey. The last few weeks we had together, right up to the day when Mikey left home for ever, were among the happiest of my life. That happiness still warms me, although now it is only the glow from the embers of a fire that was all too brief. I don't know that I would understand, or even recognise, Mikey if I saw him again. I don't believe that I will see him again. I don't believe so, but of course, I can't be certain.

And I have John, my new baby, who is only a few months old. I was pregnant the time I last saw Mikey. How he knew that, I can't say: but he was right. John is named after Mikey's father: a gesture that Mikey would probably not appreciate. I couldn't think of any other name. John is the consolation in all of this, the one person who gives me hope and a reason to go on. My mother quite likes him, I'm pleased to say, as long as she doesn't have to change him or feed him.

We've decided to let Beinn Caorrun. It is managed by a sporting agency that tries to rent out the house with the fishing and the stalking. So far they have not had many takers, but we hope that things will pick up. The house has been smartened up with a lick of paint and new carpets, and we've put central heating in. Mrs McLeish has come back to her cottage and still looks after the lodge and keeps the books for the holiday lets. I rang her to get her to pack up various things of mine and send them down to London, and I tried to talk to her about Mikey. She just kept repeating that she didn't know; that there was no saying.

I have never been back to Beinn Caorrun since that dreadful night a year ago, and I have locked the door on the flat at Helmsdale Mansions for the time being. I'm living with my mother and baby John and the chihuahua called Ned, at Stanton St Mary. We fight like cat and dog, of course, but my mother is lonely and needs the company. I have decided that, even if I drive her mad, she likes having me at home. It is understood that the arrangement is just for a while. We sit and drink a lot of white wine together in the evenings and I have started smoking again. Ned the chihuahua sits on my mother's lap: he doesn't trust me, the little sod. Baby John is as good as gold: he lies in his cot, or in my arms, his dark grey eyes taking it all in. There is something so calm about him. He rarely cries.

So my mother and I puff on our cigarettes and chat and sip away, almost every night. We talk about my father, about Charlie Summers, about village gossip in and around Stanton St Mary. We never talk about Mikey.

Sometimes, if I can get a babysitter, we go down to the Stanton Arms on quiz nights. My mother thinks it is very democratic of her to mix with the people from the village. In fact, it helps with the loneliness, and she can enjoy a gin and tonic, even if they won't let her smoke her cigarettes inside the pub any more. I rather enjoy these evenings. They are good fun, and we can forget our troubles for a while. The vicar, the Reverend Simon Porter, is the ace in the pack in the village quiz team. His knowledge is encyclopedic. He can answer questions on almost any subject: football, celebs, classical antiquity or modern politics. One evening, after a particularly resounding victory over the team from a neighbouring village, it occurred to me to ask him something that might really test his knowledge. It just popped into my head, when my mother and I were sitting at the same table as him after the quiz had finished. I said, 'Simon, does the word Lamia mean anything to you? Is it a country, or a disease, or a person?'

'Lamia? Nothing at all, I'm afraid,' he said. Then he scratched his ear and said, 'No, I'm forgetting my education.'

The vicar rarely missed an opportunity to remind us that he was a Wykehamist. 'Lamia,' he repeated. 'It's a classical Greek word: it means "greedy". The ancient Greeks believed that there was a female demon called Lamia. It was part woman, part serpent, and drank the blood of men, if it got the chance. It's mentioned somewhere in the Old Testament too, howling in the ruins of Babylon. And Keats wrote a poem by that name; not one of my favourites, I'm afraid. What on earth made you ask about that?'

'I must have heard it somewhere,' I said. 'How clever of you to know the answer, Simon. I was really having a bet with myself that I couldn't ask a question you wouldn't know the answer to.'

He smiled complacently, then stood up and said, 'Mrs Bently? Elizabeth? One last drink before they close?'

I saw my mother surreptitiously slip a folded ten-pound note into his hand.

Soon it was time to go home. That night I thought, as I did most nights: poor Mikey. What nightmares did he have; what imagined horrors did he share his mind with? I could never begin to imagine the darkness he must have lived with. Maybe, after all, any medication, no matter how grim, was better than that.

I looked up 'Lamia' on the Internet and downloaded the Keats poem from a virtual library. It was an illustrated edition: there was a picture of a woman in a long green dress, a suggestion of the vampire in her dark eyes and full red lips. The illustration was Pre-Raphaelite in intention, if not in execution. I read:

> She seemed at once, some penanced lady elf,
> Some demon's mistress, or the demon's self.

I miss Michael, I miss Mikey. I miss them both dreadfully. I don't know whether I will ever get over it.

I think starting to smoke again has helped me lose weight. At least, something has. I'm quite thin now, which is good. There's a little grey in my hair that has appeared recently, but the local hairdresser keeps that at bay by colouring it every few weeks.

I'm still in touch with Mary Robinson. We speak on the phone now and again. I've promised to run up to London one of these days and have lunch with her. She told me last time we spoke that Grouchers is being wound up. One of the members is a property developer and has made a very generous offer for the site which, in the circumstances, most members feel they ought to accept. The idea is that the present building will be torn down and the site redeveloped as a block of flats. All its morning rooms, and dining rooms, and marbled loos will disappear into the jaws of a JCB. So the club will cease to be, but the members will all get a nice cash dividend from the sale of the leasehold. Mikey's estate too, I suppose.

Charlie Summers wrote to my mother the other day. I couldn't believe it. I never saw the letter itself, but I know my mother turned pink, then white, then pink again when she read it. She laughed, and then became rather tearful. She showed me the enclosure. It read:

A unique opportunity to invest in one of the few Dutch vineyards producing premier cru quality wine

Chateau Kloof is, at present, known only to a small number of connoisseurs of fine wines. Although its output comes from only a few hectares, it produces several thousand bottles a year of an intense beetroot-coloured wine, with an unusual and distinctive aroma that has reminded many who have tried it of a great St Emilion.

In order to make it available to a wider public, it has been decided to offer the future output of wine to investors. Units can be purchased at £1000 each, and each unit entitles the investor to . . .

I didn't bother to read any more after this; I got the general idea. Japanese dog food and Dutch wine: Charles Edward Gilbert Summers, Master of Wine (for so he had signed himself at the foot of the prospectus), was nothing if not creative. When I discovered my mother had actually sent Charlie a cheque I became very angry with her.

'But darling,' she said, 'he's had such a run of bad luck. He really deserves to be put back on his feet. Besides, he sent Henry Newark a case of this wine, and Henry said it was unlike anything he'd ever tasted. I'm sure he'll succeed this time.'

Then we had one of our little rows, but that is over now and we are speaking to each other once again. I worry that, one of these days, Charlie Summers may turn up here. He's one of those men who are without shame. Henry Newark did pay off his debts, as I foretold, so he won't get thrown into debtors' jail if he comes back to

Stanton St Mary. But there are a lot of people who won't speak to him, if he does return, and I'm one of them. If Charlie comes back to this house, I don't see myself staying here a day longer.

It's cold down here in Gloucestershire in these dark January days. Stanton St Mary lies in a frost hollow and last night we had a fall of snow, although it's thawing now. This morning, when I went to check on John and drew my curtains, mist was rising off the melting snow. The sky was a gloomy grey. The day looked so cold and unwelcoming, I almost changed my mind and went back to bed.

Then, with a jolt – as if my heart had stopped beating for a second – I saw that there was a dark-haired girl standing in what my mother calls our 'park', a few acres of pasture beyond the garden. She was slim, and stood very upright, and she wore a long dark green dress but no coat. She must have been freezing, standing there, but she stood absolutely still, her arms by her sides. I thought she was looking up at the house. I thought she was looking directly up at me.

I knocked on the window but either she didn't hear, or else she took no notice. I decided I had better go and ask her what she wanted. After all, there's no right of way across that pasture. I pulled on a jersey and a pair of jeans, and went down to the back door where I had left my wellington boots. I went outside to speak to the girl, but she was no longer there. I scrambled across the ha-ha, and into the pasture, to where I thought she had been standing. Snowdrops were poking their way through the thawing snow here and there. I couldn't find any footprints. Of course, the snow was melting and patches of bleached-looking grass were beginning to appear, so perhaps her footprints had melted too.

Or perhaps I had just imagined her. I looked around. There was no hurrying figure that I could see in the fields or the woods. Then a warm wind bent the tops of the trees and ruffled my hair, and stroked the side of my cheek. The wind spoke of the coming of spring; of a new year; new hopes, new fears.